ROLLER SKATE SKINNY

J. L. MICHAELS

ISBN: 978-1-08-092732-6

DEDICATION

This book is dedicated to my family. Without you, there would be no meaning in my life.

PROLOGUE

He is pale white, sitting in the driver's seat with his shoulders high. His body is stiff as a corpse, his knuckles popping from strangling the steering wheel. I can almost see the gears clicking in his mind, shifting, turning. There is so much I want to say to him, but I don't know where to start. We have been living parallel lives for far too long. It wasn't always like this. We were close once. Now he hasn't turned his attention my way since we left home. And we have been on the long road known as the Trail of Tears for hours.

"Are you sure about this?" I ask him, faintly.

Please say yes.

His grip tightens about the steering wheel as the red sun beats against the earth. It is hotter than it has been in weeks, surprisingly hot in fact. Steam rises from the asphalt like water against burning coals. For some reason it reminds me of the sound of static. For a second, I hear flies.

The space between my legs tingles, so I rub my hands against my thighs. That is when I take note of the blood under my fingernails. It is dry and flaking. My hands still throb from the pressure of the cord that was wrapped around them. I feel the spiraling sting radiate through my arms and neck.

If that is not enough, the tooth in the back of my mouth begs to be tongued. It is on a thread of gum. I can feel it. So, I shove my fingers into my mouth to get a better sense of the situation. Instead, I accidently yank the tooth out. Right away there is a rush of blood. I taste something metallic. The flavor reminds me of a copper penny. Blood slides down the back of my throat to sour in my stomach, while I roll the tooth between my fingers and stare at it blankly. The only sound I hear is the soft hum of tires against pavement.

It's over, right? He's gone.

Praise God, he's gone.

Only, it doesn't feel over.

My partner decides to look at me. It is impossible to ignore the sadness in his blue eyes. There is confusion there as well, with fear and rage as the binding force.

"I'm sorry," I say without consideration. There are no other words I can impart. And to a degree, it is the truth. I am sorry. "You know that, don't you? I never meant for this to happen."

I only dreamed of it day and night.

My partner turns his attention to the road once more, so I look off into the distance in the other direction. It is picturesque outside with the sun in its golden glory casting buttery light over the land. There are birds in flight, grouped together in a v-pattern as they make their way toward the gray hills miles away. I study them in the manner a curator might study a painting and am filled emotion. In fact, I am drowning under the weight of it.

"You could have changed your mind," I tell my partner coolly as my eyes follow the birds.

And maybe you should have.

A long silence ensues until he finally breathes, "No. Please, God, no."

5

Immediately my head snaps forward, and I follow my partner's line of sight to the grouping of police cars down the road.

"What do we do?" I ask him in my softest voice.

"Stay calm, Delilah," he says. But I am not the one who looks panicked. And his grip tightens about the steering wheel.

"What if they try to look in the trunk?" I whisper as if the men in the uniforms down the road can hear us.

This isn't happening.

My partner flashes me a dirty look. He is angry. I understand. But now is not the time.

"Maybe we should turn around?" I say.

"And what? You don't think they'll notice? No. Just let me do the talking."

Without argument, I throw on a zippered sweat jacket to cover my bruises and lacerations then pull the visor down to flip open the mirror. Of course, I look like hell with my battered face. Adding even more concealer than I did before I left the house, I cover all of the evidence that I can.

But if they look too close—

"Your neck," my partner says after he scans me quickly with his eyes.

There is a line of black and blue marks around my throat. It is tender to the touch, but I dab concealer over the bruises anyway. Then I zip the zipper on my jacket up as high as it will go and adjust my hair. With my knees close to my chest, I throw my arm across my knees and neck, clasping the hood of my jacket to hold everything in place.

If I can just hold it in place long enough to get through this—

"Don't say a word," my partner reminds me as we slowly approach the checkpoint.

There are three cop cars in front of us. A quick scan

of the area reveals five police officers standing in various positions along the typically barren road. Two of the officers appear to be inspecting vehicles off to the side.

A car moves through the bottleneck, and we inch forward a notch. Another car moves through, and we inch forward again. Before long, we are next in line, my heart hammering inside my chest so hard it feels as though it might break a rib. And all the while, I hear the rush of blood in my ears.

"Don't let them open that trunk," I say once more.

"Be calm," my partner replies without looking at me.

Don't let them open that trunk.

The car in front of us is released seconds before the officer in charge waves us forward. She is a dark haired woman, small in stature, thin, Latina. Her eyes are far too inquisitive for my liking, her uniform near perfect with its creases.

"What is going on here, ma'am?" my partner asks her in a steady, clear tone.

The name on her tag says Gonzalez. "Where are you headed?" she replies, icily, without turning her eyes our way.

"North. We're going north to visit friends."

"Visit friends?" she says as she glances at my partner then shifts her attention to me.

Every particle in my body ignites with fear as she studies me for three long seconds.

My partner leans forward in his seat to obstruct her view and says, "Yes, ma'am. They live about forty-five minutes up the road in—"

"License, registration, and insurance," Gonzalez says curtly as she checks the notepad in her hand as though it holds instructions.

My partner turns to me to retrieve the items from

the glove compartment. At first, I just sit there like an idiot. A wave of heat washes over my body as ripples. It is the same sensation I felt as a child, the one that paralyzed me when I stood at the top of the stairs outside the quivering green door. Gonzalez and my partner are waiting with impatience. I can see it in their eyes, feel it in the air.

Move your hand.

Move your goddamn hand!

I lean forward to open the glove compartment to search for the appropriate paperwork. Every ounce of my strength must be utilized to keep my hands steady and hold my jacket in place. It is a balancing act.

Where the fuck is that envelope with the insurance and registration? This is my car. Where is it? C'mon, c'mon, c'mon.

While all of this is going on, a second officer steps around to the rear of our vehicle. He is tall and bald, muscular. In fact, he is so muscular that he shuffles along the pavement stiffly. His movements catch my attention. It is like he is a mechanical doll or a tin man. I cannot read his nametag from where I am sitting. But I am less worried about him than I am about the creature at the end of the leash in his hand. The German Shepherd looks young, barely more than a pup. Of course, that doesn't mean the dog doesn't know what it is doing.

My partner and I share a glance as the K9 heads toward the back of our vehicle. I don't know dogs. I don't know the difference between drug dogs and cadaver dogs or if they are trained in the same manner at the academy.

Please, dear God.

I cannot move. My mouth is dry, my throat on fire.

Everything seems to be happening in slow motion— Gonzalez blinks; people step out of their vehicles at the side of the road; the tin man officer reaches the back of our car; the Shepherd makes his first pass...

I hear the sound of flies. It picks up volume.

I cannot breathe.

But then a third officer, a female with tight blond hair and a severe facial expression, calls out to the muscle bound man in blue. "I need you over here, Tony," the third officer says. And the mechanical doll with his trained pup shuffles away.

"Today," Gonzalez hisses.

And my partner says, "Delilah, the paperwork."

It is like a snap of a finger.

Locating the white envelope with the registration and insurance in it, I hand the paperwork over to my partner, who hands it over to Gonzalez.

"And your license?" she says, distractedly, while examining the documents.

My partner extracts his license from his wallet and gives that to her as well. "If you don't mind me asking," he says to Gonzales. "What's this all about?"

Instead of replying, Gonzalez calls our information in through the radio that is attached to her shirt at the shoulder. "Last name Maconwood."

We wait, and as we do so, I glance through my rearview mirror to see what is happening with the muscle bound officer and his dog.

A voice comes through the line of the two-way radio. It is hard to make sense of the words.

A second later, Gonzalez says, "Thank you for your cooperation," and shoves the paperwork through the window of our car.

I want to breathe a sigh of relieve, but it is not yet over. We are still in enemy territory.

"Does that mean we are free to go?" my partner asks her.

"Just a second."

C'mon, this is taking too long.

The muscle bound officer and his dog are now returning.

A tick clicks by on a clock somewhere in the distance.

And another.

And another.

There is blood in my mouth.

Tick.

And black and blue marks under my jacket.

Tick.

My bloody tooth sits in a plastic cup between my partner and me.

Tick.

While what we put in the trunk grows riper and riper still.

Tick.

I squeeze my partner's hand.

Tick.

And the hound makes a soft whining sound.

Tick.

Gonzalez and the mechanical officer hold eye contact.

Tick.

But I know who I am now.

Tick.

For the first time in my life, I know who I am.

Tick.

Tick.

Tick.

CHAPTER ONE

As the red sun sinks behind golden black mountains and diminishing light casts a fine woven tapestry over the land, I stand outside on the balcony, one hand on my elbow, the other on my mouth, and realize something. A day will come when my husband sits across from me at the table and in his usual voice with its usual lilt say, "Explain to me what it is happening here, Delilah. Why are you the way that you are? Because I don't understand. What is wrong with you?"

Reentering the bedroom, I watch my husband as he dresses for work. He is as handsome as the day we met, with his scruffy beard and icy blue eyes. Ian flashes me a pity smile. He knows what is in store for me today. I'll be heading to the center of the city, to that rotted tooth hollowed out by political incompetence, criminal activity, and failure. My destination lies deep in the valley, the long road to its center flanked by towering mountains that seem to move, fold in on themselves, when the light plays tricks. Light reaches the valley later than it does the hilltop for some reason. Sometimes it doesn't reach the valley at all. I will not be traveling to the city for fun, not that fun could be had in such a location, but for the reading of my mother's will.

Standing in front of the full length mirror, the

chrome framed one that resides next to the bedroom door, my husband Ian stops putting on his tie long enough to give me his undivided attention. "Are you sure I shouldn't make a call?"

Am I sure?

"No," I tell him. "I'll be fine. Besides, it will just be the four of us."

"Delilah."

"Ian."

"It's not too late. I can get out of my meeting."

After I shake my head no, he places his hands on my arms and rubs me like he is drying me off after I've come out of the shower. I pull away to sit down on the bed. "We're overextended already. Let's stick to the plan."

He kisses me on my forehead and turns his attention back to his tie, finishing up the knot. "At least you will have the rest of your family there," he says right before flashing me a smirk. "That'll bring you comfort."

"Ha-ha."

Ian grabs his jacket off the occasional chair and kisses me on the cheek before studying my face. "What is it? I mean what else is it, Delilah?" When I do not respond, he adds, "You don't make it easy, you know. And I'm not a mind-reader."

"Go to work," I tell him.

He grimaces. "Don't forget what I told you about lawyers," he says playfully before exiting the room.

Mr. F. That is what I will call the lawyer handling my mother's case. Dark pools of late night briefs and a struggling practice circling coal colored eyes. Mr. F conducts business out of a shack on a slab of concrete in the heart of the rot. His business is fringed by two others, one of which on the verge of closing its paint stripped doors. Although trash cannot be seen on the street at first glance, it must be there, somewhere. The place reeks of something foul. At least that is what I remember most about the last time I was in the neighborhood. The very air surrounding the buildings leaves a film on the skin, much like exhaust fumes.

I climb into my car and turn down the radio. It takes a total of twenty-seven minutes for me to travel from my house to Mr. F's practice. Or that's how long it usually takes. Today the traffic is heavy. Angry people flash angry gestures then zoom off like the cowards they really are.

I am a coward as well. That fact does not escape me.

Clicking my signal, I pull into the turning lane. A single driver blocks the entrance to Mr. F's establishment. This middle-aged woman with gray stretched from the root pretends not to see me. She keeps her eyes straight ahead. But I know that she knows I am there. All she has to do is roll forward a few inches to let me pass, but she won't do it. This is all that she has, her one moment of control in the day. I get it.

Every particle in my body ignites as if touched by the wire of a galvanic battery. Instead of screaming, smashing shit in the vicinity, I utter a curse under my breath, something no one can hear but me.

I am alone.

Sometimes I wonder what would happen if I disappeared completely. Would anyone notice? The mark I have made in this world is so small, at best a dot of a ballpoint pen.

Fucking move, you stupid cunt!

The traffic light turns green, people step on accelerators, and cars rush forward. The way clears. I pull into the parking lot of Mr. F's establishment, my hands shaking visibly.

A deep breath gets me out of my car. Another gets

me through the door of Mr. F's practice.

A young woman greets me with a sadness that shrieks she is dying inside. Her smile isn't fooling anybody.

"They're waiting for you," she says. The young woman has the face of a twelve year old but the body of one freshly legal.

Fucking lawyers!

I follow the child into the room down the corridor, where the rest of my family is already waiting.

Family.

I use the term lightly.

Though the funeral was days ago, their eyes are red rimmed, their skin splotchy. It is different for them than it is for me. They had a mother, a real mother, someone who stuck around and took care of them when they were sick. The only unwanted person in this room is me.

I am the rejected.

I have three siblings. In chronological order, it goes like this: Bailey, Lillian, James, and me. I am the youngest. A gap of twelve years separates my brother and me.

My sister Bailey flashes me a smile. No one else bothers. Bailey is compact and pale of skin and hair, much like Lilly. I am tall, olive in complexion, and my hair is such a dark shade of brown, it is often mistaken for black. James' features fall somewhere in between, not that he considers himself one of us.

"What's going on?" I say.

Before anyone can answer, Mr. F steps into the room to invite us into his office. Not the conference room. Apparently we are not worth the space.

The minute I step into Mr. F's white walled box, I am accosted by the stench of cheap pine spray and day old French fries. There is a scented oil plugin attempting but failing to cast a Hawaiian Breeze scent in the corner as well as a pair of stinking running shoes by the door. An old grandfather clock clicks with the passage of time against the far back wall. Its pendulum swings hypnotically. And all the while, my stomach tightens.

I should not have come.

"Please," says Mr. F. He waves his hand over the chairs. "Have a seat."

The best ones are claimed before I can even get close, so I end up under the air conditioning vent.

Funny how you can be alone in a room full of people.

The air conditioner clicks on. A rush of air assaults me. Shivering, I pull my sweater tighter about my chest, shift to the side where the air blows less forcefully. It will not be long before my fingers turn purple, maybe my lips as well. I have always been sensitive to the cold, much like my father.

Why am I here?

A few minutes pass. Silence spreads throughout the room with thick resolve. It heightens all other sounds— venting, ticking, breathing, coughing, shifting, knees hopping, feet pendulum swinging, fingernails tapping restlessly upon scraped varnished arm rails.

Mr. F clears his throat. He is a middle-aged man with speckled gray-black hair and poorly fitted glasses that shield coal colored eyes. Some find him appealing. I do not.

"How much do you think?" my brother whispers in greedy anticipation.

Mr. F fiddles about in his desk drawer. He is looking for a pen. There are three in a wire cup near his calendar pad and one on the verge of jumping off the cabinet's ledge, but I remain quiet.

One drawer closes and another opens. My family grows increasingly restless, tossing looks at one another.

Mr. F coughs and wipes his mouth on his forearm. Spit glistens as a linear streak across his wrist. He doesn't care. He is not the man who drew up my mother's will. He is just filling in for the old guy.

"Be patient with me," Mr. F says as he continues to rummage through his drawers. "I will be with you in a minute."

Meanwhile, I take a look around the room, primarily at my family members. These are the players in my life or at least they are supposed to be. But I don't really know them. And they don't really know me. If I had to describe how we are with each other, I would say we are place settings. I am a blip on their radars, a quick little ping on proverbial screens, easily missed with a blink. They are the same for me. Of course, I am the youngest. And there is a gap of twelve or more years adding to our separation.

Leaning forward in his seat, my brother says something to Lillian, who responds with, "Definitely."

There is no money, you fools. No real money anyway. She died in a crummy apartment.

My focus shifts to the large glass window behind Mr. F's desk. When the traffic light turns green, cars hasten by and the windowpane vibrates. When the light turns red, cars stop and the glass settles to calm. This sequence of events repeats itself over and over again.

The sky is a strange shade of purple, pale and thick, darkening to foundry gray. It is late in the afternoon. My family is the last order of business, shoved in like a sliver for abrupt extraction.

"Ah-hah!" Mr. F cries. He holds up the pen as if it a trophy then slams the bottom drawer of his desk shut and rests his elbows on his calendar pad. "Let's get started."

The anticipation is palpable.

Mr. F opens the file on his desk and reviews the top

16

two documents. You would think he would have taken care of this before calling us into the room, but apparently our time is worth nothing. A gulf forms between his thick black brows. He looks at me—and only me—for an extended beat. There is something in his odd expression that I don't like.

"Before we begin," Mr. F says, "I would like to express how sorry I am for your loss. My partner and I extend our deepest condolences. From what I am told, your mother was a lovely woman."

No, she wasn't.

"Yeah, well, thank you," my brother hisses. "Now can we get on with this?"

Mr. F fingers the corner of the document in his hand before closing the file. "Your mother was institutionalized at one point. Is that correct?"

Silence returns to the room.

Bailey breaks it first; however, it is only after the quiet permeates the space and changes moods. "She was found competent enough to handle her own affairs. I mean she had problems, but—"

Lillian sniggers, while my brother questions, "Why?"

Mr. F looks my way once more. Now I know that it is something.

What?

And then it comes. Slow and exaggerated. Delivered in the form of sound waves formulated by thin pale lips.

Everything goes quiet for a beat.

Then Mr. F says, "As you know, I was not the attorney who drafted your mother's will and testament. There is always probate. You can contest."

Voices play in the air. I hear my own, faint, barely detectable over the others. "Wait, what are you saying?" I breathe.

"This can't be right," Bailey says. "And even if it is, he has a point. There is always probate."

"Are you saying my mother forgot my name?"

Dahlia.

She put Dahlia instead of Delilah on the paperwork and didn't have my married name.

That fucking bitch!

Lillian's laughter escalates.

My brother follows suit.

The pendulum on the grandfather clock swings.

And all the while, the lawyer rattles on about my options.

There is too much noise.

My attention turns to the quivering windowpane behind Mr. F's desk. When the traffic light turns green, cars hasten by and the windowpane vibrates. When it turns red, cars stop and the glass settles to calm. I am arrested by the window. Or rather I am arrested by the childhood memory it conjures.

The memory of the quivering green door.

I hear the sound of commotion, smell the foul odors, see color. There is a pink-eared bunny on the other side of the green door. A pink-eared bunny set in a basket of lime green grass sitting next to a glass turtle ashtray on a table. The day I left that bunny behind is the day everything changed. And now I am back there, on the stairs, alone.

Mr. F's office reeks of smoke and smokers; though, no one in the room ignites. I cannot breathe. The air is thick with stagnation.

Lillian's laughter becomes a cackle.

Voices merge, distant, dreamlike. They pound against my temples.

The smoke forms a cloud that consumes the room.

Using the arm rails for support, I stand up, slowly.

Look around the room, slowly.

Walk to the door.

Bailey materializes at my side. Out of the tunnels of my eyes, I see her mouth move, but I cannot make sense of her words. The ringing in my ears is too loud.

I cannot be here.

Stepping into the hall to get away from what is happening, I attempt to make my escape, but Bailey follows me. "You have to understand," she says. "Mom was sick."

It repeats in my head. *Mom was sick.*

"She remembered your name," I say.

"Delilah—"

"She remembered theirs."

Exiting the building from the side, I am immediately accosted by traffic noise and exhaust fumes, filth and decline. The sky is such a strange shade of purple that it reminds me of gifting cellophane. I feel light-headed.

A small stone bench that overlooks a pitiful patch of yellow flowers offers reprieve at the front. I take advantage and rest my bones.

Bailey sits beside me. "We can fix this," she says.

"Fix what? There is nothing to fix. It's done."

For a long while, Bailey says nothing. Finally she says, "Then I'll give you half of whatever I get."

I turn to face her. "You think this is about the money?"

"No."

"Because I don't give a shit about the money, Bailey. Do you hear me? I don't want it. Keep it. I don't want any of it."

"Delilah."

"Take it all. It doesn't matter. I am not going to fight you. Tell the others."

"Calm down, Delilah. You're getting emotional."

And everyone knows emotion is the enemy.

Bailey and I sit in silence. Time clicks by on the clock.

The traffic light turns red. A line of metallic slows to a stop in front of the curb. I inhale and exhale. Both actions take effort.

"How do you mean so little to the one person in the world you are supposed to mean the most?" I ask my sister. It is a thought more than a question.

Bailey places her hand on mine. The act is soft and gentle but unnatural, which is why she retracts the kindness a moment later and rests her hands on her lap. "I'm sorry, Delilah," she says in a low voice. "It probably doesn't make any difference, but I'm sorry."

I have heard those words before. I have heard them many times. And they have never, ever meant a fucking thing.

CHAPTER TWO

When Mr. F informed me of my mother's lapse in memory, my first reaction was doubt, then confusion, then indifference, all in a span of seconds, with rage sewn into each stage as the binding thread. I felt small. But I have always felt small, and insignificant. From the day I entered this world, drew my first breath and screamed. And now, as I sit here on this bench with my head hung low, I feel even smaller.

It is hard not wonder about my intellect. Is it subpar, or is it that I am innately flawed as a human being? Others understand what I do not. They know how to navigate this world in a way that I cannot. A few years ago, I would have been able to go home and find comfort in my husband's arms, but something has changed between Ian and me. Quiet dropped into our lives, between our lives, and stayed like an unwelcomed guest. The transformation happened slowly, so slowly in fact that I failed to notice it happening at all. I wonder if maybe he would be better off with someone else.

Dahlia instead of Delilah.

The stone bench that at first offered reprieve presently feels hard and cold and prickly. Traffic fumes stick to the gloss on my lips like flies to a trap, transforming accidental licks of my tongue into the foulest of metallic flavored swallows. It is like sucking on a filthy penny, a bitterness that causes my eyes to water. Still, I would rather watch the traffic go by here, on the bench outside Mr. F's office, than face what I cannot figure out how to fix at home.

My mother is dead!

She's dead.

I am alone.

When I think about my mother, I think about something young and dark and red—cap of short brown hair, cognac eyes with specks of green and gold, full pomegranate lips. She could stop traffic on the street. It was the angles of her face and the grace in which she moved. Her olive skin bronzed perfectly in the summer sun, her legs stretched on for miles, and wherever she went there lingered a trace of lavender.

I cannot see her in my mind's eye anymore or make out the features of her face. She is merely color.

Perhaps she is more to Bailey, who for some inexplicable reason suffers to remain in my company. While Bailey stares at the festering rot known as the heart of the valley, I cannot help but wonder how it is possible that we are related, much less siblings. Bailey is nothing like me. None of my siblings are. The only thing that Bailey and I have in common is our eyes, which are a light shade of glacial green.

Go away. Please.

Each second that ticks by on the clock increases Bailey's impatience. I can feel it. She turns her attention to the traffic and focuses on the moving automobiles as though intrigued, but I know what she wants.

"Bailey?" I say.

"Yes? What is it, Delilah?"

"Never mind."

She wipes her eyes with the back of her hand then looks away as though embarrassed by this display of emotion. It is normal, I think. She is normal, or as normal as anyone in my family can be. It is right to feel the loss of a parent. Yet I feel nothing. Actually, there is a buzzing under my skin, like something electric set on low.

Instead of focusing on it, I ponder how my mother's mind worked. A click that set off a spark. A spark that flared the synapses.

Bailey shifts positions on the bench. She looks at me sideways as though attempting to read my thoughts. "We should probably go inside," she says, finally.

We probably should.

My fingernails plunge into the skin of my palms. They sink deep then deeper into my flesh until they draw blood. It isn't much, but again I feel nothing. Only emptiness.

Pushing herself onto unsteady legs, Bailey says, "C'mon, Delilah. It's getting late. And they're waiting."

"Are they?"

"Delilah?"

"What?"

"You know what? This isn't their fault. They had nothing to do with it."

"Of course," I reply, but the words half stick in my teeth.

My other siblings are content to let me walk away from the inheritance. After all, money and material objects are what matter most. I am the unwanted.

Returning to the stone bench, Bailey sits next to me and touches my hand the way she touched it earlier. There is impatience in the act, though. The sensation reminds me of electrical current.

The others are waiting.

The money is waiting.

And greed and impatience hold hands.

"You go on ahead," I say.

"Stop it," she snaps.

"Nobody is keeping you here, Bailey. It's fine."

She looks out at the cars again. "Why can't you give me a break, Delilah?" It is only after a pause that she stares me down and sharpens her tone. "Delilah?!"

My teeth clamp shut. "I said it is fine, Bailey. What more do you want? I'll be in in a minute."

Standing with her hands clipped neatly around her hips, Bailey drops her head back and looks up at the darkening sky. Dusk has arrived. And night is approaching fast.

"It's okay," I tell her. "Really. To be honest, I need a moment alone."

Just go.

She studies me for an extended beat. "When you're ready then," she says.

Before she makes it to the door leading to Mr. F's practice, she stops and turns back around. "What about the money, Delilah?"

I sigh. "What about it, Bailey?"

"Do you want me to talk to the others?"

"No!" I say, coolly. "I don't want it. Any of it. You can tell them I am not going to contest. It is all theirs. Now would you please just, you know. I mean...please."

"We are all having a time of it here," she tells me. "You are not the only one."

I'm not?

"Is that right?"

"Yes, Delilah. That's right."

"Great, I'll be in in a minute."

The next thing I know, I am in my car, alone with

my hands on the steering wheel, knuckles whiter than the paper on which I write this now. I have no memory of getting up from the bench or walking across the parking lot or opening my car door. I have no memory of climbing inside the vehicle or curling my hands around the steering wheel in a 10-2 position, squeezing my veins closed. I have no memory and yet I am here.

The silence feels like noise. It is deafening.

I shake the steering wheel. *Fuck, fuck, fuck!*

Dropping my head low, I try to clear my thoughts. They are rapid and disjointed. I don't know who I am anymore. But then again I've never known. Figuring it out is like breathing under water. It's impossible.

Dahlia instead of Delilah.

When finally I push myself into an upright position, I am surprised to find something strange in the middle of the parking lot. Leaning forward, closer to the windshield, I narrow my eyes for a better look. At this point, most have gone home for the evening, everyone except for my family, Mr. F, and a few hard working stragglers. The parking lot appears larger in its near empty capacity. It feels isolated, like an island unto itself. And at its center, directly in front of me, maybe twenty feet away, is the green door, unattached yet perfectly erect, practically spotlighted with dusk as its backdrop.

"No, no, no, no, no, no, no," I say.

There is a fucking green door held up by air in the middle of Mr. F's parking lot!

I close my eyes and open them again, hoping I slipped into a micro-sleep. But the door is still there.

It begins to vibrate, slowly at first, as though with the shutter of a single knock, then faster and faster, more intense.

My car key jams into the ignition by its own accord.

The engine of my four door utility vehicle roars to life. White with tinted windows and heavy black tires, this is the car of six million real estate agents. It's so fucking common. I am a copy made on low ink.

I am nothing.

After being jerked forward and back, I ram into a pile of broken pallets, tree cuttings, and other improperly disposed of materials. The pile comes to life in the way that it claws at my rear bumper when I attempt to leave it behind. The clinging branches remind me of human bones, like those of the undead, digging, clawing after their prey.

Finally, the broken pieces of wood give up the fight, fall haphazardly on the side of the parking lot, separated from the rest of the discarded.

Another door materializes.

And another.

And another.

Soon the doors appear everywhere.

I hear music and voices and violence.

There is a flash of color, movement.

I see the stairs that lead to the green door.

And my father's angry face.

His hands about my mother's throat.

Her gnashed teeth.

Everything is color.

Reacting without thought, my foot hits the pedal. I am propelled straight into traffic. It is bumper to bumper rush hour now. Direction is irrelevant. I fly down the road without thought or consideration.

The light turns red. I stop with automatic, almost mechanical obedience, but it feels strained, as though my nerves have been scraped bare and struck by electrified pins.

The earth opens up in front of me. A green door

rises out of the ground, slowly, as if ejected by hell.

Another rises out of the median.

One materializes in front of my vehicle.

And one materializes behind.

The stench of rotted food and cigarette smoke pours into my vehicle's main compartment. I cannot breathe, much less see past this bizarre nicotine web. Somehow, perhaps instinctively, I sense the light change. Again my foot hits the pedal; however, the traffic does not proceed as it should.

Slamming on the breaks, I veer into the adjacent lane and am thrown forward and back in my seat with violent force.

A horn scolds me from behind, while a voice I have never heard before yells, "What the fuck is wrong with you? Get off the road."

What the fuck is wrong with me?

More horns blow.

Curses echo in the valley.

Speeding down the road, I land beside a 60s truck that has been upgraded in appearance by a fresh coat of cherry red paint. My eyes follow the bold color straight to the owner of the vehicle, who is sitting neatly behind the steering wheel like a propped up doll.

I stare at the driver.

And the driver stares at me.

Then everything stops.

The whole fucking world stops.

"My pink-eared bunny," I breathe.

My pink-eared bunny life-size and holding eye contact with me.

Maybe if I hadn't left him next to the glass turtle ashtray on the table behind the dirty green door...

Another bunny catches my eye, this one in a sedan,

and another and another. Bunnies everywhere.

Horns blow.

Curses linger in the clouds.

Nasty words float to the heavens.

I yank the wheel and skid into the parking lot of an old abandoned warehouse. The place used to make foam pillows until the owner passed control of the facility to his incompetent son. Now the place sits as a remnant. To the east of the warehouse is a fence bent like a wilted flower, and to the west a gaping hole.

With the engine still running, I expel myself from the vehicle and stumble hastily to the rear of the car, where I cling to everything and anything for support.

I cannot breathe.

My mother is dead.

I cannot see straight.

She is dead and forgot my name.

I cannot feel.

Perhaps we are one and the same.

Young.

And dark.

And red.

I drop to my knees.

CHAPTER THREE

A train station resides behind the old foam factory, not directly behind it but within walking distance, or maybe a few hundred steps farther. I grab my keys and my wallet, nothing else, and take the shortest route from one point to the other. The ground is soft and at times difficult to manage, but the puddles have dried, and if my clothes get dirty, they get dirty. I don't really care.

My shoes mark the territories they touch with an imprint, except when I stumble and fall, which happens more than once; then the imprint created is not of my shoes but of my hands and knees. It reminds me of the clay imprints I made at the summer programs my father forced me to attend as a child. He did not send me to those programs to improve my social skills or develop my creativity or encourage my growth, as he sometimes claimed, but to get me out of the house and as far away from him as humanly possible. And when the programs failed to remove me from his presence, he simply locked the door.

The divots in the ground cause me to trip and fall yet again, and with my hands and knees set in the dirt, sinking ever so slightly, slipping into the swale, I recall not the summer of my youth but the winter when the snow was so thick and unforgiving it climbed high up to my thighs.

Of course I was smaller then, younger, so my perspective may be a little skewed. Either way, the snow was tall and it was cold—*painfully* cold—and the fact that we had little money on account of my father never accomplishing more than factory work ensured I did not have the right kind of clothes to stave off the bite. The hostile weather did not stop my father from locking the door that day either. Even as I stood outside on the icy porch, banging and begging, desperately pleading for him to let me in, my fingers aching and purple, my ears so raw they felt like they were going to split, even as I told him that I was going to wet myself if he did not open the door, which by the way happened, my father refused to allow me inside to thaw. He claimed it was for my own good. I needed fresh air, he said, and friends—*any fucking friends*, to be exact—since I had none.

That was just one of the differences between my brother and sisters and me. I was raised by a single father, while they were raised by two parents. My mother hadn't packed up and disappeared until I came around. Plus, my brother and sisters had friends, people who would open their doors on cold winter days. I didn't. I was the rejected. Me and me alone. The only one who stayed was the one prone to stinking of beer and engaging in violence.

It is not that my father had hate in his heart. I don't believe that he did anyhow. Even at his absolute worst, when his drunken hands unleashed their dreadful blows, when the brutality escalated to nightmare, hate never seemed to be the driving force. It was misery. And fear. More importantly, perhaps most importantly, it was that I reminded him of her.

Young. And dark. And red.

I remember the day I figured this out. My father and I were in the midst of an argument. It was just the two of us living at home. My other siblings had moved out already.

I was thirteen years old, no longer a child yet not yet an adult. The argument between my father and me became heated. He made comments about my mother that stuck like a knife. In my anger, I said quite coldly, "You are not my father. I've never had a father or a mother or anyone else for that matter. And it's because of you. You are a miserable old man. That is all you are, all you'll ever be. I hate you. I. Hate. You."

I hate you.

In that moment, brief though it was, I witnessed something I had failed to notice before. It came through in my father's blistering gray eyes and in the inexplicable shift of his shoulders. The sadness. The regret.

Later that same night I could not sleep. I felt guilty, so I slipped out from under the covers and tiptoed down the hall to my father's room, which resided at the far end. When I lifted my hand to knock, directly before my fingers hit the door, something caused me to stop. For an extended beat, I remained very still, simply listening to the strange noises on the other side of the door. I don't know why, but I felt this incredible urge to peek inside my father's room. There, I found him with a dark haired woman.

This woman, this unknown person in my house at the dead of night, had short black hair and a sharply boned spine. She was naked from the waist up, covered with a blanket from the waist down. The woman was straddling my father, and in her hand was a long thin shaving blade, the kind that barbers use. I knew what I was doing was wrong. The thoughts in my head kept screaming for me to turn around and go back to my room, but I didn't. Instead, I remained fixed in position and watched as this woman, this stranger, lifted the blade in her hand above her shoulders, not so much high as high enough to provide force, then bring it swooping down to slice my father's backside bloody and raw. I will never forget the wet sharing sound.

Right away my father cried out from the pain.

"Shut up," the woman whispered harshly as she yanked his head back by his hair.

I wanted to run and hide, return to my room; however, a wave of heat enveloped me, and I could not move. My father's backside was red. The world was red.

"Wait," my father said after the woman slapped him. "Wait."

The woman tossed the blade to the side before sinking her fingers deep into his hair. Then she yanked his head back once more. With her mouth close to his ear, she said, "Shut up or she will hear you. And you know what I will do to you if that happens."

What?

My father grunted but did not cry out again.

Still, the woman said, "Shut up." She paused briefly before adding, "Say it."

"I don't understand."

"Say what I'll do to you."

My father did not respond.

"Say it," the woman demanded more forcefully.

"It's too tight," my father replied, faintly.

"You say it right now or I swear to—"

"Stop," my father said.

I am not sure how long I stood there in the minimal light watching my father with this strange woman. Too long, I suppose. And when I did return to my room, I closed the door quietly behind me, climbed into bed, and pulled the blankets up over my head. All night I lay there, sleepless, thinking on what I had seen. Something very adult was sparked inside me. Something odd. And it has never really left.

Presently, on my hands and knees with my fingers in the dirt, I feel as alone in the dark as I was on the night I witnessed my father get his ass sliced to shreds by that woman, as alone as I did when I stood at the top of the stairs outside the dirty green door.

Dahlia instead of Delilah.

Picking myself up off the ground, I brush off the dirt and the stickers and make my way to the train station once more. The bunnies are gone, and the green doors. Even the electricity under my skin has faded away.

When finally I arrive at my destination, a little worn for the wear, the memory of my journey from the warehouse to the station already in the process of being dyed in the machine of vague recollection, my skin feels moist.

I board a train—*any* train—and take a seat. The cushions feel warm and soft and welcoming, velvet to the touch. The fabric is blue and red with traces of white. A draft forces me to wrap my sweater tighter about my chest, but I do not feel uncomfortable, not as I did in Mr. F's office. It is more that I am exhausted.

"Keeping oneself sane is tedious work," I whisper.

The statement is not one that originated with me but with a nineteen year old girl who attended the same college as me. For some reason, it stuck in my head.

Keeping oneself sane is tedious work.

The brakes release and the train rocks slightly. Then the train jerks forward, kicks a little, and picks up speed. Soon the wheels click against the track to create a cadence. My mind wanders. I see yellow flowers and pale lips, grave stones and traffic lights. Then I see a green door and a pink-eared bunny, and blood.

There is always blood.

The skin into which my fingernails dig breaks, and my palm fills with a sticky wet sensation. It takes a minute for the sting to register. When it does, I am quick to react by wiping my hands on my dress pants. They are my most expensive pair, but it doesn't matter because I have never been materialist.

Right about now I notice the woman in the seat several rows in front of me. She is on the left hand side, neatly positioned facing my direction. The line of sight from me to her—or her to me—is a straight diagonal, only slightly obstructed by rows of seats. She is not a striking woman, or at least not in the conventional sense, yet something about her causes her to stand out in the space. Whether it is her silky hair or pomegranate lips or exotic flavor, I cannot say. She certainly holds herself with confidence. After a while it dawns on me that the woman's lips are moving and have been for some time. Nothing registers.

What is this?

The train clicks, there is a slight jolt, and I am pushed an inch forward and back in my seat. The windows tremble as the wind outside whips at the glass. There is something dreamily dizzying about the moment. No one else is around, at least not as far as I see, but I am not searching.

The woman's mouth moves again.

"What?" I say, faintly.

"I said stop looking at me like that," she says. And suddenly her words are crystal clear.

The woman places her hand on the seat in front of her and leans forward, partially into the aisle. This closes the gap between us by a few inches. "Right. Now. Please."

Immediately, warnings go off in my head. I should not engage this person. I know this the same way that I know silence is safe. For whatever reason, though, I say, "How am I looking at you?"

"Like that."

"Like what?"

"The way you are looking at me," she spits. After knitting her sickly thin brows, she adds, "You're staring."

"Am I?" I had not realized.

"It's very rude."

Bitch.

"Is it, though?"

I have never been the type to poke at snakes. Confrontation is something I typically avoid; however, I don't feel much like myself right now. And what happened with my mother's will is still firing through the neurons of my brain.

Dahlia instead of Delilah.

The woman on the train is quick to respond. She snarls, "Yes. So please stop."

My fingernails dig deep then deeper into my palms. Leaning forward in my seat, I place my elbows on my knees, and I stare this unpleasant woman down. Her features are attractive enough when set alone but when added together, like a language translated, something is lost. I cannot stand her face.

"What's wrong with you?" she says after a long pause.

What's wrong with me?

I have been asking myself that same question since I was six years old.

Instead of attempting to give answer, I take a deep breath, sit up straight, and look away.

That should be the end of it, but it isn't. The woman starts up again. "People like you—"

"People like me?" I reply without turning my

attention her way. The glass window next to the seat in front of me begins to vibrate. It is dark outside. Beyond the window is black.

"What is your name?" I ask the woman before giving her my undivided attention.

Of course, she does not respond.

"Your name, what is it?" I demand.

"Why do you want to know?" she says.

There really isn't a reason.

The hum of the train and the inside lights against the outside darkness add a dreamlike feel to the moment. Isn't it odd how in the confines of our own minds, nothing constrains us, yet in the real world, we hold back?

The woman and I maintain eye contact for what feels like a long time but probably amounts to seconds.

"Do you want to hear something funny?" I ask her.

She shakes her head, confused.

"My mother died."

There is a long pause before the woman replies, "I'm sorry to hear that."

I'm sure you are.

"Are you?" I say.

"Yes, well, the loss of a loved one is a terrible thing."

"Loved one," I say, faintly.

Ha.

The woman melts into her seat, and for a time, it is quiet. Then she furrows her brows and says, "Wait, how is that funny? Your mother's death? I don't understand."

I shrug. "We cremated her body a few days ago. And today I learned that she forgot my name. Just couldn't remember it, I guess. Like I was never born."

Dahlia instead of Delilah.

The woman tips her head as a confused dog. "What do you mean she forgot your name?"

I do not respond.

The train slows to a stop. The woman gathers her belongings, stands still for a moment, then walks over to me. Her eyes drill through the top of my head. After an extended beat, I extend my neck to look up at her.

"This has been—"

"What?" I say, coolly. "What has it been?"

She considers her answer. "I'm not sure, actually. Strange."

A second later, the woman exits the train to disappear from my life forever.

I collect my keys and my wallet off the seat beside me and exit the train as well. Right away I am hit by a cold wind blowing in a north-easterly direction. The ocean is nearby, the stench of death caused by red tide heavy in the air. Darkness has spread like ink on linen.

"Excuse me," a man says from behind me.

I turn around. The man is tall and muscular with light brown skin and light brown eyes. He looks mixed race.

"I didn't mean to eavesdrop," he says, "but I overheard your conversation with the other woman."

It surprises me to realize that there was another on the train. I don't know how I failed to notice, especially one so handsome.

An awkward silence fills the space between us.

"Anyway, it sounds like you could use a drink? There is a bar around the corner, if you are interested," he says.

Am I interested?

"You're asking me out for a drink?" I say.

The man laughs. "If you'd like, yes."

He is cleanly dressed and healthy in appearance, but I am married.

Still, I imagine his mouth on my mouth, his hands

on my body. This is the kind of man who knows how to fuck a woman properly; I am sure of it.

Maybe if I was another person.

Dahlia instead of Delilah.

CHAPTER FOUR

To wake in the middle of a starved night is much like emerging from the swamp of a nightmare, when the whispers have not quite departed or the sickness run its course.

My hand reaches over to paw and pat the other side of my bed, only to find that my husband is not there. The sickness is inside me now as a wash of cold heat. He tucked me in after I returned home from the train station; however, I wasn't in the mood to talk, so he respected my wishes and disappeared.

Ian.

Ian probably wanted to know more about the circumstances surrounding my mother's choices for her will. Instead of sharing those circumstances, I simply told him that she left us nothing. It was a strange thing to do, keeping the truth from my husband. I don't know why I did it, maybe because we have been living parallel lives. Or maybe I have known for quite a while that hope is a dangerous thing.

Clothes and sheets soaked with perspiration, I pull the covers to the side. The cool air hits like a punch. The chill penetrates my skin and bones. Sharp as a knife, it forces me to hold still for a moment.

I check the clock. The broken green lines say it is

3:00 AM. Of course it is 3:00 AM. The witching hour. It is dark in the room, not quite pitch black, but menacing enough to slow a person down.

Where are you?

I do not like the dark. I've never liked it. It feels like a threat, like someone or something is waiting for me in the unseen places. If not for the streetlight illumination spilling into the room to provide visibility, I might be afraid. But then again another emotion is at play here, and its volume is on high in my head.

"Ian?" I call, softly, almost as though to evade being heard.

Walking toward the master bathroom, I nudge the door open with my knuckles, slowly, quietly. "Ian, are you in there?"

He does not respond.

I check the room anyway.

Then I wipe the sweat off my brow with the top of my wrist and proceed into the hall, where the streetlight illumination fails to reach. Although it is dark, something inside me keeps me from switching on the light. Hardwood floors send a chill up through my feet and creak from the strain of my weight as insult.

"Ian?" I say, faintly.

Again, he does not answer.

There is a staircase at the end of the hall. I make my way to it and descend one step at a time. When I reach the bottom, I swallow hard and proceed to the living room, where I walk along the edge. I pass my husband's dirty dishes, the ones he left behind on the end tables. How many times do I have to ask the man to clean up after himself?

How many times?!

Finally, I reach the kitchen; however, I do not enter

the room. Instead, I stop short at the door. I cannot see my husband at this point, but I hear his voice and the voice of another.

A woman.

There is something guttural, carnal, in the sounds that follow, something that brings my insides to a boil.

With soft hands, I push the swinging door open to soak in the sight. My first reaction is pain, then sorrow, then outrage, with hate as the binding thread. A part of me wants to turn around and flee, close my eyes, forget what I am witnessing. But the other part, the newly ignited part, is sick of all the bullshit, of the long line of wrongs. And the other part demands a different kind of response.

Like a mosquito drawn to an electrocute trap, I am compelled to watch the transgression happening in front of me. Blue-white light from my husband's computer satiates the tunnels of my eyes, while his movements create flickers reminiscent of a candle. His back is currently facing me, his pants and underwear down around his ankles. It makes no sense that he is in the kitchen like this. No sense at all. Couldn't he have gone in the bathroom or his office? Didn't he consider the possibility of me waking and finding him?

Where is his decency?
The sonuvabitch.

"Like that?" he says in a low voice.

The girl on the other side of the screen has long dark hair and flawless sun-kissed skin. "That's right," she replies, seductively. "Like that, baby. Don't stop. You got it. Keep going. Keep going. That's right. Now how about me? Tell me what you want from me, and be nasty about it."

She is prettier than I am. Younger.

The tile floor burns like ice. Ian is all I have in this world. He is all I've ever had. And here I am watching him fuck without fucking someone else not ten feet away. The moment feels savage; it reels me back to the green door and the pink-eared bunny that I left next to the glass turtle ashtray on the table.

Why did I leave my pink-eared bunny behind?

What the hell is wrong with me?

On the table in front of my husband are a box of tissues and a bottle of lotion. Ian grabs the lotion and pumps a few squirts into his hand then opens his knees and, leaning back in his chair, takes hold of his penis to work the shaft.

"Take those off," he says to the woman on the other side of the computer. "Your clitoris...Play with your clitoris."

"This is you, baby," the girl on the other side of the computer says. "Your mouth. Your tongue. Can you feel it? My God, what you do to me."

My fingernails dig into the palms of my hands.

"Harder," she says. "C'mon, baby, like that. Harder."

She spreads her legs wider in front of the camera, wets her fingers in her mouth, and slides them over her thin toned body, all the while writhing, moaning, caressing her breasts with her free hand. Then she plunges her fingers deep into her vagina for my husband and I watch.

Only, no one notices I am here. I am invisible. I am always invisible.

Am I invisible?

With clumsy hands, my husband attempts to grab the tissues off the table but knocks them over instead. Just as the tissues are about to hit the floor, he manages to snatch a few from the box.

"Are you close?" the woman says. Her fingers pick up speed.

How her daddy must be proud.

"Because I am. I'm so close, baby," she tells my husband while panting like a dog.

The next thing I know, I am standing in front of Ian with the knife I snatched off the plate that he left behind on the end table in the living room.

Ian elevates in his chair, surprised to see me. "Delilah."

Immediately, I drop to my knees and without wasting a beat take him into my mouth. At first he does not know how to respond—the caught and reward conflict. But then, as I continue to give him oral sex, he melts in his seat and places his hand on my head as though to guide me.

The sonuvabitch.

I slide my underpants off and kick them to the side. Then I straddle my husband, the way that strange woman straddled my father so many years ago.

As I kiss Ian deeply, my long hair drips over his hands and wrists, forearms.

He cups my face between his fingers and kisses me in return. We know each other well from years of marriage. Our bodies find their rhythm quickly. Soon, there is nothing but the sound of labored breaths and slapping skin.

Ian throws his head back. His eyes are closed, but I want him to see me, to know what he has done.

After all, I am the rejected.

I am the unloved.

The jettisoned.

And it is his fault.

My husband moans. His fingers curl, tighten about my waist. I feel the pressure of his hands pulling me close then closer still. And right at the point when he is about to ejaculate, when his pleasure is at its peak and the smell of semen is on the verge of lacing the air, I bring my hand around the way my father's woman brought her hand around so many years ago, and I jam that dirty steak knife deep between my husband's ribs, so deep the fucker gasps for air.

Ian's eyes snap open. He cannot breathe.

Calmly, coolly, I whisper, "Like that, baby."

Only, it is not my voice anymore. It is the voice of the woman on the other side of the computer. She says it again. "Like that."

Now I realize that I haven't moved an inch. My husband is jacking off to porn. And the woman who is getting him off is the one doing the talking. The rest is in my head.

I don't know what to do. Hell, I don't even know who I am anymore.

Who the fuck am I?

Dahlia instead of Delilah.

Unable to stand the sight of my husband for a second longer, I return to my bedroom and crawl under the covers. For a long time I lay there, alone, sleep refusing to offer reprieve.

When my husband returns to our room, he falls right out, probably from exhaustion.

The next night it is the same and the night after that. In his office. In the bathroom. One more time in the kitchen. The acts always differ, the women as well, but each new image adds a memory to the box—The Stranger, The Cold Climax, The Hutchence.

My husband's needs are insatiable.

And when he is done, he always slides into bed next to me, kisses me on the forehead, and goes to sleep. No detectable signs of guilt.

One random night, I lay there fuming. I can't take it anymore, so I climb on top of Ian, straddle style, and wait for him to feel the pressure of my body upon his. A few seconds later, his eyes pop open, and he studies me for a beat before he says, "Delilah."

"I want to know why," I say.

The gears clicking in his brain are practically visible. He is putting the pieces together and knows that I know. *That's right.*

"What are you talking about?" he says, regardless.

I do not answer.

Ian pushes himself onto his elbows, while I slide off to sit on my heels at his side.

Then, throwing the covers back, he gets out of bed and walks to the window, where the streetlight illumination washes over him more powerfully. The moon adds a silvery glow, highlighting his rippling muscles.

"Are you bored with me?" I ask him.

"What? Don't be ridiculous, Delilah."

"Have we been together too long?"

"Delilah."

A short silence ensues.

"My mother just died, Ian. She. Just. Died." Actually, it was two weeks ago, but his timing is for shit.

"You said yourself that you didn't even know her."

I shake my head, disgusted.

Closing the gap between us, he crosses the floor. "I'm sorry, okay."

Oh, you're sorry.

"I only meant—"

"When I agreed to marry you, I asked you for one thing, Ian. One fucking thing. Not to be like all those others. Do you remember that conversation or did it slip your mind?" At no point do I raise my voice.

The wall of silence between us gains a new layer.

Ian sits on the end of our bed, his fingers close to my leg yet falling short. "What do you want me to do,

Delilah?"

"Nothing. I don't want you to do anything, Ian."
After a pause, I add, "Actually, I take that back. You can
leave. Yeah, I want you to leave."

"Delilah—"

"Now, Ian. Go." When he fails to complete the task,
I repeat myself, only this time louder. "Go."

Pushing his fingers through his hair, Ian shakes his
head. "This is what I'm talking about, Delilah. This is the
problem between us."

Oh, this is the problem.

"We don't communicate," he says.

Well, no shit.

The room quiets.

"Delilah—"

"I can't even look you," I tell him. "You're just like
all the rest."

Ian takes hold of my ankle. "I'm not. And you know
it."

I kick his hand away.

Then he stands up and takes a few steps toward the
dresser before he says, "I'm sorry, okay? What do you want
me to do, Delilah? I fucked up. I'm sorry."

But I have heard those words before. I have heard
them many times. And they have never, ever meant a
fucking thing.

"I love you," he tells me.

I simply reply, "Get out."

Grabbing his pants and his shoes, my husband exits
the room. And as he proceeds to leave, I cannot help but
wonder if this is what it means to be loved.

Is it?

A second later, the front door downstairs slams shut,
and the walls tremble.

I crawl under the bedcovers.

When I roll over onto my side, blinking my last blinks for the night, I see my pink-eared bunny, life size, staring back at me. And I fall asleep.

CHAPTER FIVE

It is a strange thing to fear death yet long for it most hours of the day, a thing that leaves you bewildered. And the mind secretes all kinds of trouble when it is disturbed.

Waking, I bury myself deep in the covers, much as the dead bury themselves in the cold clay of the earth. My bones feel heavy, my eyelids as well. There is a chill that penetrates right to the marrow. Time clicks by on the clock, and I drift in and out of sleep, until finally the morning is spent and the afternoon arrives.

It is not want that gets me out of bed, but vibrations, untold quivers that are felt but never seen. I have no plan for the day. In fact, I have no plan for the future. Everything I do is mechanical, visionless. Each act clings to vague recollection rather than establish its own new memory. The world around me enters as a haze, and I have forgotten my childhood dreams.

Did I ever have any? I cannot remember.

Packing my belongings without consideration, I place two suitcases at the bottom of the staircase then perform a perfunctory sweep of the house. Though it is smaller than I would like, my home is a pleasant place, secluded behind black iron gates, set at the far end of a well-manicured subdivision. It is a home of rich granite countertops and antique white cabinets, polished stainless steel, and fashionable stone tiles. High ceilings and an open floor plan make it feel larger than it is, but the closets are no wider than a jewelry box, which sometimes causes my temper to ignite. My husband and I are the shining example of dead center middleclass.

My husband. Ha.

I used to pray for this kind of home as a child, particularly on those nights when I could not sleep and the cockroaches scurried across the floor in our stinking apartment. The sound of breathing, snoring, would play in the air. Sometimes it would be as loud as a jungle. With my hands clasped tight, close to my chin, I would push myself under the covers, deep then deeper still. My eyes peered out at the horrid world, while I feared the day one of those cockroaches would come for me. Even now I dream of a crawling, scuttling creature creeping its way into my mouth or laying an egg in my ear. There were so many cockroaches in my childhood house. They were all around—deep in the cabinets, behind the refrigerator, under the sink, hidden in the laundry room—scampering, scurrying. The memory gives me the shivers. I scratch scalp.

Sitting on the bottom step of the staircase of my current place, I stare blankly at the wall directly in front of me. It is the wall that separates the entry hallway from the stove side of the kitchen. Over the sink is an opening. To the left of the staircase is the foyer and to the right is the formal dining room and living room, which are connected by open space. There is also a small dinette area off the kitchen. It is adjacent to the foyer. From the entryway, before the staircase, there is an extremely small hallway that leads to the garage door then beyond to a half bathroom. The second floor is made up of three bedrooms and two bathrooms, one of which the master. Lulworth Blue is the color on the walls. The paint has been there awhile. Too long. It is starting to get drab, much like my marriage.

The air suddenly feels thick, the smell lacing it stale. I feel a strange need to clean, so I wash the dishes and put them away and fold the clothes and wipe down the countertops and vacuum the floors and mop the tile and disinfect the toilets and take out the trash. I even do a vinegar rinse of the washing machine and clear out the garbage disposal. Every pore in the air stinks of chemicals, but that does not stop me from cleaning some more.

And when it is done, when there is nothing left for me to polish or disinfect, I focus on myself and scrub my hands raw, first with soap and water, then with a scouring pad. Finally, I scrape out my fingernails and clip them so close to the skin that my fingers bleed. It takes the pressure of my palm to finally stop the flow.

On the bottom step of the staircase once more, I sit in the quiet. Eventually, my husband materializes with a bouquet of calla lilies in his hand and a well-rehearsed apology. He enters through the front door and, seeing me waiting, remains motionless for a beat. It is difficult for me to look at him. He is still a handsome man with blackish-brown hair, icy blue eyes, and thin muscular build. His eyes drop for a moment. When he lifts them again, he takes a breath then closes the gap between us with well-paced steps.

After I stand, he takes two more steps to invade my space.

Who the hell does he think he is?

There is an awkward delay before Ian delivers his speech. The delay is extended for him to look over at my suitcases. His expression changes, saddens.

Good.

Then his mouth moves. I hear the sound of his

voice. Actually, I feel his voice more than I hear it. Either way, nothing truly registers. There is almost a foreign quality to what my husband is saying. The translation is lost.

Thrusting the calla lilies into my hand, he continues to add layer upon layer to his mountain of excuses. He and I have been married for seven years—seven long years—and we were together three years before that. Never in all that time did I appreciate flowers as a gift. I have mentioned this to him on multiple occasions, if only to save us the money. Trimmed and tidied like a cadaver, what are cut flowers but the dead neatly prepared for viewing? Ian should know this—he should know me—but he doesn't.

He doesn't know me!

And of course I don't really know him either, as evidenced by his nightly show.

Still, he thrusts those flowers into my hand with the expectation that I will react in a positive manner. What he gets, though, is the opposite. I take those calla lilies and fling them as hard as I can across the room. Then I plow past my husband and my suitcases to snatch my keys off the hook by the front door in preparation to leave.

Ian is not a violent man so much as a physical one. He clutches me by my arm and with a rough pull swings me around to face him. With two smart moves, he pins me against the wall, caging me like an animal between his arms. We are in the foyer now. My head is an inch from the entryway painting, a dark piece I selected the night after my father succumbed to his last heart attack.

"Stop," he says.

"You stop, Ian," I reply. Of course, I recognize that I act like a child sometimes.

"You've made your point," he tells me.

I've made my point. Ha.

His face is so close to mine, I half think he is going to kiss me.

"Do you hear me, Delilah? You've made your point."

"Have I, Ian? Well, I guess everything is fine then."

Ian does not respond. He is a large man, not heavy but broad shouldered, 6'1" in height. He takes up space.

"Move your arm," I hiss.

"You can't be serious. Where will you go, Delilah? You're making more out of what happened than necessary."

I knew he would say that. They all say that.

Outside the birds are chirping and fluttering their wings. Someone honks a horn in the distance. I hear people walking past our house. But inside the temperature in the room is rising, and it is only my husband and me.

Ian studies me at length. "Delilah—"

"I'm not interested in hearing anymore of your excuse, Ian. I know your lies."

"Why can't we talk about this like adults?" he asks.

I swear every word out of his mouth sounds scripted. It makes me want to punch him in the face.

"Move your arm, Ian."

"Delilah—"

"Move your goddamn arm."

At no point do I raise my voice, but my tone sharpens considerably. After all, there are calla lilies on the floor.

Fucking calla lilies!

"You know I have never cheated on you," he says. "Never."

That is a matter of perspective; however, I refuse to argue the subject. Instead I simply reply, "What a shining example of husbandly achievement. How proud you must be."

The lines on his face deepen as his expression thickens to a scowl. "Is that how it's going to be then, Delilah?"

"Yeah. Why not?"

I should slide out from under his arm by way of the side, grab my keys, and head for the door. For whatever reason, though, I allow him to keep me trapped. It is a strange sensation that I am feeling, like this is my comfort zone, having another exert power over me, and yet there is a bubbling underneath pushing me toward resistance.

Silence fills the space between us, heavy, lingering.

"Have you ever considered, even for a minute, that maybe this is not entirely my fault?" he says.

Not his fault.

I click my tongue.

"No, hear me out, Delilah. We haven't exactly been burning up the sheets of late. Or more like a while. I mean how long has it been?"

"Let's talk about fault, Ian," I snap. "Was I the one in the kitchen with the lotion? I can't remember. Remind me."

Ian's eye twitches. It is a telltale sign that he is angry. The vein on his neck bulges a little as it pulsates with blood, and his cheeks flush red. He is frustrated. I frustrate him. I know this, just as I know what is going to happen before it happens, even though it has never happened before. There is a vibration that signals it coming. I do not move an inch for fear that it would be in the wrong direction.

Squeezing his fingers into a white knuckled fist, Ian draws his arm back and releases, smashing his hand through the wall. My teeth rattle in response. And now there is a hole in the sheetrock.

A second later, realization washes over my husband's face. His eyes, which were hard and flat the moment prior, return to their usual softness. They fill with remorse.

"My God, Delilah, I'm sorry," he says as he backs off a little. "I shouldn't have done that. I don't know why I did that. I am under so much pressure lately. I'm sorry."

"Move your arm, Ian," I demand, because I am still caged.

Ian does not respond.

I sharpen my tone. "Ian, move your goddamn arm!"

"Okay, I know I fucked up," he says, "but this is crazy."

"Is it, though?" I reply.

"Why are you like this, Delilah? I don't want us to be like this. Give me a chance."

"Move your arm."

"What is wrong with you?" he spits, and a knot forms in my throat.

What is wrong with me?

It's always me.

We stare at each other at length.

Then my husband nods faintly as if he has come to a decision. "You know what? I'm done with this ridiculousness," he tells me. "Do you hear me? You're not going anywhere."

"Is that right?"

"People screw up, Delilah. It happens all of the time. But I love you. You know that I love you," he says.

Another long silence ensues.

"And you love me, Delilah. Pretend all you want. But you damn well do."

Do I?

The memory of us sitting outside Peter Pop's Ice

Cream Shop on Seventh Street, eating ice cream and laughing so hard our bellies ached, flashes through my head. It was our second date, mid-summer.

"Are you sure about that, Ian?" I ask him, coolly.

The quiet heightens all other sounds—humming refrigerator, clicking ceiling fan, chirping birds, rushing cars.

"Move your goddamn arm," I spit.

But Ian is a stubborn man. He leans closer to whisper in my ear. "You're being unreasonable, Delilah. You know that you are being unreasonable. Everyone does it. It's not a big deal."

I want to claw the skin off his face and gouge his beautiful blue eyes out with a spoon.

"Maybe to you, Ian. But to me..."

His breath is warm and moist on my neck. I smell the mint of his toothpaste and the faint medicine scent of his mouthwash.

But we haven't been burning up the sheets.

After a long pause, Ian pushes himself off the wall, grabs my keys and my suitcases and walks them upstairs. When he returns, empty handed, he takes me by my arm and leads me into the living room, where he sits me neatly on the couch. Then he pulls the occasional chair around to position himself in front of me. "Alright," he says. "Let's hash this out."

Neither of us utters a word.

It grows late then later still. Eventually, Ian pushes the chair back to its original location and fixes us something to eat. I refuse the food, shoving my plate to the side on the coffee table. He picks up the remote, clicks through the channels, and settles into his seat. This is our routine. The TV solves everything.

"I can cancel my business trip," he says right before

55

he shovels a wallop of food into his mouth.

"Why would you do that?" I ask him.

Ian turns the volume down on the television.

"I think you should go," I say. "Yeah, go. Consider it a trial separation."

His reaction is immediate. He leans forward with his elbows on his knees and his hands dangling toward the earth. At first he doesn't look at me. He doesn't say anything. He is too angry. But then his head lifts, slowly, and he holds me in his glare. "Give me a fucking break. Are you serious, Delilah?"

My expression answers for me.

Ian shakes his head. "You know what? Fuck it. Whatever."

He throws the remote, not so much at me as onto the couch. It ricochets and hits my leg.

Then Ian darts up the stairs and slams the bedroom door behind him. The ceiling trembles in response.

An uneasy quiet sets into place. I roll over onto my spine and stare at the knockdown plaster ceiling. There is a cobweb in the corner, but the spider that made it is inexplicably missing from view. Presumably it is hidden in a crevice somewhere, where others do not venture to go.

The sound of the television reaches my ears and draws my attention to the screen. I cannot hear my husband at all. He is noiseless in our bedroom.

I wipe my eyes with the top of my hand. The knot in my throat has thickened to the point where it is choking me. Ian is there, while I am here. I don't know him anymore. Hell, I don't know myself.

What is happening to me?

After a deep breath, my fingers crawl to the remote. I hold it for a while, watching without watching flickering images on the television screen. It is nothing but color.

I hear footsteps and the slamming of a door. Then I pull the old red throw blanket off the cushions on the couch and rest my head on it. Clinging to the tail for comfort, I curl up like a fetus. Communication is impossible. It's a heavily spiked cactus. The more you touch it, the more it hurts.

Keeping oneself sane is tedious work.

I turn the channel.

CHAPTER SIX

It is a little known fact that James Glenmore Westgrove, founder of the company for which I presently work, obtained the funds to begin his enterprise by conning his eighty-four year old grandmother out of her life savings. And as his business grew and flourished and the benefits rolled in by the truckload, James Glenmore Westgrove enjoyed the spoils of his deceit, while his sweet little grandmother suffered the great humiliation of being deposited against her will in one of the worst nursing homes in the county. The night Grandma Westgrove died she had a pressure wound on her back six inches in width and one inch in depth. Lying in her own piss and shit for hours, contracted into disfigurement, Grandma Westgrove was found by an intern. Three people attended her funeral. James Glenmore Westgrove was not one of them. Of course neither was I. But I am pretty sure the grapevine gossip is accurate on this one, as evidenced by the fact that the man is a dick.

Whatever the truth, James Glenmore Westgrove is the person I work for now, the owner and leader of the company that provides me with my living. When I allow myself to think about that, a sickness rises into my chest. But I am not concentrating on that now. I am staring blankly at the computer screen in my office, the same screen I have been staring at for hours, hating the only man I have ever truly trusted.

"We haven't exactly been burning up the sheets," I whisper.

The sonuvabitch.

The acid brewing and bubbling inside my stomach burns as hot as a scratched nerve. I can feel it in my throat.

The worst part, the part I hate to admit, is that Ian isn't wrong. Sonuvabitch or not, we haven't had intimate relations in months, more or less because every time he rolls over with that look in his eyes or climbs on top of me with sex on the brain, every time he brings up the topic, my body immediately shifts into autopilot and sings with resistance. It closes in Pavlovian response. The pleasure and the mystery have bled out over years of marriage, the passion as well, much like the connection and the communication between us. Sometimes I do what some call my wifely duties, but a lot of the time I employ the skill I have mastered above all others. Avoidance.

We haven't exactly been burning up the sheets. The fucker.

The thing my husband fails to recognize is that it is no different for him than it is for me. I see it. I feel it. But for the fact that he needs my body parts to achieve his goal, I could disappear from the equation altogether. The passion between us has dipped to an all-time low. Yet Ian complains and complains. If he took a moment to examine the situation a little more closely, as he damn well should, he might be surprised by the truth. Of course, truth is the first thing he opted out of in our relationship. The minute he turned every kiss into a semen deposit warning, the minute he tired of putting effort into pleasing me in that department—and I know I am exceedingly difficult to please—the minute it became solely and endlessly about him, sex became a chore for me. It became work. And after years of courtship and marriage, I'm fucking tired.

"Burning up the sheets," I whisper through gritted teeth. "Burning up the goddamn sheets."

I should have clawed his eyes out.

The door to my office is closed; however, I can still hear movement and conversations taking place in the hall. It is a stir out there. My boss is close to my present location. I can hear the sound of her voice. Ms. Suzanne Kline. As far as boss's go, she is not the worst; however, she is not the best either. Everything must suit her, benefit her. And she is a rather loud person, which often gets under my skin.

"You understand what I am saying, Delilah? It's not personal," she told me the other day after our sit-down. Extending the slack due to my mother's departure, Ms. Suzanne Kline decided not to write me up for missing yet another deadline. "But I expect more from you from now on. And for the record, it is no different anywhere else. Wherever you go, you will find it is all about profit maximization."

My work world is no better than my personal one at this point, not that my work world was better in the first place. But it is even worse now that James Glenmore Westgrove, our fearless multimillionaire leader, decided to bring in a group of consultants to clean house and increase productivity. The advisors or consultants—whatever you want to call them—have been so zealous in completing their task that they've come to be called the Butchers of Westgrove.

There are three of them: Harold Kesler, Bentley Price, and Nathaniel Martin.

Kesler reminds me of a soccer dad, tall and thin, balding at the crown. There is nothing remarkable about his face or presence, except maybe the kindness behind his light brown eyes. If I am not mistaken, the kindness demonstrates just how ill-fitted Kesler is for his job. I give it a week before he's out with half our staff.

Then there is Price, the opposite. The self-important metrosexual with thick black hair and rich hazel eyes takes great pleasure in delivering bad news. The deeper the cut to our workforce, the greater the injection of energy he seems to receive. When Price comes around, heads drop and fingers scurry across keyboards. Anxiety rises to unseen levels. There is fear in the air. Price is a royal bastard.

That leaves Nathaniel Martin, who falls in between the two on the butcher spectrum. Tall, slender, and muscular, Nathaniel is well-postured, well-polished, and despite his position, well-liked. Wherever Nathaniel goes there lingers a citrusy bergamot scent, a smell that is almost intoxicating.

I don't know what it is about Nathaniel, but I find myself intrigued by him. When he is near, the air leaves the room. The mystery he creates is like sadness without a source, yet not sadness at all, the opposite even. He fascinates me, and not because he is one of the Butchers of Westgrove. It is something else, something underneath, like a vibration.

Right now, the instability of Westgrove, Gardner, and Jones is palpable. Of course, the timing could not be worse, especially given the state of my marriage.

Every aspect of my life feels precarious. Added to the fact that I don't even know who I am anymore—*Dahlia instead of Delilah*—and there is no ground beneath my feet. Ian used to be my stability, my foundation. Now he and I have not spoken in days, not since he left on his business trip. Actually, that is not entirely correct. The quiet set in long ago. It is difficult to pinpoint exactly when.

So, here I am, sitting in front of my computer at

work, staring at a blank screen, inexplicably numb. My left eye twitches after I rub it. Tears trickle out from the corners. The burning in my eye reminds me of the gift my father gave me one drunken night, an interesting starburst hemorrhage made more noticeable by the white of my sclera. The damage took weeks to heal, and my eye has never been the same since.

A knock at the door wakes me from my stupor. While I dry my eye with the back of my hand, Nathaniel Martin enters the room. He does this even though I did not call for him to come inside.

After nudging the door closed with his elbow, he crosses the floor to land directly in front of my desk. Nathaniel is carrying two coffees, one for him and one for me. I don't know why, but it feels strange to be alone with him. I wish he had left the door ajar. My muscles tighten.

"How can I help you?" I say.

There is something about Nathaniel that picks at my brain. I can't quite place it.

With a click of a button, I pull an old spreadsheet up on my computer, hoping all the while Nathaniel does not get close enough to see that I have not done a lick of work all day. I am fucking up everywhere.

The failure.

The unwanted.

What the hell is wrong with me?

"Iced macchiato from Vinnie's?" he says before extending his arm to hand me one of the coffees.

Goddamn, he is a fine looking man!

Although I do not know what to make of his generosity, I accept the drink and respond with a hesitant, "Thank you."

Nathaniel walks around to my side of the desk, the side closest to the window; he half stands-half takes a seat on the edge. With his leg bent at the knee, he nudges my supplies over and nearly causes my files to spill off the corner. My curiosity is sparked by the brazenness of the act. After all, who makes himself comfortable like this? He doesn't know me. We're not close.

Nathaniel wets his lips lightly with his tongue, which causes his mouth to shimmer as though glossed. I suspect it is a habit, as indicated by the chapped outline.

I am attracted to him. I won't deny it. He is broad shouldered with finely chiseled features and sandy blond hair. Although he is masculine in manner and makeup, there is also something distinctly feminine in his look. Perhaps it is the shape of his lips, which are fuller than most, or his perfect porcelain skin.

"Delilah," he says. "You don't mind me calling you Delilah, do you?"

Do I?

"Let me ask you something."

Nathaniel has never used my first name before. It almost sounds strange coming from his mouth.

I wait for the question in silence.

He seems to read my thoughts. "Oh, I hope you don't mind me sitting here like this. It doesn't bother you or make you uncomfortable, does it?"

I fail to reply.

The Butcher of Westgrove is in my office. He is in my office and sitting on my desk, not two inches away from my hand. And there is no easy way for me to respond to his questions. Of course, it makes me uncomfortable. His very presence makes me uncomfortable. After all, he is the Butcher, and I need my job. Plus, he has a sculpted face that makes most women stupid.

"How do you feel about the changes around here?" he asks.

How do I feel?

What am I supposed to say? That the carnage is a bit much? He should pack up his shit and go home? His partners should as well? It feels like a test.

"I don't know. Fine, I guess. Why?"

Nathaniel narrows his eyes as he smiles. Then he takes a sip of his coffee and performs a visual sweep of the room, while I fidget with my pen.

"You have one of the better offices," he tells me. "Or at least one of the better views of the cars outside."

I attempt to match his smile with one of my own; however, it feels forced.

Then Nathaniel moves around to my rear and peeks over my shoulder. "What are you working on?"

As quickly as possible, I minimize the outdated electronic file on my computer and turn the screen to the side as I say, "It wouldn't interest you. Besides, I am still in the middle of a project, so I would rather...you know."

Repositioning himself on my desk, Nathaniel says, "Will you be at Don's sendoff on Friday?"

"Where is it again? I can't seem to remember."

"The Paper Nickel."

The Paper Nickel.

I nod slowly. "Yeah, I don't know. I'm not really much for those things. Maybe."

Nathaniel catches sight of the scars on the palm of my hand. Embarrassed, I hide my hands under the desk, where the darkness protects them from further examination.

He smiles again. And I have to admit that it is a good smile, the kind of smile that makes you want to do the same.

Then he takes another sip of his coffee and eyes the art on the wall behind my desk.

"You did this?" he asks.

I nod.

"Nice." He pauses briefly. "I think you should attend," he tells me. "If only to get to know your coworkers better."

What the fuck is he talking about?

"I know my coworkers." After all, I have worked at Westgrove, Gardner, and Jones for years.

Nathaniel frowns as he studies me. "How many office functions outside of work have you attended in the last two years, Delilah?"

This is bullshit. I am paid to do a job, not socialize.

"I don't know. Why?"

A short silence ensues before Nathaniel says, "You are not so introverted that you cannot come to a going away party. After all, Don has been a loyal employee to the organization. He deserves a proper sendoff. And it is important that workers support each other. Don't you think?"

I do not respond. It is not that I have anything against Don; it's more that I find gatherings exhausting. Plus, Nathaniel is being hypocritical. How many employees has he let go that have not received proper sendoffs or support?

He walks around to the other side of the room. On the easternmost wall, there are floor to ceiling bookshelves. Nathaniel spots a book that he likes and flips through the pages. It happens to be from my personal collection— Catcher in the Rye. When I was young, I would sometimes imagine myself in Holden Caulfield's world. I would even pretend to be the roller skate skinny girl.

Light streams through the thin glass window to cut across Nathaniel's legs and shoes, while tiny dust particles float as pale golden specks in the air.

"You should definitely find a way to attend on Friday," Nathaniel tells me as he continues to finger through the pages of the book. And when finally he turns his attention to me, he adds, "It'll be fun."

There is a stone award on my desk, six inches tall and four inches wide, round with a square base. After returning the book to its rightful location, Nathaniel decides to pick up the award. He examines it briefly before he says, "How long ago did you get this?"

"I don't know. A while ago." Before my work took a dive.

"It is much heavier than it looks."

I nod in agreement. Once I dropped the damn thing on my toe and had to have the blood drained from under my toenail.

Nathaniel returns the stone award to my desk then shoves his hands into his pockets and simply stares at me. "Alright then," he says. "I guess I'll leave you to it. Time to make more of those." He lifts his chin to indicate that he is referring to the award. This is his way of putting pressure on me, I believe. "If you need any help..."

Nathaniel doesn't make it to the door before he turns and adds, "Delilah, you take your lunch at the park by the river on Mondays, don't you?"

"Usually, yes."

"Good, I would like to join you today."

Shit.

I fail to respond.

"Around one," he says. "See you then."

What can I do? I can't exactly say no.

An hour later, I am sitting on a bench in front of the river with gilded clouds overhead and the afternoon sun coppering my skin. Nathaniel is sitting next to me, slightly more than a fraction too close, while the thin aroma of watermelon laces the air and mixes with Nathaniel's citrusy scent. He looks out at the diamond crested river and remarks about how much he loves the area. Then he places what is left of his lunch to the side in order to give me his undivided attention. Of course, he is smiling. Nathaniel smiles a lot, almost an inordinate amount.

"What?" I say in response to him staring at me.

I don't know why, but the way he is looking at me reminds me of the way Ian used to look at me when we were young. I suddenly feel uncomfortable.

"We should probably head back now," I say. Then I stand to throw the rest of my lunch in the nearby receptacle, a large pale blue garbage bin bolted to two four-by-fours that are cemented to the ground.

"Delilah," Nathaniel says in a soft voice.

I take a moment before turning around. And even when I do, I do it slowly. "Yes?"

"Nothing."

He smiles. Only, there is sadness in it.

"Don't take this the wrong way," he says, "but you look—"

"What?"

"Beautiful."

Reading my thoughts, Nathaniel adds a second later, "Your husband is a lucky man."

"Yeah, well..."

We haven't exactly been burning up the sheets.

CHAPTER SEVEN

Time is the black pit of despondency. And night is its keeper. There is sound to the night, as there is sound to the cutting void, labored yet quiet, like the slow breathing of a dying child. The sound surrounds me in loneliness and monotony. It keeps my mind from settling and my body from falling asleep. Despite my protestations, my brain collects thoughts from the darkest of its layers then weaves those thoughts together into an unforgiving tapestry of anxiety and despair. I am the festering wound of all that is unwanted and unloved. I am the rejected soul, jettisoned by those around me. I am also changed. When it happened, I do not know. But I feel the difference.

The alarm rings shortly before day pours through my bedroom windows. I do not roll over and slap it off as I typically do but instead remain immobile, planted with my shoulder blades pinned to the mattress and my eyes wide open. My fingers explore the fine veining on my coverlet as well as the empty side of my bed. The alarm runs its course until it stops. Then silence reigns. And the sound of breathing—my breathing, *singular*—fills the air.

The alarm goes off again. This time I pull the covers to the side, climb out of bed, and stumble in the dark to the master bathroom, where I perform my morning rituals with machine-like efficiency. Everything I do is routine. It is mechanical. You could crack open my skull and remove my brain and my body would still function on cue. It would still complete each and every habitual task without pause. I move slowly like I am sedated.

Am I sedated?

After a shower, I brush my teeth, coat on moisturizer, and pull up my hair. Then I put on my makeup and slide into my clothes. Slipping on my shoes, I take a beat before standing in front of the full length mirror.

There is nothing about me that I like. Not a single goddamn thing. The items in my line of sight are shrouded in what looks like the gray murk of ground water; at least that is how it seems. Of course, I have on gray. The world is so dull you could scrape the lead off it with a knife. It begs the question: Was there a time life wasn't so bland? I wonder if I was ever happy, if the moments I remember with fondness were real or in a dream far removed.

No, Ian and I were happy once. We were in love.

We were, weren't we?

My eyes feel gritty. It is the one inconstant in the stream of constants. I swipe at them with the back of my hand and yawn from exhaustion even though my sleep was less disturbed last night than usual.

Sensing it is going to be a long day, I brew a batch of coffee in the kitchen and watch it percolate as the edge of the counter digs fresh craters into my spine. Then I pour the coffee into a tumbler, climb into my car, and prepare to head off to work. It is the last place I want to go right now, not that I ever truly want to go. But this is how you pay your mortgage. It is how you get your food. One's job is also what is used to measure success.

What a fucking warped world we live in!

Freedom is an illusion.

And yet I still want to be free.

The viscosity of sleeplessness slows my mind and movements. It also slows my reaction time and nearly causes me to get into a collision on the highway. If I had gotten into an accident, it would not have been my fault but that of the driver of a silver pickup. He is bastard of a man, large and dark-eyed, yelling, waving his hands. The sonuvabitch missed me by an inch, veering into my lane without regard. Then he had the audacity to pretend that I was in the wrong.

It feels like my nerves are on the outside of my body, exposed to the elements. I won't deny that I am in a precarious state. If you add a pin to the wrong side of the scales that balance me, I will completely tip over.

Horns blow.

People scream for me to get out of the passing lane.

Back at you, you stupid cunt!

Some guy in a white button down curses me out through the glass window of his vehicle, while cars whip by me with alarming speed.

I pull off onto the shoulder and strangle the steering wheel, knuckles bone white. The up and down movement of my chest is more perceptible now. The excess oxygen leaves me lightheaded, so I have to close my eyes.

There is nowhere I fit in this world.

I am the perpetual outsider.

But then a single word creeps into my head, and I say it aloud, barely more than a whisper: "Beautiful."

He finds me beautiful.

I don't know what it is; there is something about Nathaniel that makes him different. And for whatever reason, he seems to have taken a liking to me. It shouldn't matter, but it does. It has been a long time since anyone has seen me as anything other than a wife or a worker. A long time since I have heard that word, even if it is a lie. Which it is. I am not beautiful. At best, I reside at the high end of average.

After my head clears, I take a deep breath and return to the highway, where the traffic has died down a bit. The slight tremor in my hand is still there, but I am able to drive without issue. The road hums a soothing yet distant sound, like a promise that has not yet been given. The traffic lightens even more. It allows the tension in my shoulders to subside.

At the corner of my exit, I find a homeless man with a sign that reads: *Need bus ticket.* He is worn of the face and long in the tooth; however, his clothes are clean, and he holds himself like a warrior. Maybe he is a veteran. Or maybe he's just been in the thick of it. Either way, it doesn't matter. I pull a five out of my wallet, wait for him to notice me, and give him the money.

He flashes a set of rotted teeth. "God bless you," he says, snatching the money out of my hand as though he believes I might take back the charity. His teeth are as green as they are black, probably from methamphetamine use.

"Thank you," I reply, faintly, before rolling up my window and continuing on down the road.

I want to be good.

I want to be the type of person who does good.

Am I?

Because I am running late for work, all of the best parking spots are gone. The only ones left are in the dreaded garage with its shadowy center and invisible corners, unmonitored levels. The parking garage of Westgrove, Gardner, and Jones is the place where a serial rapist targeted three women a few years ago. No matter the weather, the garage feels cold and damp, dark, and it stinks like moldy wallpaper.

My right eye smarts from the grit that has wedged itself deep under my eyelid. Again, I swipe at my eye with the top of my hand then blink profusely as the tears swell and drip down my face.

The smell of precipitation is in the air. After exiting my vehicle, I walk over to where I can look out at the darkening clouds and take note of how they threaten to fill the valley like a basin.

Sometimes I like the rain. I like the tinking sound it makes against glass and metal. The rest of the time, though, it only makes the world cold and dark.

Today feels like it is shaping up to be a dark day.

Everything is gray, the people of Westgrove, Gardner, and Jones included. They are hustling and bustling, swarming about like flitting flies. And it is all thanks to the Butchers. The very air inside the building is heavy as lead.

Still, Nathaniel thinks I'm beautiful.

Does he want me?

Will he try to keep me from harm?

Is he the type of man who jacks off in a kitchen?

A part of me wants to explore what the comment means.

Taking the elevator up to the fifth floor, I cut around the center cubicles to make a beeline to my office. My goal is to arrive unseen, but of course Jane Furlough is waiting for me in the hallway. Leaning with her hip against my office door, she has her arms crossed over a clipboard.

Jane is a plain woman, not ugly, just unremarkable with short dark hair that she consistently cuts into a traditional mom style. Her eyes are lackluster brown, her lips pale and small, made smaller by the facial expressions she favors. There is an insignificant beauty mark under the corner of her lip on the right side.

Although I would not call us friends so much as acquaintances, I like Jane. She is a sweet person. Never in the history of humanity has there existed one less inclined to cause harm.

Actually, Jane does gossip a bit from time to time. But it is only to connect with others, not to spread hate. At least, that is how I see her. Jane is a gentle soul. A pinprick of cruelty can bring her to tears. Today, though, she looks invigorated, if not outright chatty.

"Good morning, Jane," I say as I push my office door open to let us inside.

Jane follows me into the room. Although she is not heavy, her heels against the carpet make an echoing sound.

I drop my keys into my bag and my bag into one of the desk drawers then sit down behind my desk, while Jane closes the door behind us.

Moving slowly toward the end of the room, Jane's facial expression gives away her thoughts. She wants something. I can tell. Instead of making her struggle, I say, "What can I do for you, Jane?"

As if on cue, she flashes a smile. "You can say yes, Delilah." Then Jane sets her clipboard on the chair to her right and bites her bottom lip. "I know how you hate workplace functions, but I would be grateful if you would put that aside and come with me to Don's sendoff.

Oh, no, not another one.

"I don't want to go alone or with anyone who is going," she says. And after a pause, she adds, "Please, Delilah, I need you there. If only for support."

"It isn't mandatory, Jane."

As the words exit my mouth, an idea tickles the rear of my brain. What if someone else put Jane up to this?

I'm probably reaching.

Of course I'm reaching.

Rounding the chair in front of her, Jane sits down. Unlike Nathaniel, she keeps it professional by remaining on the opposite side of my desk. The computer monitor partially obstructs her view, so she scoots her chair to the side, once, then twice, until I am completely in her line of sight and she is in mine.

"All set now, Jane?" I say, teasingly.

"You know what I have been going through at home, Delilah," she tells me. Of course I do. Despite the fact that I have never asked Jane a personal question, she tells me everything. I even know the name of her favorite childhood pets—Leviticus and Nazareth.

"You mean the fact that you are married to a man-child?"

"Exactly," she says.

I want to help her, I do, but I hate workplace functions.

"Delilah, please," she says to drive her point home.

A conflict brews inside my stomach. Jane is a nice person; however, every cell in my body is screaming in resistance. "Why can't you ask Carmen or Ginger or someone else?"

Jane scoots forward in her seat. "Carmen is out of town."

"Ginger then?"

"There is no one else, Delilah," Jane tells me. "And if you do this for me, I promise I will never ask for another thing. Not one."

Only, Jane hardly asks for anything now, so the promise does not amount to much of an incentive.

"Why do you want to go so badly?"

"To get out of the house. Have some adult time." After an extended silence, she adds, "I just want to be normal."

Normal. Does it really exist?

"The thing is I am sort of going through some stuff, Jane," I tell her.

"Do you want to talk about it?"

A shake of my head serves as my response.

There is a migraine forming at the base of my skull. It runs up the side of my face. Pressing my fingers against my temples, I clamp my teeth shut; however, it only serves to exacerbate the problem.

"You can bring Ian," Jane says, as if the act will make all the difference. "A lot of spouses will be there, I think."

"He is away on a business trip," I reply coolly as I shift some files around.

Jane's expression changes, but she chooses not to ask questions. Instead, she says, "Don's sendoff is at the Paper Nickel." A community favorite with waterfront views, live music, and Hampton style nautical atmosphere.

"Jane—"

"I need this," she tells me as she places her hand on my desk. "Jim and I, well, we...Please, Delilah."

The dull throb inside my head becomes an aggressive hammer. I want to be alone. I need to be alone. *Go away.*

"Let me think about it, Jane, okay?"

Rather than push, Jane picks up her clipboard and heads for the door. Stopping short, she turns around and adds one last, "You'll let me know then?"

I nod.

"By the end of the day, Delilah?"

"Jane."

"Alright, alright."

As the door shuts behind her, I drop my head into my hands and close my eyes. The pain has already spread from my temples and base of my neck to my entire skull, while the muscles of my shoulders continue to stiffen. Fishing my cellphone out of my handbag, I check for messages.

There are none.

I swipe at the grit in my eye with the back of my hand before attempting to work.

Then Jacob Wallace decides to pay me a visit. Wallace is average in almost every way, maybe 5'10" or 5'11", with dark brown hair. He has a square, masculine chin and a bottom lip that is noticeably larger than the top. Usually, Wallace and I get along, but today he is all teeth and noise. I am being given an earful about some electronic files that I moved without his permission, not that I needed his permission in the first place. He is not my boss, though higher in the ranking system.

Everyone in the building is on buzz now. The presence of the Butchers has made the atmosphere tense.

But he thinks I'm beautiful.

"How many times do I have to repeat myself, Delilah?" Wallace says. "You know what's going on around here."

And on and on he goes. Only I stop hearing him on account of the ringing in my ears. It sounds like flies. I don't remember leaving my seat, but I must have done so because I am standing in front of Wallace, whose lips are smacking together in a way that reminds me of my father.

The anger.

The scowl.

When men raise their voices around me, it creates a separation of a kind. And every once in a while, like presently, I am thrust back to the day I left my pink-eared bunny next to the glass turtle ashtray on the table behind the green door. The only difference is my memory is not of my bunny but color.

I feel like I am going to fall down the stairs.

The hammering inside my skull strengthens.

My fingernails dig fresh tunnels in my palms.

And all the while, there is a pungent, fermented odor saturating the air. The stench grows stronger and stronger still, until I can hardly breathe. I am choking on the putrid stink.

Looking past Wallace, I see green polish slide from the top of my office door to the bottom then puddle and spread across the floor. Peering down a long black tunnel, I find the green door vibrating, slowly at first, then with increasing intensity. Sickness rises from my stomach into my throat.

The doorknob rattles.

And rattles.

He is waiting for me on the other side. I know this because I can feel him out there.

My pink-eared bunny wants to get in.

There is a faraway noise. The sound of violence, pain.

Then, from a distance, I hear my name.

And hear it again.

As the voice calls out to me, I feel the pressure of a hand on my forearm. Suddenly, I am plunged into the present moment. Jacob Wallace is holding me by my arms. The green door is gone, and the polish on the walls and floors. Wallace is standing so close to me I can feel his breath on my skin.

"What just happened, Delilah?" he asks. "Should I get you some water?"

My skin feels clammy.

The room looks abnormal, like it hasn't been set back into place correctly.

Everyone is against me.

I am the unwanted.

I am the unloved.

"Do you need to sit down?"

Tearing my arm away from his grip, I say, coolly, "If you don't mind."

"Sorry," Wallace says. "I am just trying to help."

"Yes, well, it has been a long day, Jacob. I'll be sure to let you know before I move the electronic files again." After a pause, I add, "So, are we done here?"

Only, Wallace doesn't leave. Instead, he eyes me strangely.

A knock at the door breaks the tension.

Nathaniel Martin materializes without anyone inviting him into the room. "Do you have a minute?" he asks me.

My response is slow in the coming. I nod.

"We'll talk about this later," Wallace says.

"No, it's alright, I got it," I reply.

A second later, I am alone with Nathaniel, and he is looking at me the way Ian used to look at me when we were young.

Does he really find me beautiful?

"I figured you could use a hand," he tells me. "I sort of heard the two of you down the hall, not that I usually get involved. Anyway, I was wondering if—"

My cellphone buzzes on my desk. "I'm sorry, Nathaniel, but I have been waiting for my husband's call all day." For several days.

Nathaniel excuses himself from the room before I pick up the phone. "What do you want, Ian?"

"You're angry?"

"You think?"

It is awkward between us now.

"We need to work this out, Delilah."

Closing my eyes, I sit in the chair behind my desk and, with my elbows on the top, rest my forehead against my hand. The bottle of painkillers in my desk drawer is empty.

"What happened to us?" Ian asks.

It takes a moment for me to answer. "The hell if I know."

"Do you ever think about when we first met?" he says. "Our first date? The heater in my truck?"

His truck.

"You loved that truck."

"Yeah. Yeah, I did. Never found one like her again."

My response is immediate and cold. I can't help myself. The images of my husband's extracurricular activities are too fresh in my head. I can practically smell the semen in the air. "Maybe you shouldn't have traded it in then."

"Delilah—"

"What?"

He does not respond for a long time. "So, this is what you want? For us to be separated?"

Even though it was my idea, it feels like a sledgehammer to my chest. "Yes, Ian. It's what I want."

"Delilah—"

"I have to go," I tell him. My voice cracks a little.

"Can I call you later?"

"I'm at work. I have to go."

Before Ian can say another word, I hang up the phone. Then I march over to Jane's office and, bursting through the door, say, "We're on for Friday night."

It takes a minute for Jane to process my statement. "Great, yeah, wonderful. I'll drive. Eight okay?"

After a nod, I close the door behind me.

Moments later, I head to the parking garage, where it is cold and damp. Outside the sky is leaden. With the engine of my car running, I clutch the steering wheel and, feeling a torrential downpour well on its way, close my eyes and cry.

It can't get any worse, I tell myself.

Right?

CHAPTER EIGHT

The male spider mite, when given the opportunity to choose between a live female sexual partner and an infected dead one, prefers the dead. I feel as though I have a million spider mites scurrying under my skin right now.

Jane and I are not far from the Paper Nickel, maybe ten minutes or so. She taps her fingers against the steering wheel before she puts on her blinker. The radio is on one of our favorite stations. We are rock fans, lovers of music from the 1970s and 1980s, as well as the music of today, even though I am sick of hearing Nickelback and Linkin Park.

Jane looks at me sideways. "You should wear your hair down more often," she says as she yanks the wheel to round the corner of Idle Lane and 6th Street. The girl is heavy on the gas and doesn't slow for turns. I have to hold the door handle in order to keep from sliding toward the driver's seat. "Seriously, though, Delilah," she adds a second later, "you look amazing."

I cannot say that I agree with her assessment. My makeup does little to nothing to hide the purple pools under my eyes. And my eyes themselves are bloodshot from lack of sleep. If I have anything going for me, it is my hair, which is hydrated by product, the long tendrils dripping over my shoulders to the center of my back. I am a mass of dark curls.

Looking out the passenger window, I take in the sight of the evening. Cars and buildings and lights flash by as whips of color. It is a strange night. There is a quiet over the land. I can feel something in the air, something deep in my bones. It penetrates like the bite of the cold.

It can't get any worse, right?

The song changes on the radio. Jane turns up the volume. Honestly by Stryper comes on. Right away my attention shifts to the audio system, and I experience a sharp pang in my chest.

Ian used to love this band. In my mind's eye, I can still see him in his favorite graphic Stryper t-shit, joking around. He would wear that thing all the time, wear it to holes. The song conjures up the memory of Ian and me sitting in his old pickup truck. The radio was on then, too. Ian turned up the volume the same way that Jane turned it up a moment ago. Smiling, he began to sing, softly at first, but then louder and louder still. What a horrible voice he had, and has presently. Things were different then. Ian was different, lighter, sillier. I was different, too. We laughed so hard that night my gut nearly split, and I peed a little in my pants.

I wonder what he is doing right now.

My fingernails dig new tracks in my palms. I smell the faint scent of blood. I don't want to think about Ian anymore. I don't want to think about the past. But I can't stop remembering how he used to paw at me—tickling touching, caressing, grabbing, pulling—and the way he would reach over and brush his index finger softly down the side of my cheek and neck.

What happened to us?

Of course, I already know. He traded his old pickup truck in for a brand new four door with shiny rims and better gas mileage. *The sonuvabitch.*

It starts to drizzle outside. Jane flips on her windshield wipers. Back and forth the rubber blades go to create a swooshing sound that gives a dreamlike feel to the moment.

I close my eyes and see my husband pulling bedcovers over the top of us on a rainy day. Curling up beside me in bed, close then closer still, my husband whispers in my ear. I feel his breath warm and moist on my skin, see us walling ourselves up in our bedroom and binge watching our favorite shows as the day wastes away. And I see us making love until our bodies ache and we collapse from exhaustion.

Only those days are gone. Now Ian beats off to porn, while I sleep alone or lay wide awake fighting the thoughts in my head.

Jane slows to a stop in front of a traffic light. A second later, the drizzle transforms into a full-fledged rain. I like the sound of it against Jane's car. I like how it forms baby pools on top of her hood. The world can be dreamily dizzying sometimes.

We proceed.

The rain picks up speed; however, the storm is short lived. It turns out to be nothing more than a tossed a water bomb.

"Delilah, did you hear me?" Jane asks.

After her voice registers in my head, I look her way.

"Are you okay?" she inquires. "You don't seem like yourself. What's going on with you?" When I do not reply, Jane adds, "What is it, Delilah? You can talk to me? You know that, right? You've been distant lately."

Lately?

"Have I?" I say.

We hit another traffic light, which turns green in a

beat. Jane shoves her foot against the accelerator, and we are propelled down the road toward our final destination.

The lights on the Paper Nickel catch my eye before we actually arrive there. Jane makes a left to pull into the establishment's parking lot. The place is packed from end to end. In fact, it is more than packed; it is overflowing. Even the bare spots on the grass have been taken. So, Jane and I drive around in search for a place to park her vehicle. When nothing materializes, we drive around some more.

"Maybe it is a sign," I tell her.

"Don't be silly, Delilah," she says.

No sooner do these words leave her mouth than a couple holding hands exit the restaurant and make their way to their car, a shiny blue Jaguar.

Jane leans forward in her seat, ready, impatient. She isn't going to let anyone get her spot. A stalker in expensive boots. She follows the couple to the last row on the right.

Then we wait.

And we wait.

And we wait.

Apparently, the two are not in a rush to surrender their parking spot.

Jane slams her hand again her car horn.

"Jane!" I say, surprised.

"What? It's rude."

Fair enough. It is.

When finally the couple stops playing around and leaves, Jane pulls forward to reverse into the open space. She then cuts the engine on her vehicle and prepares to exit the car.

I hesitate, however, slowed by the image near us. There is a streetlight casting a long accusatory finger in the form of a shadow our way. The shadow is pointing directly at me. I cannot move. It feels like the universe is warning me of something awful to come, something destructive or deadly.

Failing to notice any of this, Jane hops out of her car and stands in front of the vehicle, leaning against the side.

Popping the passenger door open, I get out of the car as well, only gradually. My ears are immediately assaulted by a mixture of music, laughter, conversation, movement, dishes, and inebriation. The cacophony makes my muscles tighten and my mouth go dry.

I shouldn't be here.

I know I shouldn't be here.

Jane drops her handbag onto the hood of her vehicle then rummages through the center of the bag for some lip gloss.

"You look great," I tell her, and I mean it. She must have ironed her hair before picking me up because it is glossy smooth, like silk. Jane has on her good jeans, too, her best jeans, and a sweet little blazer along with a rather expensive trendy pair of three inch brown leather boots.

"Thank you for coming out tonight," she says. "It means a lot to me, Delilah."

If I were to have a friend in this world, other than Ian, then Jane would be my person. But I'm not great with friends. I am not great with people in general. They take work.

Still, I feel for Jane. She is in a marriage where she is the single mother of a grown man as well as two children. I'm not sure who has it worse, her or me.

Smiling, I nod.

I follow Jane up the stairs of the Paper Nickel and into a cloud of body heat and conversation. Right away there is a parade of faces staring back at me. Mops of hair separated into clumps. Eyes. Teeth. Noise. Movement.

The stimuli are overwhelming my senses.

Jane and I have to nudge our way around this person and that person, our bodies brushing against strangers in the process.

We proceed deeper into the room. No one moves out of the way. If anything, the space tightens. And all the while, my palms sweat. My heart hammers violent beats against the bones of my chest. I feel the blood in my veins, coursing.

Jane takes us straight back to the far end of the building, then out onto the patio where fresh air offers a moment of reprieve. The majority of the Westgrove, Gardner, and Jones employees are not outside. They are inside at the main bar or in the room with the live music. But there are a few out here, scattered about in human clumps.

I perform a scan of familiar faces. I work with these people every day yet know nothing about them. It might seem strange if not for the shield put up by business walls, cubicles, conversations, acquisitions, collections, and electronic files.

"Jane, maybe we should go back inside," I say because I suddenly feel uncomfortable. At least the live music offers distraction.

She looks at me sideways. Instead of responding verbally, she takes me by the hand and smiles. "It is only one night, Delilah," she tells me. "Relax. Enjoy yourself."

Enjoy yourself.

The patio is the most popular spot at the Paper Nickel, mainly because of its waterfront view. Typically umbrellas shield tables from the scarring burns of the sun, but it is evening now, and the umbrellas are closed up for the night. The sky is a deep shade of ink black. Ten foot iron posts boast fabric that pools at the bottom and flutters softly in the breeze. I look around. The rain seems to have missed the Paper Nickel altogether. Everything appears dry and clean, white and blue and beautifully crisp.

There is a small bar at the far end of the patio. It looks portable, a chunk of wood and bamboo set at a diagonal in the corner. Behind the bar, manning it, is a hard-edged woman with a pixie cut and thick black bracelets. Over her left breast of her cotton white tee shirt is an embroidered emblem that reads: Paper Nickel.

"There they are." Jane says right before she yanks my arm out of its socket.

The next thing I know, we are standing in front of the table of Westgrove, Gardner, and Jones employees. At first, I fail to see Nathaniel. Others are blocking him from my view. But then Nathaniel stands up to greet us, and something odd tickles in my stomach, scratches at my brain.

I shouldn't be here.

It is interesting to see my co-workers outside of the office. They look different, more relaxed. Most are dressed casually yet somehow remain polished in appearance. I glance around the table. And glassy eyes stare back at me.

Nathaniel attempts to offer me his seat, but Jane says, "Oh, no, that's okay. We'll take that spot over there. Thank you."

She grabs my hand again and leads me to the small opening lodged between the table and exterior wall of the main building. It is like navigating through a triangle of rock during a storm. We have to fight our way past legs and handbags, hisses and moans, until finally reaching the opening and plopping down in our respective seats. Now Nathaniel is across from me, one seat over, directly in front of Jane. I can feel his eyes on me as I try to look at everyone else but him.

Beautiful.

When I finally muster the courage to lock eyes with Nathaniel, he smiles. It is a good smile, the kind of smile that makes you want to do the same.

"Have you eaten?" Jane asks me. "Because I'm famished."

Jane is always famished, though. Her metabolism is phenomenal.

My stomach tightens into knots, while my palms smart from having been assaulted by my fingernails. I do not reply to Jane's question but instead examine the crowd at the Paper Nickel. The place is packed from end to end.

"At least the weather is warming," Ginger says.

But the night still holds a chill. It is the precarious time between seasons. The flames on the citronella torches flicker in the wind, while swarms of moths and other bugs surround exterior white lights.

The table at which we are seated fits twelve with no current openings. There are four on one side, four on the other, and two on each end. Starting on the left across from me and running clockwise, we have Yvonne, Nathaniel, Fredrick, Sabella, Ginger, Elizabeth, Milo, me, Jane, Don, Chino, and Eve. The rest of our coworkers are in different locations around the restaurant. I saw them when Jane and I entered the building.

Ginger turns her attention my way. Then she focuses on the table, while Elizabeth sips on a Long Island Iced Tea, and Eve appears to be searching for a more interesting group to join. There are rounds of empty and half empty glasses all over the place. I can smell the sick stench of liquor in the air, along with that faint but detectable odor of death in the ocean.

Why have I come?

"Can I get either of you a drink?" Nathaniel asks before pushing himself into a standing position.

As a child of an alcoholic, I am not a big fan of spirits. However, at this same time, in this place, and given the whirlwind in my head, not to mention the spider mites under my skin, I decide to partake. Plus Jane eggs me on by saying, "Go on. You deserve it, Delilah. Enjoy yourself."

Then Jane turns to Nathaniel and says, "Nothing for me, thanks. I'm driving." A second later, she adds, "Actually, make it a diet Coke. Thank you."

I haven't had a drink in years. I haven't had a need. So, I ask for recommendations.

"Seven and Seven," Ginger says. "Trust me." It is also called a highball.

I nod for that one.

Before Nathaniel walks away to take care of our orders, Yvonne pushes her chair back dramatically and says, "Aren't you going to ask me what I want?" Her tone is harsh, snappish.

Everything stops.

Then a slow smile washes over Nathaniel's mouth, even though there is something detectibly contrary in his eyes. He looks at me before returning his attention to Yvonne. "Sure. What can I get you, Yvonne? A Seven and Seven as well?"

What was that look about?

For an extended beat, Yvonne simply sits there, daggering Nathaniel with her stare. That is until she snatches her handbag off the ground and storms off to disappear in the crowd.

One of the men at our table cracks a joke. I don't catch which one. Everyone laughs except me.

An hour, I promise myself. *That's it. One hour and you can go home. You can do an hour.*

"Well, folks," Elizabeth says. "It's been a pleasure, but I think it is time for us to be hitting the road."

"We've only just arrived," Jane replies.

"Yes, I know. You'll have to forgive me," Elizabeth says. "Milo and I have early plans. Don't we, Milo?" Elizabeth pulls her purse strap over her shoulder before adding, "You coming, Ginger?"

Milo never breathes a word, but Ginger says, "Oh, yeah, okay."

The next thing I know our party is reduced to nine.

And Frederick changes seats for more room.

Then Jacob Wallace shows up to slap himself in the chair across from me. He looks different in his casual clothes, less intimidating, more appealing, almost boyish. His eyelashes seem thicker, longer, darker. In this atmosphere, under this light, he is upgraded to handsome. But I can smell the liquor on his breath a mile away. I can smell it across the table.

Just the person I want to see.

Wallace eyes me for a beat before he finally says, softly, like the conversation is only between us, even though there are others around, "I didn't expect to find you here."

"And I didn't expect to find you."

The conversation at our table begins to lull, so in an attempt to bring it to life once more, Wallace decides to tell a joke. "Here it is," he says, his eyes fixed on me. "Okay, listen, listen. There is a black woman, Asian, Mexican, and Caucasian heading into a hotel."

I look over at Fredrick, who is African American. Fredrick slowly sets his beer bottle down on the table and sits a little straighter. He also leans forward slightly in his seat.

"The Maître D' sees the four, runs to the kitchen, and says, 'Get me some watermelon, rice, enchiladas, and tofu. Make it quick.' Then the Maître D' returns to the front and—"

Nathaniel arrives with the drinks. Thankfully everyone forgets all about Wallace's joke, even Wallace.

"I heard you are staying on permanently," Wallace says to Nathaniel after Nathaniel settles into his seat.

"Yeah, maybe, I don't know," Nathaniel replies. "I'm thinking about it." He looks up and smiles at me.

Now it makes sense that Nathaniel is here. He is on the verge of becoming one of us, while the other Butchers are at home, uninvited, or packing their bags to leave. And even if Nathaniel wasn't becoming one of us, people like him. It is his charisma, his confidence.

Jane has been laboring over the menu this whole time, almost since we arrived. "I think I'm going to have a burger," she says, finally. But when she tries to flag down a waiter, she can't find one, so she grabs her cellphone and her wallet, leaves her purse on her chair next to me, and heads off to put her order in at the portable bar.

Meanwhile, I take a sip of my drink. A highball is supposed to be composed of an alcoholic base with a larger portion of soda. Mine tastes like pure alcohol, save for a hint of mixer.

"Where's what's his face?" Wallace asks.

It takes me a second to realize that he is talking to me. "You mean my husband? He's out of town on a business trip."

"He travels a lot, doesn't he?" exotic Sabella says. And I am surprised that she knows this. "I imagine it must be difficult. I would hate jumping from hotel to hotel."

Difficult, yes.

Rather than respond, I take another sip of my drink.

Wallace laughs.

"What?" I say.

He shakes his head, scratches it.

Then Jane returns. And right away I know that something is wrong. "I'm sorry," she tells me. "The sitter is sick and so is Lela." Lela is Jane's youngest, a curly head mini-monster with the sweetest giggle in the world. I don't hold it against her for having a name similar to my sister's. (Lela and Lillian.) "She is running a 102° fever," Jane adds. "Any chance you can catch a ride home with someone else?"

Nathaniel immediately offers his services.

Jane thanks him before I have a chance to accept.

"I'm so sorry," Jane says again before leaving. Then she hugs me against my will, and my entire body tightens in response.

"Don't worry about it, Jane," I reply in effort to be kind. "Let me know if you need anything or if I can be of any help."

Eve and Chino follow Jane out the door a few minutes later. The numbers around here are dwindling, not only outside, but inside as well. Now there is some negative space.

A game starts up. It's where one person gives the name of a celebrity then the next person uses the first letter of the celebrity's name to give the name of a different celebrity and so on down the line.

Sabella says, "Alexis Arquette."

The men grumble in unison, crack a few jokes.

Then Wallace says, "Audrey Tautou." But it creates an argument because no one knows who the actress is.

To break up the dispute, I say, "Tom Cruise." And the game gets underway once more.

In fact, Don is quick to respond with, "Charlize Theron. You know the one from that gorilla movie."

As the game continues, I drain my cup and Nathaniel gets me another, this time without asking.

Eventually Don and Sebella disappear and most of the others at the Paper Nickel. When I suggest that it is time for Nathaniel to take me home, he says, "Absolutely, whatever you want. One more drink, though, okay?"

I am buzzed. I know I am buzzed, possibly on the line of something more. I haven't eaten all day. My stomach is growling. But the kitchen is closed. It is late. Still, there is nothing waiting for me but a dark empty house with a sad empty refrigerator in a pitiful empty life. So, I do not argue the matter. And I will be honest, I like the attention. It feels good to be wanted; it takes away the sting.

Nathaniel gets me yet another drink. This one is strong, much stronger than the others, like pure alcohol with no mixer. The pixie behind the bar has been replaced by a handsome man with thick blond hair and light brown eyes, who smiles and nods as he wipes down the counter. Then the bartender waves to Nathaniel, the cloth still in the blond's hand.

I take a sip of my highball.

And another.

And another.

And another.

CHAPTER NINE

Centruroides sculpturatus is a light yellowish colored scorpion native to Southwest North America. It is a nocturnal creature, a night dwelling predator stealthy in nature, with a waxy exoskeleton that protects it from harm. The tiny hairs on its body are sensitive to vibrations, terrain, and prey, but that is not what sets it apart from other creatures. It is its venom, which induces vomiting, numbness, and pain. Some say the scorpion's sting is like being touched by a galvanic wire or hit with an electrical jolt. The *centruroides sculpturatus* can slip through a crack as thin as folded paper. And it pretty much always hunts at night.

Rain scents the nighttime air. The world around me is a blur. One minute something is there and the next it is gone. My peripheral vision is distorted as though someone has dropped a gossamer cloth over the sides of my eyes and clipped it at an angle to give me a small breath of tunnel vision. I cannot remember how I got here or who brought me. I don't even remember if I agreed to come.

The stench of alcohol is detectable in the breeze, even though the crowd has thinned to stragglers and the tables have all been cleared. I do not like alcohol. It reminds me of the past, of days I folded up neatly and placed in a box then shoved into the farthest corner of my mind. A few of those memories leaked out over the years, but for the most part the box held true to keep me intact.

I do not drink alcohol often. In fact, it is only on rare occasions that I partake and maybe every once in a while when my husband and I go to a comedy club, or at least that was before we got married.

It is the smell. I don't like the smell, the way it sickens my stomach and floods my body with unwanted emotion.

Nor do I like the taste, sweet or tangy or something in between, which is why I still don't understand what possessed me to gulp so much down.

Fredrick is gone. When he left, I cannot say. It could be an hour ago or it could be a minute. Time is fleeting now.

Jacob Wallace and Sabella are gone, too.

Actually, that is not correct. They are still outside on the patio in the back of the Paper Nickel. That is if I am not mistaken.

I am the one on the way out the door.

The pressure of someone's grip is on my arm. I look at the hand upon me and follow it up to the person leading me through the center of the Paper Nickel, past tables and chairs, workers and dishes. Nathaniel keeps me from falling down.

Where is Ian right now?

Why is he not here with me?

The interior bartender has finished wiping the bar with a cloth. Under the light, it glows with a buttery wet sheen.

Nathaniel and I exit through the double doors at the front of the Paper Nickel then step out into the night. As soon as the cool crisp air hits my face, I pull away. In the process, I stumble and fall, scraping my palm on something sharp and protruding on the handrail.

Suddenly I am on my knees and hands with the cold of the concrete permeating my skin and the chill of the early morning hour deep in my marrow.

What is going on?

Nathaniel laughs. It is a good laugh, the kind of laugh that makes you want to laugh as well, infectious. I enjoy the sound.

"You alright?" he says as he yanks me onto my feet and snakes his arm around my waist. "What am I going to do with you, young lady?"

I do not respond.

He leads me down the stairs and into the parking lot of the Paper Nickel. I haven't slept in days. My eyelids feel thick, my legs heavy and lazy. I want to lie down, but Nathaniel won't let me. He keeps insisting we go on.

Where is my Ian?

Nathaniel's car is at the far end of the parking lot. It is three spots east of the thin patch of woods beyond the grassy knoll, away from the road. I stumble and crack my elbow on asphalt, hitting at just the spot for nasty electrical prickles and accompanying jolt.

Nathaniel helps me up again. "You're alright," he breathes. His lips brush softly against my earlobe, and I feel his breath on my skin, warm and moist.

The sky is like liquid oil, thick black with no visible stars. It reminds me of dark matter, axons and energy, mystery and danger. I cannot focus on it too long or I'll get dizzy.

Looking over my shoulder I see the exterior lights on the Paper Nickel. They are small and growing smaller yet brighter at the same time, like someone pumped up a charge and flipped a switch to create points of bright white blinding light that, if you are not careful, will burn holes through your retinas.

With one hand on my arm and the other on my waist, Nathaniel spins me around and sets me against something cold and hard and metal. The surface is not flat but separated by curves and glass. It takes me a minute to realize that I am pinned against his custom black SUV, his body the binding force. I have seen this vehicle before. I have seen it in the parking garage at Westgrove, Gardner, and Jones, a pristine beast of chrome and ink, never a visible smudge or scrape anywhere.

My sweater soaks up the rain water like a sponge. I do not remember it raining, at least not while I was at the Paper Nickel. But it must have happened because the car is wet and there are tiny puddles on the ground, which shudder when you walk near.

"My knees feel gritty," I say. "I want to lie down."

It is like I have been kneeling with my fingers buried in the sand. Everything is coated and grainy.

A fine threadlike sensation burns through my hands when I brush them over my jeans. I catch my breath on account of the pain. Then I look down to examine the injuries and run a soft finger over my wounds, feeling the sticky wetness of blood in the process.

"You're alright," Nathaniel says. "Now stay still for me while I get my keys."

The sonuvabitch didn't come.

Everything registers in my brain as color—red, black, gray, green...the orange-yellow glow of the streetlights, the faint silver extension of the moon, the white gold of my wedding ring.

My lungs feel confined in their cage or maybe it is the sharpness of the crisp air. I am not sure.

Slowly, I begin to slide toward the earth. The sound of my skin against the metal reminds me of a squeegee on glass, yet Nathaniel somehow manages to keep me propped up like a ragdoll.

He turns my face his way with pressure from his fingertips. "Can you do something for me, Delilah? Can you stay on your feet?" he says. "I need you to stay on your feet."

Nathaniel talks to me like I am a child.

I am not a child.

I have never been one.

"You know what it's like," I tell him. "It's like..." But I cannot finish my statement because I have lost my train of thought.

In an attempt to open the driver's door, Nathaniel unfastens his grip and immediately I drop to my hands and knees, hitting the ground so hard it jars my insides and causes my teeth to smash together in a traumatic fashion.

I am so tired. I don't want to get up.

Nathaniel squats beside me. "I need you to help me here, Delilah," he says. "Do you think you can do that?"

Help.

Before I answer, though, he presses his lips against mine and kisses me, gently, softly, something quick, meaningless.

"I think maybe it's me," I tell him. "I don't know."

He pulls me up onto my feet and pins me against his car once more. I am wedged between the vehicle and Nathaniel's body with no room to move. The rain water works with my flesh in such a way as to create a leaching, where my exposed skin sticks to the metal and stretches as I slide.

My eyes drop and I see a bare, bloody toe. It is my big toe on my left foot. The skin under the spot where my toenail should be is hanging off by a thread, shredded to pasta, and the tip is coated in dried blood.

"Let me go," I say as I push Nathaniel aside. "Let me go. Where is my shoe?"

Ian, help me find my shoe.

Nathaniel swings me around. "Calm down, Delilah," he says. "It's right here. Look, see, I have it. Everything is fine."

The next thing I know his tongue is in my mouth. It is a real kiss this time, long and deep and wet. My spine is against his car, his body firm against mine.

Nathaniel smells the way a man is supposed to smell, clean and masculine yet with a citrusy bergamot scent, but there is something that makes my stomach turn.

I pull away.

"Where is Jane? We can't leave without Jane. I have to find her." My voice does not sound like my voice but something cracked and sluggish.

Nathaniel laughs. "What am I going to do with you, Delilah?" he says.

"I don't know what you mean."

He studies my face for a beat before pulling on one of my ringlets like a bell. Then his hand slides behind me to the small of my back, while his mouth finds my neck and his erection presses against my thigh.

Nathaniel slips his hand up under my shirt then into my bra as I turn my attention to the liquid oil sky and keep my eyes fixed. The sound of breath is all around me. It is everywhere. I am doing these things, but I am not doing them. It is more that I sort of allow them to happen.

Nathaniel brushes his thumb softly over my nipple then reaches down to apply pressure, pulls me in close, then closer, his body firmly against mine, the two of us melding into the car. Again, there is no room to move.

The taste of his lips is one I do not recognize. It is the taste of liquor, I imagine, maybe scotch or bourbon, something strong, a man's drink, a drinker's drink, something that belongs in a crystal decanter by a leather couch in a room full of books or on an episode with rich white men.

"You're so beautiful," he breathes.

The compliment makes me feel wanted and confused.

Suddenly, we are on the other side of the vehicle and the passenger door is open. Nathaniel places one hand on my arm and the other on my head to guide me into his SUV, not so much forcefully as dominantly.

"Where is my shoe," I say when I feel the sensation of my bare foot on the cool car mat. "I need my shoe. I can't leave without my shoe."

He holds it up in front of me and, while leaning across my chest, tosses it onto the backseat, along with my handbag. Then he closes the door.

Nathaniel rounds the vehicle to slide in behind the steering wheel on the driver's side.

The sound of the confined space reminds me of being on an airplane. It is like having gauze in my ears or my ear in a seashell. Everything is cloudy.

Before jamming his key into the ignition, Nathaniel turns his attention to me again and runs a slow hand southward over one of my ringlets. He leans over and, before kissing me on the mouth, says, "You have the most beautiful eyes, Delilah. Has anyone ever told you that?"

Yes. My husband.

Glacial green with a hint of blue.

"I don't feel well," I say.

Nathaniel jams the car key into the ignition. "If you are going to be sick, I need you to tell me," he says while looking straight ahead. Facing me he adds, "Are you going to be sick?"

I do not respond.

A knock on the driver's side window surprises us both. Jacob Wallace is there, standing with his hands in his pockets, bouncing from one foot to the other in the cold of the night. He gestures for Nathaniel to get out of the car, and Nathaniel complies. The two then engage in what looks like a heated conversation. But I am not interested because my eyes are fixed on the small patch of woods a hundred feet away. They settle on the darkness between the trees, where the light of day never seems to touch.

I don't know how much time passes; it seems like a little as much as it seems like a lot.

The driver's door opens and Nathaniel slides into the car, resuming his spot behind the steering wheel.

Wallace is no longer around. I look for him, but I don't see him anywhere. He must have gone home.

"I don't feel well," I say, faintly. But Nathaniel cannot hear me over the sound of his own voice, which registers in my brain as muffled and distant. "Are you listening? I don't feel well."

My name finally captures my attention. Nathaniel says it again. "Delilah? Delilah, look at me. Are you going to be sick?"

Where is Ian?

The passenger door opens and an arm snakes around my waist. It pulls me from the vehicle and hauls me over to the grassy knoll, where I drop to my knees but fail to vomit.

I want to be sick. It would be a relief to get it out.

"You're alright," Nathaniel says, even though the earth is spinning far too fast on its axis.

The next thing I know I am on the ground in the woods with a canopy of leaves blocking my view of the liquid oil sky. Everything is moist and cold and sticky.

There is a sour musty scent in the air. It is the smell of the woods at night, the odor of dangerous creatures.

Nathaniel is on top of me, his mouth against mine.

He tugs at my jeans, then tugs some more, trying to pull them down. There is a sense of urgency in his actions. Then he unbuttons and unzips his own pants with that same urgency.

I feel the weight of his body on top of mine. In certain places, it crushes me, but I do not say a word.

I never say a word.

Not one fucking word.

Reaching between my legs, Nathaniel runs his hand up until he finds the spot he is looking for. As he jams himself inside me, he fills my mouth with his tongue.

"You're so beautiful," he says. And I am confused.

The sour fermented stench of alcohol fills my nostrils.

My head falls to the side, where it is assaulted by sharp rocks and other debris.

Everything is wet and slimy and soiled.

Splintered twigs slash like razors at my exposed skin.

It is so dark I cannot see more than a faint outline of shapes, silhouettes.

The sound of the night is suspended in lieu of Nathaniel pounding his flesh into mine and the guttural noises he makes in the process.

Then the final thrust arrives with its dirty strain.

Nathaniel moans loudly.

Satisfied, he collapses on top of me and, after a second, rolls off onto the forest floor.

I smell the faint ammoniacal scent of semen. Its molecules cling to the receptor cells in my nostrils to form what will eventually become a trigger.

With the slow motion of someone beaten, I pull up

my pants. My muscles are angry now. They are resistant.

Nathaniel gets to his feet and fastens himself together. Standing above me, he says, "Let's get you home."

I do not remember the drive, other than the darkness and a few flashes of passing light.

The next morning I wake in my bed with my sheets covered in perspiration, vomit, and tiny red dots from dribbles of blood. My jeans are torn at the knees and blood soaked, fused to the wounds under my kneecaps. Threads of skin dangle off the side of my left toe. My toenail is gone except for a small bent overhang, which is coated in filth. I try to pull what is left of my toenail off, but the severity of the pain stops me cold. Tiny bruises litter my skin, along with fine hair-like razor sharp slashes. My hands ache from scraping asphalt.

In slow motion, I lean forward with my knees over the side of the bed. A leaf falls out of my tangled web of curls, then another and another. I pick a few more out before acid rises into my throat and I am forced to make a mad dash for the master bathroom.

Flipping up the toilet lid, I drop to the floor and puke my guts out into the toilet bowl, at first all fluid, but then something awful, something unknown, the texture of tomato skins. My chest rises and falls quickly as I heave. And when it is done, or rather when it is put on hold, I rest my arm on the toilet seat and my head on my arm, breathing heavily.

After a while I collapse onto floor, where the cold of the tile offers a moment of reprieve.

Every living and dead part of my body throbs.

I puke again.

And again.

Stuff comes out of me from both ends.

Never in my life have I been so sick. It is like I am being torn apart from the inside out, like my body is trying to get rid of something foreign, something that does not belong.

Please, God, help me.

Beads of sweat form above my brow. I swipe them off with the top of my hand. I am drenched in perspiration. If you wring out my hair, it would still be oily wet.

Slowly, carefully, I begin to peel off my clothes. First I remove my shirt, muscles smarting; then I remove my jeans. The flesh around the wounds on my knees tears along with the scab in the process. I suck air in through my teeth in response. My eyes well up from the pain. Then I lie on the cool hard tile in nothing but my underclothes.

The light in the bedroom hurts my eyes, so I stretch out my leg and kick the door shut.

I am alone and have no one.

Time clicks by on the clock. The morning is gone. I feel myself surrender to the guilt and the shame. It consumes me.

Tears begin to slowly slide down my cheeks to puddle in the suprasternal notch at the base of my neck. Some call this spot the hollow, the dip between the collar bones. It seems fitting.

I sink into the cold hard stone, well on my way to fossilization, and feel completely, utterly, agonizingly hollow.

When I roll over to face the cabinet, I am not the least bit surprised to find my pink-eared bunny waiting for me. He stares at me from the same level.

"Don't look at me like that," I say.

A swell of emotion washes over me like the slow beat of a death drum. My chest aches as though it has been hit with a sledgehammer.

I should not have left my pink-eared bunny next to the glass turtle ashtray on the living room table. What happened was my fault. It was all my fault.

Everything is my fault!

It's my fucking fault.

Fingers point. People yell. I am still that child. I will always be that child, yet not a child at all, trapped in an inexplicable state of suspension.

My bunny is the cause and the solution, the threat and the shield. I don't know what the fuck he is. Nor do I know who I am. What I am. The movies and the books have it wrong. Nothing is clean, pure, nothing wrapped up neatly in a bow. It is all a tangled mass of shit.

"Please, don't looking at me like that," I say again, faintly, to my pink-eared friend.

I begin to weep.

CHAPTER TEN

In the realm of Christendom, forgiveness of sins, especially mortal sins, is given to the penitent in the form of absolution. It is through absolution the sinner is relieved of guilt and shame. But what many do not understand, what they do not realize, is that forgiveness is not granted to all. It is not furnished arbitrarily to those who seek it. In fact, speaking to the apostles, Jesus said, "Those whose sins ye forgive are forgiven; those whose sins ye retain are retained."

They. Are. Retained.

My eyes spring open not with the gradualness of sleep but with the promptness of registered alarm. I am still on the bathroom floor in my underwear with my skin scraped and bloodied and my toenail covered in filth, hanging over the edge of my toe. Small twigs and leaves are still planted in my mass of curls. My chest feels as though it has been hollowed to the bone. There is a presence I sense in the room, like an unspoken jury, unseen, set to deliberate on whether or not I should be condemned. The chance of forgiveness does not seem to be in my favor, at least not given my history.

I am the unwanted.

I am the unloved.

I am the rejected.

Please, Father, please forgive me.

Rolling onto my back with my knees twisted to the side, I stare up at the eggshell white ceiling and examine the shapes and tiny imperfections in the plaster. There is a web located in the corner of the room so fine it is nearly imperceptible. The web is exactly like the one in the living room, possibly from the same spider, the one presumably hidden in a crevice somewhere, down where others do not venture to go. With my shoulder blades pressed against the cold tile floor, I blink slowly and think about absolution. Where will I fall on the line? The very thought makes the acid in my stomach churn.

Please, God, I can't.

The floor is like a bed of nails digging into my bones. I take a deep breath and roll over onto my side then use my hand for support to peel myself up off the ground. Because of the shape I am in, I cannot move quickly. Once in a sitting position, I pause briefly then slide across the floor to rest my head on the edge of the garden tub. Finally I push myself onto my feet, knees close to buckling from the weight of my body. The puking has left me dehydrated and weak, and I ache everywhere from wounds and remorse.

Nathaniel's voice keeps playing in my head on repeat. I cannot shut it off. "You're alright, Delilah. You're alright."

What have I done?

Bracing myself against the counter, I cup my hand under the faucet and scoop out a handful of water to drink. My mouth tastes like vomit, so I rinse it and spit what is left in the sink. There is puke in my hair and crust on my skin. The stench of sickness is all over me. It is everywhere.

With sluggish steps I cross the room to the shower

and set the water temperature to scalding. After a minute or two, a plume of steam rises above the glass. The steam moistens the stale air and fogs up the mirror, coating it with tiny droplets that slide down like tears.

Just let me die.

I remove my bra, then my underwear, and toss them both to the side with a plan to discard them later. Then I step into the shower and am assaulted by the sting of hot rushing water on my wounds. Every nerve ending in my body ignites, but the pain is only temporary. I soon adjust.

Leaning with my head and my hand against the stone tile, I close my eyes. The disgust I feel for myself is tempered only by ineffectual will, yet I do not cry. The last of my tears for the day are still drying on the floor.

Please just let me die.

My skin turns a new shade of heated pink as the scalding water washes away the blood and the filth, which circle the drain before disappearing.

There is a loofa sponge hanging from a rope off the shower rack. I grab it to scrub my body. I use my hands and fingernails as well, picking small leaves and twigs out of my hair in the process. The lacerations that litter my skin smart at the introduction of soap, but it doesn't matter. I scrub and I scrub. I scour until my fingers are pruned and the water runs clear and cold, until my skin is raw, dotted in clusters of red, and I can scrub and scour no more.

Then I shut off the water and step into the cold, naked and shivering. I wrap myself in a bamboo cotton blend towel Ian bought me to prove he was listening one day.

Ian. What I am going to tell Ian?

My long loose curls drip down the center of my back. Despite all of my effort, I still feel unclean.

Returning to my bedroom, I am struck by the stench

of vomit and blood, sweat and dirt. The entire room reeks of sickness, so I throw on a fresh pair of underwear and a long nightshirt; then I put on my rubber gloves, peel off the blanket and sheets, and scrub the stains out of the mattress.

Once everything is washed and bagged, thrown in the trash and deodorized, I stand in front of the bed and stare at the giant wet mark. There is a hairdryer in the storage closet, which I obtain in an attempt to dry the spot. It takes too long; I start to scream. Then I force myself to calm down, flip the mattress, slap on a fresh set of linen, and exchange my nightshirt for a different one.

Suppressing my tears, I crawl under the covers and pull the blanket up close to my chest, the way a child would pull a doll in close and hold it for security.

Nathaniel's voice surfaces in my mind once more. "You're alright, Delilah. You're alright."

I cover my ears.

Stop!

For the rest of the weekend, I remain in bed, wrapped in the blankets, getting up only to relieve myself in the bathroom. The first time stings my privates.

Hours drift by, and the days bleed into each other.

When Monday rolls around, I call in sick and spend the afternoon distracting myself with television and sleep. Later in the day, a terrible thought takes up residency in my head. I try to push it away because it adds anxiety to my suffering. It won't leave, though. The scratching is incessant.

Dear God, please make it stop!

"You're alright, Delilah. You're alright."

Tuesday morning I pace the floor with the fingernail of my thumb lodged between my teeth, and I contact my gynecologist for an appointment.

"Is that the soonest you have," I say to the clerk who does the scheduling. "No, no, it's fine. I'll take it. Thank you."

Because I cannot afford to miss another day of work, I dress and pull my hair into a sloppy bun, leave the makeup untouched on the vanity, and climb into my car to head to my job, absentmindedly skipping my morning coffee and breakfast.

The outdoor parking lot of Westgrove, Gardner, and Jones is full, so I have no choice but to park in the dreaded parking garage. With my head low, I make a beeline to the elevators and another beeline to my office.

Nathaniel is standing near the break room. He barely acknowledges my passing. I half wonder if he is planning to show up in my office later so that he can speak to me in private.

What will I do if he shows up?

Once I am alone and not so neatly settled behind my computer, Jane enters the room without permission. "Where have you been?" she says in her most motherly voice. "I almost drove to your house last night. Why haven't you been answering my calls? You look terrible. Oh my God, Delilah, are you still sick?"

"I'm fine, Jane," I tell her without lifting my eyes from the computer monitor. "But I'm very behind, so do you think maybe we can talk later?"

Jane studies me at length. Feeling the weight of her stare, I give her what she wants—my attention.

"This afternoon then," she says slowly and moves toward the door. Before exiting, Jane changes her mind and pivots on her heel. "Are you sure there is nothing I can get for you? Something for your stomach? Some tea?"

Go away, please.

"I really need to work," I tell her.

But Jane still does not leave. "You're not mad at me, are you?" she says.

"Why would I be mad at you, Jane?"

"Because I basically left you stranded on Friday."

Yes, you did.

My answer is immediate and absolute. "No, Jane, I'm not mad at you. I'm behind." Then I nod at the files on my desk to indicate the meaning of my statement.

"You look so thin," she tells me as she steps deeper into the room. "Your clavicles look like handlebars."

As calmly as possible, I set my hands on the desk. "Jane, please can we talk later?"

No sooner does Jane leave the room than a beautiful young blond materializes to take up more of my time. The blond is all legs and breasts, lips and hair. I do not know her name, but I recognize her face. She is the twenty-two year old intern working the floor as part of her school requirement.

"I'm sorry to bother you," she says in her perfect voice with its perfect lilt. "But they asked me to gather everyone into the break room."

"Who is they?" I reply.

The beautiful young intern blinks at me slowly.

Fucking hell.

"Never mind," I say. "I'll be there in a minute."

The meeting is actually in the cafeteria at the far end of the hall. It is a large room with plenty of space, tables, and chairs. Vending machines line one side of the wall, while two large trash cans reside at the front corner. Every chair in the room has already been taken, and people are standing in various locations as they wait. To minimize my presence, I step to the side, which is shielded somewhat by the door.

"What is this about?" I say to the man standing next

to me. He has been with our company for years, but I cannot remember his name.

"Mr. Tamaka is retiring," he says with his voice a hair above a whisper.

"Retiring or being pushed out?"

"Pushed."

As soon as the announcement is made, a wave of whispers spreads across the room like wild fire. If Mr. Tamaka, who has given the best years of his life to our company, can be pushed out of Westgrove, Gardner, and Jones, then no one is safe. The tension in the room turns to lead.

Then Wallace arrives and stands next to me with his arms folded over his chest and his eyes fixed on the speaker. Without turning his attention my way, he says, "You were out yesterday."

No kidding.

"Was I?"

He gives me the once over. "You look like shit."

I could care less.

"Did you even iron your clothes this morning?"

No. And fuck you.

I don't respond.

The crowd reacts positively to one of Mr. Tamaka's jokes even though it isn't funny and does nothing to assuage fears.

A few minutes later, the crowd is released and Wallace grabs hold of me in the hall. He pulls me to the side and says, "You need to be careful, Delilah. They are going to be doing another round of cuts."

"Where did you hear that?"

"It doesn't matter, does it?" he says. Then he adds, "Delilah, about the other night—"

"I have a lot of work to do, Jacob."

Nodding faintly, he releases me. We go our separate ways. I spend the rest of the morning trying to distract myself with work. Every second that ticks by on the clock enforces the fact that Nathaniel feels no compulsion to address what happened between us. It is like it didn't happen at all. It was meaningless.

I am meaningless.

I don't matter.

I am nothing.

Pathetic.

I don't even know who I am anymore.

Dahlia instead of Delilah.

Nathaniel is a person who matters. He is an important man. And people who matter can do whatever they want to the people who don't. And even if that weren't the case, I remember what they did to that girl in school, the one who pressed for things to be different. Of course, that girl didn't matter.

And neither do I.

My brain chews on the events that transpired outside the Paper Nickel as my fingernails dig tracks into the arms of my office chair. Maybe I should confront him, force him to help me make sense of what happened between us. Nathaniel needs to explain, if only because I can't make sense of the situation myself. The world is on tilt. It is flat. And I am falling off the edge.

Please, God, please.

Before I can figure it out, Jane returns to take me to lunch. When I try to argue, she cuts me off with her motherly voice. "I am not taking no for an answer, Delilah. Now grab your bag and let's go get something to eat."

Because my mind has grown cloudy from lack of sustenance, I do not put up an additional fight but follow Jane out the door. We walk to the retro diner two blocks away, a cool place with Formica countertops and mini jukeboxes at every table, chrome all around. A waitress with mousy brown hair and wide spaced eyes seats us at the booth in the rear by the window. She takes our orders then disappears behind the kitchen door.

Silence sets in to make the situation awkward. Jane alleviates it by saying, "So, tell me what has been going on with you."

My mouth goes dry. "How is your daughter, Jane? Better?"

It is the right question to ask because it immediately sends Jane on a tangent.

There is a bell above the door to the restaurant that chimes every time the door opens. As Jane continues to rattle on about her family, the bell rings.

Looking up, I find Nathaniel not twenty feet away. The beautiful young intern with porcelain skin and youthful glow enters a second later. It takes me a moment to realize that the two are together; though, I am not sure if they are there as a couple.

A waitress with short black hair cut close to her scalp seats Nathaniel and the intern at a table on the other side of the room. I have a clear view of them, but somehow they fail to notice me in return.

I am invisible.

Am I invisible?

Then Jane's voice registers in my head with the hollowness of distance. It registers again, this time with clarity. "I lost you there for a second," she says.

My cheeks flush with warmth. "Sorry, I have a lot on my mind. Where were you again?"

Jane follows my line of sight all the way to Nathaniel and the intern. "Did he drive you home the other night?" she asks without a shred of alarm or question in her tone.

It takes conscious effort for me to keep my eyes on Jane rather than drop them to the table. Somehow, though, I manage.

"He is very handsome," Jane says, and I know it is a fishing expedition. "Don't you think?"

Turning my attention to the mini jukebox, I flip through the songs and reply, "I don't know, Jane. If that is what you like. Do you have a song that you want to hear?"

Fifty cents later, the jukebox is playing random music.

Jane glances over her shoulder at Nathaniel and the intern once more. "Well, I think he's handsome," she says. "You know he's the one filling Tamaka's position?"

Now I am wide awake. "Where did you hear that?"

Before Jane has the chance to reply, our waitress returns with our orders, and Jane starts pushing her salad around with a fork. The scraping sound mirrors the scraping of my nerves.

Meanwhile, Nathaniel and the intern fill the room with laughter. The intern's laugh is sweet, almost hypnotic. She is someone, lovely, important.

Jane stabs at a tomato then shoves it into her mouth. The juice dribbles past her lip.

Through the dark tunnels of my eyes, I see the intern place her hand on Nathaniel's arm and Nathaniel lean forward in his seat in response. Then the two reengage in conversation, oblivious to everything around them, including me.

That fucking sonuvabitch.

Now Jane shoves something crunchy into her mouth. She chews like a horse. Like a goddamn horse.

The flirtation between Nathaniel and the intern escalates.

With a slow hand, I bring my fingertips up to my

lips. I can still feel the pressure of Nathaniel's mouth against my mouth and the moisture of his breath on my skin. I can taste the liquor he consumed—scotch or bourbon, something strong, a man's drink, a drinker's drink, something that belongs in a crystal decanter by a leather couch. The sour stench of alcohol is in the air. It is thick as key lime pie. My throat feels as though it is closing. I cannot fill my lungs with air. Vomit rises into my throat. I cannot think.

I hate him.

The bastard.

I fucking HATE him!

The pain is torturous. It is more than I can bear.

Let me die, God.

Let me fucking die.

I am the unwanted.

I am the unloved.

I am the jettisoned.

Throwing my napkin on the table, I say, "I am sorry, Jane, but I have to go." Sliding out of the booth, I toss some money on the table to cover the cost of the food and add, "I have to get back to work."

"Wait, what? Delilah," Jane says, but it is too late; I am already at the door.

The next thing I know I am in my car with the engine running, staring at a massive structure of stained concrete. My head throbs, and I feel the pressure of tears swelling in my eyes. The sensation of dirt on my skin is overwhelming. There is so much dirt. I want to scrub my skin bloody and raw with my fingernails.

I am empty.

I am used.

But most of all, I am angry.

I'M FUCKING ANGRY

CHAPTER ELEVEN

Some believe that what you put out into this world is what you get in return, a form of God's just deserts. So, if you spread hate and negativity, stir up trouble, then hate and negativity, trouble, are what you receive as a result. When I think about that belief and how I fit into the fold, my breath catches a little in my throat. Considering who I am—a relatively quiet, keep-to-herself kind of person, a person who gives easily—I have no choice but to conclude that the problem is innate. There is something wrong with me. And it is something so ugly, so perverse, others pick up on it and respond. But then again I do not see how a little boy's actions can ever warrant him being locked in a cage for years or how a little girl, desperately in need of her mother's love, can be abandoned into the hands of violence and marked by namelessness.

I am the nameless.

I am the unwanted.

I am the unloved.

And apparently, I am not worth a second thought.

While my anger over the diner incident has subsided to a large degree, replaced by a deeply entrenched melancholy, I think about these things and more. Fresh storm clouds roll in from the east and, as they do so, the rain intensifies outside. Strong gusts of wind rattle the windowpanes like prisoners behind bars screaming for attention. Standing with my arms folded over my chest and my fingertips on my lips, I stare out the sliding glass doors and watch as the smoke purple sky finishes its transformation to liquid oil. Thanks to the weather, the grass in my yard is balding and the six foot wooden fence needs another protective coat. But there is comfort in the hypnotic sound of the rain. The anger that filled me earlier in the week has died down, yet I still feel something I know I shouldn't—a thread of hate stitching its way through my soul. It is like poison of the most virulent kind coursing my veins, spreading quickly to wreak havoc.

A veil of blackness settles in over the land and, as it does so, I am reminded of the space between the trees outside the Paper Nickel, the way my eyes failed to capture everything except faint shapes and silhouettes. I see those shapes now. It is like staring out the wrong end of a telescope, its lens draped in murky cloth. And all the while there is a lingering thought in my head that I simply cannot shake. I wonder what the storm is doing to the place between the trees. Is it washing the evidence away, washing it clean, drowning threads of cloth and strands of hair, separating molecules of body fluid, or is it creating tiny pockets of proof that will later push up from the earth with the daisies, along with the worms?

That indecent bastard.

Maybe I am still angry.

Resting on the arm of my living room couch, I press my fingers against my temples then attempt to rub the knot out of the base of my neck. There is no one in the house now, no one except me. The television is off, most of the lights as well. From the kitchen there is a clicking sound followed by the soft hum of the refrigerator. Periodically that hum gets overpowered by cracks of thunder and violent shakes of glass. The storm is heavy outside, lashing ferociously as a whip. I do my best not to be afraid. But then again I have been afraid my whole life. There is little else I have known during my time on earth.

What else?

What. Else?!

Extracting my cellphone from my pocket, I play Ian's message for the third time. "I'm sorry we keep missing each other," he says. "It is not on purpose." He pauses briefly on account of someone in the distance distracting him. He and that someone make conversation I cannot quite hear. Then Ian comes across the line clearly once more. "Anyway, I am about to get on a plane. You know how it is, Delilah. I will call you as soon as I touch ground at the airport. I have been thinking a lot about what is happening with us, and I want you to know that I love you. I really do. We are going to make this work."

Despite the fact that his words sound cleanly scripted, the last line of his message repeats in my head.

We are going to make this work.

I cannot say I am so confident.

The rain is starting to calm, but not the wind.

Staring out at the veil of black, I feel empty. It is like my mind is blank and my body numb. I am here, but I am not really here. A part of me wishes I was gone all together, erased from existence by the tail end of a pencil. At least then something new and beautiful could be created in my place, and the ugliness that surrounds me on a consistent basis will disappear into the background.

The phone vibrates in my hand a second before I attempt to shove it into my pocket. It is a strange sensation, the electronic quiver. I see Bailey's number on the screen and am briefly lifted from the haze of self-pity and remorse.

"Bailey," I say hastily into the phone.

Only it is not Bailey on the other end of the line. It is my sister Lillian. She and I have never been close.

"Why are you calling me from Bailey's phone?" I ask, to which I do not receive an answer.

Lillian and I engage in meaningless small talk, the kind of talk that matches our relationship. She complains about her job and how she works for a cult then goes on about the weather and how she is ready for a change. There is an invisible wall between us, impossible to mount. We are strangers connected by blood. Despite this, despite the long held strain in our relationship, at some point during Lillian's lengthy monologue, her voice grating in my ears, a shift occurs. Misery takes hold in lieu of the numbing emptiness, and I break down and cry. I cry and I cry. Then I reveal a small piece of myself.

Of course, Lillian's response is automatic. It is mechanical. She is a metal shell, as well as a skilled interrogator. Actually, she is more than an interrogator. Lillian is a closer.

I confess everything.

A long silence ensues.

Too long.

I know I made a mistake. It's clear to me now. But it is already done.

Lillian takes great pleasure in speaking her mind. She takes even more in making me feel like shit.

"Lillian, are you there?" I say.

I can hear her breathing.

"Lillian?"

"What do you want from me, Delilah?" she replies, coolly. "Do you want me to tell you it wasn't your fault?"

The long dark finger is pointing in my direction

again. And the knot at the base of my neck rises higher into my throat. I knew better than to share anything with Lillian. She broke my toys when we were little. She whipped me without reason.

Why would I expose myself and tell the truth?

What the hell is wrong with me?

All I can say is, "No. That's not—"

"Because I can't do that, Delilah," she says. "Based on what you told me, everything you told me, you need to take some responsibility. Honestly..."

The knot prevents me from giving answer.

"And do you want to know why? Do you want to know why, Delilah? It is because you did this with your choices." There is a bloated pause before she adds, "You're a grown woman. Take responsibility for your goddamn life."

In the heat of the moment, in the sting of what feels like a betrayal of confidence, I go on the attack. "At least Ian and I were separated."

"How convenient," Lillian says, incredulously.

She enjoys feeling superior, as evidenced by her mocking tone. *That bitch.*

"What's that supposed to mean?"

"I think you know, Delilah."

That fucking bitch.

Now I am on my feet leaning against the glass door staring out at the ink black night and feeling the cold against my skin. There is not a single star in the sky.

An awkward silence takes hold to increase the space between us. It feels like I am in a confrontation with an enemy.

Then Lillian says, "I was calling to ask you to brave the storm for game night, but in light of whatever this is, I think you should stay home and figure your shit out. In fact, Bailey is standing right next to me, and she agrees."

It bothers me that Bailey knows the truth and now thinks less of me. How could she not?

I am less.

I am nothing.

Or at the very least, I don't know who I am anymore.

Dahlia instead of Delilah.

"You had me on speaker phone?" I say.

What a cunt.

Instead of waiting for a response, though, I hang up the phone and shove it into my pocket.

Curling up on the couch in the living room with my knees to my chest and my arms around my knees, I run through the conversation in my head. There is a click in the kitchen followed by the hum of the refrigerator. The house feels big now. It feels enormous.

Windowpanes rattle.

Walls creak.

I see Ian staring back at me from a picture frame.

And reflected in the glass is my pink-eared bunny.

I cannot be here anymore, so I grab my keys off the rack, climb into my car, and drive down the slick, winding roads of the valley. Then I go up suicide hill and down the dark mountain behind the supermarket I used to work at as a teenager. The valley is a microcosm of the state in seasonal flux, but it is hard to recognize this on account of the unforgiving black. The only visible light is the faint glow that comes from the headlights as I approach the highway and the widely spaced lampposts on the roads.

Somehow, and I am not sure how, I find myself outside the only church in town open at this time. The place is just over ten miles away from my house, up the road from the library, separated by soft welcoming lights. I sit in the parking lot and stare at the building. With its towering cathedral and stone turrets, stained glass windows and gothic mullions, it stands as one of the most beautiful churches in the United States. Two stone vessels filled with holy water flank the entrance inside, and when you disturb the water's calm with a dip of your fingers, the veins in the marble move, bend in strange hypnotic directions. Personally, I favor the colossal wooden doors and cardinal red candles, but it is the thick vaulted custom made arches that really draw the eye. During the day, when sunlight enters through the stained glass windows, the congregation room takes on a heavenly golden glow; the furnishings glisten with a buttery wet sheen. But it is late now. The place feels eerie. And I am the only one here.

Once inside the building I have my selection of pews. I walk to the front and pull down the third rest on the right then kneel with my head bowed low before a carved statue of the crucified Christ. It has been some time since I have visited a church. The weight of this knowledge does not escape me. Suddenly I am overwhelmed with emotion, with guilt and shame. Behind my eyelids, I see images of my life layered one over the next, melting into each other. It is all color. Only color. Like the green of an apartment door or the pink of a bunny's ear.

With my hands clasped and my head bowed low, I pray the Lord's prayer. In fact I pray it over and over again like a mantra. It is His promise that I cling to now.

Come unto me those who labour and are heavy laden; I will give you rest.

I am tired.

I am so fucking tired.

The next thing I know a hand is on my shoulder stirring me to awareness. My eyes blink thickly as light slams against my retinas. Then I follow the hand on my shoulder up to its owner and say, "Father O'Neil."

He looks like every other priest in our neighborhood—old with white thinning hair and an Irish ruddy face, tall and thin, except for his swollen belly, which he typically hides under thick robes.

"You need to wake up now, dear," he says. "Morning mass starts in an hour."

I sit up straight and feel the heat of embarrassment on my neck. Sleeping on the pews is not exactly promoted. I wonder how I made it through the night without being asked to leave.

"You are more than welcome to stay," Father O'Neil says before leaning forward and adding softly, "but we have places for this kind of help. We have shelters, my dear."

He doesn't recognize me.

It's been too long.

"No, Father," I say, wondering if I look like a homeless person in my tattered yoga pants. "I'm fine. Thank you."

As soon as Father O'Neil disappears in the back, I gather my belongings, nod at the choir setting up at the front, and leave before the crowd arrives. I do not belong here. In fact I feel foolish; though, I do not know why.

There is a strong chill in the air outside; however, the day is bright, shining. My eyes need a moment to adjust, so I shield them with my hand as I climb into my car. Then I watch a few families funnel into the church. The family with the young girl in her little blue dress holds my attention the longest. It is the way she looks up at her mother with love and admiration. The girl has long curly hair similar to mine.

Dahlia instead of Delilah.

A troubled sun ascends a troubled sky as I drive for home.

Ian's plane touched down about an hour ago. According to the message he left on my phone, he is ready to talk.

Now I am afraid.

Closing the front door of my house, I peel off my clothes and jump into the shower. Usually the steam helps clear my head. But I can't get past Lillian's voice. "Take responsibility for your goddamn life. Your choices…"

My fingers prune.

The water runs cold.

I step out of the shower and into the frigid air then wrap myself in a towel. Grabbing my cellphone off the vanity, I sit on the bedroom floor, wet, dripping. Coiled up close to the bed, I rest my arm on top of the mattress while my ribcage presses against the side awkwardly. For a prolonged beat, I do nothing. My hands tremble. My fingers turn a light shade of purple. After a while I take a deep breath, swallow my fear, and make the call.

Ian picks up on the third ring. His voice immediately brings me to tears. "What is it?" he says.

I can barely get out the words: "I have to tell you something." My voice cracks a little under the strain. "And it can't wait."

In truth I should give Ian the courtesy of delivering this news face-to-face, but I need it done and I need it done now. The guilt and the shame are eating me alive. The only way to be free is to confess.

"Delilah, I know we haven't been able to connect, but I am supposed to have a meeting with George in twenty minutes," he says. "I'll be in again on Monday. Do you think we can—"

"No." My response is so quick, so strong, its significance is unmistakable. "It can't wait, Ian."

He takes a beat before replying, "What's going on?"

Suddenly everything I had planned in my head is like a tangled mass of yarn, knotted and impossible to unravel. I am mute.

"Delilah?"

"I did something," I say but can hardly get the words out.

"You did something?"

"Something stupid."

My fingernails make new tracks in my palm. And a long silence ensues.

"Ian, are you there?"

He knows.

I know he knows. I can feel it.

"I don't want to talk about this over the phone," he says.

"I'm sorry, Ian. I need you to know how sorry I am." Then I swipe my eyes with the back of my hand and refuse to let another tear fall. It's time to steel myself, handle the situation.

"You're sorry?" In my mind's eye, I see my husband pacing the floor of his hotel room. He has his fingers buried deep in his thick hair and a miserable expression on his face as he chews on my unspoken confession. "You're fucking sorry, Delilah?" There is a swollen pause before he adds, "Who?"

"It doesn't matter. Someone from work," I say, slowly.

"From work. Someone from work. Who?"

"You don't know him."

"Fuck you, Delilah." The statement is delivered in a calm tone but carries the weight of rage.

I hear the squeak of Ian's bed as he sits.

"Why are you telling me this now, while I'm away?"

I do not respond. Instead I think about how careless

we have been with each other. Like a load of wash removed too early and hung crookedly on wire hangers, the threads of our marriage were bound to get frayed.

"Ian—"

"I don't want to hear it," he says.

Another silence ensues.

Then he says, "Tell me what happened."

The fear inside me seizes control of my mouth. The cactus spikes are sharper than ever. Ian deserves the truth—he deserves the whole truth—but I cannot give it to him. In any case, it wouldn't make a difference. Look what happened with Lillian. She is right about me. I am a worthless piece of shit. There is nothing I can do or say to change that, so I simply reply, "What does it matter?"

"What does it matter?" Ian makes the statement more to himself than to me. "Are you serious?"

I do not respond.

"Delilah, tell me what happened."

There is nothing more I would rather do than engage in a lengthy monologue, plead my case, but the warnings screaming inside my head are far too loud to ignore. They are telling me to remain silent. After all, look what happened after I opened my mouth that night on the stairs outside the quivering green door, and then there is the case of that girl from school who tried to make a difference, and Bailey, and Lillian...

No.

People think the truth solves everything. Naïve people. In my world, the only world I have ever seen or known, the truth tends to make things worse.

"Please, Ian," I say.

With his voice low and stern, he replies, "Tell me, Delilah."

"It is not a good idea, Ian."

The silence that ensues is so long I start to wonder if he has hung up the phone. "Ian, are you still with me?"

"I want his name," he says.

I do not reply.

"Delilah?!"

With my eyes closed, I say, "Stop asking."

"You're telling me no?" he says, coolly.

"It is never going to happen again and telling you more will only cause additional damage. I've done what I could."

"So that's it?" he says. "Are you punishing me for what you saw in the kitchen?"

"I wouldn't do that."

"You wouldn't do that?" Again, Ian mumbles, making the statement more to himself than to anyone else. It almost sounds like he is mocking me. "Fuck you, Delilah."

Another silence ensues. This time it doesn't get broken with conversation. Ian hangs up the phone on me.

Pulling my knees close to my chest, I wrap my arms around my legs and stare at the wall. A line from the bible, from John 20:23, plays in my head.

Whoseever sins ye retain are retained.

I think about that for a long time.

They. Are. Retained.

CHAPTER TWELVE

Sigmund Freud theorized that dreams reflect a person's deepest wishes. Most often these are repressed desires, sadistic or masochistic or something in between. I cannot say I agree with his perspective, mainly because my dreams of late have all been nightmares accompanied by stress and suffering. They have all been fears pigmented in deep dark hues, shifting, merging, creating a lasting sense of dread. Right now, for instance, I am in a sterile room with the floor smeared in blood and viscous fluid. My teeth are gnashed together tightly, my knuckles drained white, and my fingers are grasping the pale blue sheet beneath me so violently, squeezing it so fiercely the blood to these appendages is all but cut off. And when I wake it is not to the feeling of wish fulfillment but to a body coated in sweat. My hands are trembling, my heart pounding against my ribcage. It is three o'clock in the morning, exactly three o'clock, the witching hour, and I feel as though I have been touched.

But then again, maybe I am masochistic.

Pulling the covers off, I throw my legs over the side of the bed and pace the floor. There is a racetrack of speeding thoughts in my head that leaves me in a state of agitated anxiety. It feels as though the nerves on the inside of my body are now on the outside, exposed to the elements, ravaged by them. The sound of my footsteps against my bedroom floor creates a cadence of distress, echoes of echoes. I cannot shake this feeling I have or the thoughts wildly burning through my skull.

Stop!

Fucking stop!

Time clicks by on the clock. And before I know it, three o'clock becomes four, four becomes five, and five becomes six. I cannot call in again, so I take a beat then tear open my closet doors and throw on the first skirt I see, unironed. The shirt that I select to go with it only partially matches. I enter my master bathroom and pull my hair into a messy bun then sit quietly until I climb into my car and set out not to work but to the local drug store. The purple shadows under my eyes are heavier than usual. I stare at them in the rearview mirror. There is not a stitch of makeup on my face to hide my flaws.

I am ugly.

So goddamn ugly.

Automated glass doors open in front of me. I head inside the store to the far end of the building, third aisle on the left. Slowly I walk the aisle until I catch a glimpse of what I am looking for then scan the available products on the shelf. There are five different choices of pregnancy tests from which to choose. It is too early. My adult brain knows it is too early, even if yesterday was the first day of my missed period. Regardless, I read the backs of three or four of the boxes to get a feel for which one will be the easiest to use as well as provide the most accurate reading. The first is a stick with an indicator that turns blue. The second creates a pink line in a small oval window when the test returns as positive. The third is a dipping stick, which changes color based on the results. I grab the test that turns blue and pay the cashier at the front.

"Can you point me in the direction of your restroom?" I ask the young man behind the counter. There is an open economics textbook resting face down on the stool behind him, which leads me to believe he attends the local junior college, a paper mill.

What a fucking waste.

The young man looks at the pregnancy test then at me once more. "It's out of order," he says, "but there is a fast food place next door. I doubt they would mind if you use theirs."

Before he has the chance to bag my purchase, I snatch the box off the counter and exit through the automated glass doors. The early morning rush has started to get way, the air thick with exhaust fumes and traffic noise. I can practically feel pollution form a fresh layer of film on my skin.

The restaurant is a little over fifty feet away from the drugstore, the two establishments separated by a thin median of small, poorly kept bushes. Although it is cool outside, I toss my sweater onto the passenger seat in my car before heading over. There is only one gap wide enough between the bushes for me to pass, so I make my way to that section. Otherwise, I would have to walk all the way around the median, and that is something I do not want to do.

I feel the crunch of leaves and straw beneath my feet and a branch reach up to catch hold of my arm. The branch slashes through my shirt to scrape the top layer of my skin. Sucking air in through my teeth, I stop to untangle myself from the bush and examine my injury in the process. The cut stings like mad but is relatively minor. My shirt is torn, its threads a little frayed, and a spotted line of blood is soaking through the light colored fabric.

There are two entrances to the fast food place, one

on each side of the building. At the front is a large play area surrounded by floor to ceiling tinted windows. Placing my hand over my smarting wound, I enter the building through the side door closest to the drug store then stand still for a moment as I assess my surroundings and determine where to go.

What are you doing?

A large wooden sign with an arrow points me in the right direction. I walk past the registers at the front to the opposite side of the building, where another wooden sign, one that looks as though it has been hanging there since the 1950s, resides above the restroom door. I half feel the chains holding the sign in place will snap the minute I step under it but proceed anyway. Aside from the employees and little old couple enjoying their meal in a booth by the window overlooking the parking lot, the place appears to be empty.

I push open the restroom door and am immediately hit with a stench that makes my eyes water. Looking right, I see a woman changing a baby on a makeshift plastic table. The diaper is clearly the source of the rancid smell; though, the restroom itself is in nasty condition with paper on the floor and a coating of filth. I step deeper into the room and let the door close on its own behind me then walk toward the far wall and drop the pregnancy test on the counter. My arm is still smarting, so I roll up the sleeve of my shirt and place a cool wet paper towel on the cut. The sting subsides slowly.

Looking over my shoulder, I see the young mother yank her baby up off the changing table then shove the dirty diaper into the garbage bin. She sports the child loosely, almost carelessly, on her hip as she exits the room. At no point does the young woman wash her hands or ensure the diaper makes it fully into the trash. In fact, it doesn't.

Disgusting.

There are three stalls in the restroom, none of which clean. Moving from stall to stall, I examine my options. The first toilet has a bloody tampon floating in brown bloody water. The second is missing its seat and appears to be broken. The third stall has what looks to be urine on the floor. I proceed into the third, stepping carefully to avoid getting urine on my shoes. It makes for a physically awkward situation.

I place toilet paper over the seat then pull my skirt up and prepare to take the pregnancy test.

This crazy.

I know it is crazy. But I have to do it anyway.

After rereading the instructions, I slip the stick between my legs and bear down to force what little urine there is inside me onto the stick. The filth in the confined space draws my attention and I lose my balance as a result. The pregnancy test slips from hand as easily as if my fingers had been greased. Before I can catch it, it lands with a splash in the bowl, droplets of toilet water springing up onto my bare thigh. I can only imagine the bacteria and viruses sitting on my flesh close to my private parts.

"You've got to be kidding me," I say, frustrated by my own clumsiness.

What the hell is wrong with me?

On my feet, I stare at the pregnancy test on the bottom of the toilet bowl. It looks like a sunken ship with its tip half hidden under the porcelain ledge.

Someone enters the room. At this point, I am unwilling to give up my stall, so I do not move. I hear the sound of footsteps and the creaking of stall doors being forced open. A soft voice issues a complaint. Then the main door hisses, and the person is gone, having chosen to wait rather than brave this filth.

I step out into the main area of the restroom and lock the door then go about washing my leg with soap so strong in odor it stings my nostrils. Then I dry my thigh with a brown paper towel that is soft as gravel and exit the building to return to my vehicle. Already late for work, I do not have time to go through the process again, nor would I want to go through it in a place like this.

I'm going mad.

Jacob Wallace sees me as I exit the elevator on our floor at Westgrove, Gardner, and Jones. He shakes his head at me as we pass in the hall. I know what he is thinking, but I don't care. My appearance is the last of my worries at this time.

Mind your own business.

While proceeding past the center cubicle section, I notice Nathaniel standing next to the intern, his arm resting on top of the cubicle wall close to where she is seated. There is a coffee in Nathaniel's hand as well as another from the same place on the intern's desk. Vinnie's. He looks up at me and smiles.

I keep walking.

A horrible burning immediately snakes through my stomach, like a bastard child encased its placenta sac kicking violently while in wait to be born.

What happened means nothing. My feelings about what happened outside the Paper Nickel mean nothing.

I am the unwanted.

I am the unloved.

I am the rejected.

But he should care because of his position in our organization. He should give a damn. Why doesn't he give a damn? Do I really mean so little?

Of course I do.

I meant that little to her.
Dahlia instead of Delilah.

Closing my office door, I take refuge behind my desk, staring blankly at my computer screen for a long time, hands trembling, heart pounding. The sour stench of alcohol is in the air. I taste it on my lips—a man's drink, a drinker's drink, something that belongs in a crystal decanter. Thoughts fire through my brain to cause a headache to form behind my eyes. I press my fingers against my temples in an effort to prevent the pain from becoming entrenched. The nerves under my skin ping with agitation as though scraped and scoured raw.

"Okay. It's okay," I tell myself softly.

Then I pull up a spreadsheet that I know needs to be worked, but I cannot focus. The numbers begin merge. They bleed into each other.

I need to know what is going on inside my body. My period is two days late.

Grabbing my bag from the desk drawer, I head to the convenient store across the street. Mr. Bhatia, the owner, is stocking shelves when I arrive. He looks up at me and smiles.

"Good morning, Delilah," he says in his thick accent. "You're here earlier than usual today."

I am neither in the mood nor the right frame of mind for small talk, so I get straight to the point. "I need a pregnancy test. Where can I find one?"

Mr. Bhatia blinks slowly before replying, "Aisle three."

There are only two product options from which to choose. I grab the blue stick and bring it to the front for Mrs. Bhatia, a quiet woman who always seems to be staring at the floor, to ring up at the register.

"Good luck," she says softly as she hands me the

bag. But I seriously doubt her idea and my idea of luck are in alignment.

At the office, I perform the pregnancy test carefully, following the directions exactly as they are written and ensuring I take extra precautions so as not to drop the stick in the toilet again.

Then I wait.

And I wait.

And I wait.

I wash my hands in the sink, checking the indicator over and over again in the process.

The final seconds arrive and my heart slams against my ribcage as I read the result.

Negative.

A rush of relief washes over me.

I double and triple check the indicator.

Negative.

Then I lean against the counter and begin to laugh.

It's true. You're going crazy.

Less than a minute later, my laughter turns to tears. I am overcome with emotion and have to splash cold water on my face to calm down.

Patting myself dry with a paper towel, I return to my desk and get to work, as is necessary to survive. The day drifts on. For a while I feel like I am going to be all right, like I will find a way through the tangled mess I have made of my life. But then the racetrack of thoughts in my head kicks into gear once more, and an incessant gnawing begins to take shape in the pit of my stomach. Mr. and Mrs. Bhatia are nice people, but they are not exactly known for keeping the most up-to-date products on their shelves. I can think of at least three occasions when I have bitten into an expired burrito. The scratching at my brain escalates to a point where I can no longer ignore it. There is a high probability that the pregnancy test was outdated and the result wrong.

It was wrong!

It was wrong!

I am now certain it was wrong.

Plus, enough time has not passed.

My adult brain knows I need to calm down and wait, think things through, but someone or something else is tugging on my puppet strings. Here I am working like an idiot, fingers scurrying across this stupid keyboard, while a bastard child is sitting inside its placenta sac deep in my womb waiting to be born.

I cannot do this.

The knot on the back of my neck tightens. I rub on it as I remember how sick I have been over the last few days—the vomiting and the dizziness, the general sense of physical change. Although it is not uncommon for my monthly to be late, when combined with the other markers, there is no doubt something is askew.

Acid rises into my throat. I grab the wastepaper basket from the side of my desk and lean forward in preparation to puke, but nothing comes out because I have not eaten anything substantial in days.

Then I sit quietly with my eyes closed, the up and down movement of my chest rapid and audible. I cannot think with that which is firing in my head.

By the time lunch rolls around, I am in a state of pure, unadulterated agitation. I drive to the store up the street and purchase not one, not two, but three more pregnancy tests. Then I take those tests to the restroom on my floor at Westgrove, Gardner, and Jones.

C'mon, c'mon, c'mon.

Negative. Every one.

After my final trip to the ladies room, Jane catches

hold of me in the hall and drags me to the break room for Lindsay Day's birthday party. It is a small affair with only a handful of people in attendance. The cake looks as though it was purchased at the last minute, a pitiful single layer circular sheet maybe six or seven inches in width. Basically, it is chocolate frosting with a lone candle in the center for the celebrated person to make a wish. I stand to the side as everyone sings to the birthday girl, the room spinning, my coworkers' faces as well. In my mind's eye, I see a child's birthday party layered over the black space between the trees outside the Paper Nickel. The stench of alcohol is in the air, even though the people around me are consuming soft drinks. There are nothing but teeth and lips and noise. Everything is ringing. It sounds like flies.

"I'm sorry, Jane," I say, faintly, "but I have to get back to work."

Stepping out into the hall, I feel acid rise from my stomach into my throat and am forced to make a mad dash for the toilet. I don't make it, so I puke what little I have inside me into the sink in the ladies room. Then I turn on the faucet and rinse out my mouth.

Jane enters the room a moment later. She rubs my back in a motherly fashion. "You're alright, sweetheart," she says. "You're alright."

"Don't say that," I hiss.

The rubbing ceases and Jane steps back to look at me.

"Sorry," I say. "I'm sorry, Jane. It's not you."

Get it together.

Her expression softens again.

I turn around and lean with my spine against the counter. The room is spinning. Beads of sweat are forming on my brow.

Jane shuts off the faucet and says, "What is going on

with you, Delilah? Are you ill?"

I do not respond.

She studies me at length once more. "You know I am your friend," she says. "I am here for you, if you need me."

I look up into her eyes then at the floor again. It is a nice thought, but Jane doesn't really know me. She doesn't know anything about me.

And I don't know who I am anymore.

Dahlia instead of Delilah.

"It's just a bug," I tell her. "Nothing to be worried about. I'll be fine once it passes." The weight of her stare makes me uncomfortable, so I add, "I'm fine, Jane. Really. Thank you for your concern."

In my office, I pick up the phone and call my gynecologist to confirm my upcoming appointment.

"Are you sure you cannot get me in sooner?" I say to the girl who does the scheduling. "No, no, I understand. I guess I'll have to wait."

"Hold on a second," she says. I hear the muffled sound of a conversation, like a hand over the receiver as a discussion takes place on the other end. The scheduler gets on the line once more. "There has been a cancellation. I know it is short notice, but if you can make it here by two tomorrow—"

"I'll take it," I say, definitively, excited that I am going to get the answers I need.

"Then you are rescheduled," she says.

"One more thing, I'll need a pregnancy test."

"That's fine," she says. "I'll tell the doctor."

"And a STD panel. In fact put me down for everything, whatever can be completed in a day."

Then I hang up the phone and sit quietly in my office.

My mind begins to wander and, as I think about what the doctor will find, the things that may be inside me, my hands go cold. I feel the blood rushing out of my cheeks.

I really am going mad.

CHAPTER THIRTEEN

It is in the confines of the mind that madness takes hold, a slow drip so imperceptible it rarely reveals itself until it is firmly entrenched and enslaves its owner. Like a memory etched into the cortex, its removal requires a knife.

Sitting alone in the conference room as I wait on my fellow coworkers to arrive for our scheduled meeting, I think about Ian's crooked smile and the way he touched me when we showered together. I think about his morning hair, shock of locks askew, sticking up in every direction, and his blue eyes looking at me with care. I think about how he would turn on the television at night and I'd curl up in his nook until the sounds lulled me to sleep and about his ratty old truck and how he revealed his love for me with a look.

Now, even though Ian is back in town, he won't pick up the phone when I call. He is avoiding me.

"Keeping oneself sane is tedious work," I whisper. *It's impossible.*

My fingers dig new tracks in my palms. There is a swelling in my throat that leaves my mouth dry. Thoughts swim in my head. Everything the doctor told me spirals through my mind as a cyclone. The evidence has returned in my favor; I am not pregnant. And yet there is still a lingering feeling I cannot deny, the feeling of a bastard child encased its placenta sac inside my womb kicking violently while in wait to be born.

Stop!

Fucking stop!

The doctor asked why I wanted the panels done to see if I have a sexually transmitted disease. And as he stared at me with his inquisitive eyes, I felt a swell of emotion in my gut, found that I could not formulate the words. I could no more talk to this man, who in all reality is a stranger, than I could talk to my husband. So, I simply replied, "I just want them and would rather not go into more."

"Are you sure there is nothing el—" he replied.

But before he could finish his thought, I snapped, "Yes, I am sure. Thank you."

He is a decent man. Dr. Gregory Baltic. Tall with chocolate brown skin and a warm white smile, Dr. Baltic is somewhere around fifty-five years old. I have been going to him for my feminine checkups for years.

He agreed to give me what I asked for but said that I still had to wait seven to ten days to find out if I am infected. It seems like a lifetime. And even if by some miracle the panels come back clean, I will have to do it all again in six months.

My brain tells me that I will have to do the pregnancy test again, too.

The fear feels like a cage. I am trapped while Nathaniel is free to roam the halls of Westgrove, Gardner, and Jones without a shred of remorse.

It's not fair.

But when has life been fair?

My fingernails dig new tracks in the palms of my hands.

This morning I spent my time at work researching sexually transmitted diseases and scanning painful pictures, examining alarming statistics, before settling into my seat in the conference room for the upcoming meeting. And as I am sitting here, alone, my brain runs through the laundry list of symptoms I might experience. I make a mental note of what can and cannot be cured. Of the people I see in the restaurants and at the grocery store, of my neighbors and my coworkers, of the ones on the street, someone has something—crawling, itching, breaching, destroying. In fact more than one person does. Chlamydia, gonorrhea, syphilis, herpes, hepatitis, HPV, AIDS...the list goes on for miles. And I don't know if I have been exposed. I don't know what is burrowing its way deep then deeper into my tissues. All I know is that I am skinnier than I have ever been.

When I stop to think about the number of diseases out there, the probability of exposure, the space between my legs tingles. It tingles and reminds me of the fact that I don't know who I am anymore.

Dahlia instead of Delilah.

I want to know who I am.

It also reminds me of my flaws, and guilt.

But I am not the only one at fault here. Nathaniel has passed his filth onto me. Yet the fucker is worshipped by everyone on the planet.

I switch my crossed legs from one side to the other.

Doesn't Nathaniel look jaundiced in a certain light?

He does, doesn't he?

Why didn't I notice earlier?

Resting my hands on the conference room table in front of me, I study my fingernails, which appear healthy and strong. For how long, though? What is the incubation period? When will necrosis set in? Is God punishing me?

Am I going to die for my sins?

Maybe I deserve to die.

Lillian's voice is in my head, nasty, screaming. She is crying out that it is my fault. All my fault.

But I have been thinking long and hard about the matter. In fact, I have been tossing and turning in bed night after night. If it is my fault, then it is his as well. And Nathaniel will surely do it again. Not to me. But to some other unsuspecting young girl.

So, yes, maybe I do need to take responsibility for my life. But then again shouldn't he take responsibility for his?

Someone needs to make him take responsibility!

Before I walked into the conference room, I saw Nathaniel by the cubicle section on our floor. He was leaning over the intern while she was looking up at him with a smile on her face, eyes lit the way someone's eyes light up around those they care for. I do not register on Nathaniel's radar at this point. He has forgotten me.

I am the unwanted.

I am the unloved.

I am the jettisoned

Nathaniel used me.

He used me.

He fucking used me and forgot my name.

It is like I am nameless all over again, always, forever, sitting in that room with the windowpane rattling behind Mr. F's head. I am nothing. I might as well not exist.

Do I even exist?

The filth Nathaniel injected into me is coursing through my veins right now. I feel it along with the million spider mites crawling under my skin, wreaking havoc. Though I have no sores between my thighs, no obvert signs of infection, I know there is corruption there. And the worst part is I cannot wash it away. The prickling feeling between my legs will always be there, however the tests return.

I cross my legs the other way once more.

Staring blankly at my hands on the table, voices distantly stewing in the hall, Nathaniel enters the conference room and sits across from me, one seat over to the right. The air feels thicker now that we are alone again. He has on the suit he was wearing the day we ate lunch together in front of the river. It was the day he told me I was beautiful and the comment filled me with emotion.

Now, a different emotion spirals through my frame like barbwire, ripping, tearing. Is he the kind who reads then preys upon vulnerability? The kind who in a blink measured my worth, or lack thereof?

I am worthless.

"Good morning, Delilah," he says in his usual voice with its usual lilt. "I am sorry we have not been able to catch up. I hope you understand how busy I have been with the transition."

Deplorable bastard.

It is like what happened outside the Paper Nickel never occurred.

I stare Nathaniel down but do not otherwise respond.

He glances at the stack of papers in his hands then places those papers on the table in front of him before he looks up at me. Examining my face, his eyes begin to narrow. "Is everything alright?" he says.

"Is everything alright?" I mutter.

How could everything be alright?

Lillian's voice repeats in my head. "Take some responsibility for your life."

It's my fault.

Everyone will say that it's my fault.

After a breath, I add, "I've been thinking about this story written by a woman at a time when such things were not written by women. The story was of a man and a woman traveling in different directions. At a certain point, their paths crossed and the two slammed into each other. The man, being physically stronger, trampled over the woman. He left her screaming on the street like she was nothing, like she didn't even matter. Then he went on his merry way and forgot all about her. In fact, he didn't give her a second thought. Time went by. Slowly, painfully, the woman began to recover from her injuries. She grew stronger. It was hard work. Took will. Then one day she saw the man. She followed him home."

Nathaniel does not reply. However, he furrows his brows.

"Do you want to know what she did to the man who wronged her, Nathaniel?"

"Delilah?" he says. And it is like distant thunder that only now draws near. His voice gradually becomes distinct. "Delilah, I seem to have lost you there for a second."

I've lost myself.

Our coworkers begin to trickle into the room, one at a time, Jacob Wallace included. Wallace takes the seat next to mine on the left. As everyone else chats, I quietly watch the person across from me engage in pleasantries.

Is that a sore above his wrist or only a shadow?

"You look better," Wallace says in a low voice. "You've washed your hair and your color is back."

His statement only partially registers. "Is it?"

I took the time to apply makeup before leaving my house this morning, if only to prevent such comments. Of course, I still didn't bother to iron my clothes.

Once all of my coworkers settle into their respective seats, the head of our department, Ms. Suzanne Kline, enters the room and begins the meeting. She reviews what we went over at our last conference and provides a breakdown of departmental goals and shortcomings. Then a series of presentations follow, none of which pertinent to me. I do not belong here. I am lower on the totem pole than most of these others. They have only asked me here to review some numbers and projections because of an upcoming project. I am like the dog in the corner, waiting for my master's call.

My eyes run over the people in the room, one after the next. Polished, professional people.

Before learning that my mother forgot my name and Ian preferred porn over the warmth of my body, before finding out that my husband isn't going to forgive me for my transgression and Nathaniel used me without care, I would have worked tirelessly to keep up with these others. I would have pretended. But something has changed. I don't know who I am anymore. *Dahlia instead of Delilah.* And I certainly don't give a shit about this company's bottom line.

My fingernails dig deeper into my palms. I can feel beads of sweat forming on my brow. The room is closing in on me. All about there are microorganisms causing disease.

Nathaniel looks my way under the dim lights. He smiles at me with his eyes. And it is a good smile, the kind of smile that makes others want to do the same. It is infectious.

Infectious.

I want to gouge his eyes out of their sockets with a dull knife, keep them from ever smiling again.

When it is Nathaniel's turn to speak, he commands the room. I have witnessed his effect before, his charm, the way he moves across the floor confidently, utilizes his voice to draw attention. Women cackle at Nathaniel's pedestrian jokes. They blush at his ridiculous flirtations. Even Suzanne, a smart woman, perhaps the smartest in our company, falls under the weight of Nathaniel's charisma. And the men—the men succumb as well. After all, Nathaniel is a guys' guy, the type of guy who talks about football in front of the water cooler.

But I see past his falseness, past the compliments and mannerisms, the fucking lies. And as he stands in front of the room looking over at me, I suspect he knows that I know.

Eventually, the meeting releases and my coworkers exit through the single door. Nathaniel lingers behind as I collect my belongings. We are alone again. I move to leave, but he cuts me off at the pass, sort of turns me around.

"What is it?" I ask him.

"I was hoping to get in a quick word with you," he replies. When I fail to respond, he adds, "If you don't mind me saying, you look as beautiful as ever, Delilah."

I do mind.

"But you don't seem like yourself."

"Don't I?" I whisper.

There must be something in my expression because Nathaniel furrows his brows. He takes a step forward, closing the gap between us. It is a breach of my personal space, one that causes the spider mites to scurry faster. Then Nathaniel gently places his hand on my arm. As I look at it, he says, "We need to talk about what happened between us, Delilah. I hope you understand I haven't been avoiding you. In fact, I have been meaning to reach out to you all week."

I am sure.

"May I take you to lunch today?" he inquires.

My response is immediate and glacier cold. I rip my

arm away from his reach. "Can't. Busy."

"You mean you have plans with someone else?"

With a little shake of my head, I say, "No."

Nathaniel stares at me at length before he starts to laugh.

I don't think I like what that means; however, I refrain from commenting.

Then his laughter stops, and his expression grows serious. There is darkness in him that I cannot believe I did not recognize earlier. It is probably what was scratching at my brain from the start.

Nathaniel checks the hall to make sure no one can hear us. "We really do need to talk, Delilah. How about dinner?"

There is a stretch of silence, at which time the noise outside the room elevates, even though the crowd has already started to disperse.

"I honestly don't know what is happening here," he says.

"Oh no?"

"Did you think that what happened between us was something more than it—"

"Do not flatter yourself, Nathaniel," I tell him.

"Then why am I sensing so much animosity?" he says.

Animosity. Ha.

"Are you?"

He looks at his shoes before returning his attention to me. "Listen, Delilah, I like you. I do. But we need to keep things professional. So, if you thought—"

"I didn't," I say, abruptly. "Trust me."

Another awkward silence ensues.

Nathaniel smiles, but it is not his usual smile. It is forced, borderline ugly. "Please, let me take you to dinner," he says. "I would really like to discuss this like intelligent adults."

I half expect the word "consenting" in there somewhere.

"Remove your hand from my arm," I tell him, because it is back on me again.

He complies, slowly.

"Where is Yvonne?" I ask with a detectable chill.

By the expression on Nathaniel's face, I know I have caught him off guard. "Excuse me?"

"Yvonne? Where is she?"

"Why are you asking me this?"

"Did you have something to do with her losing her job or was it a coincidence that you two were involved?"

Nathaniel chews on my question for a moment before giving answer. "Did she tell you that?" When I do not respond, he studies me for an extended beat. "I did not realize that the two of you were so close."

"We're not."

Another awkward silence takes place.

Nathaniel says, "What happened with Yvonne was outside of my control. I did everything I could to help her."

Help? Right.

"Did you?"

"Yes, Delilah, I did." His tone grows increasingly nasty as our conversation continues. And the windowpanes behind him begin to vibrate.

He needs to take responsibility.

"Yet here you are, while she is gone."

"I am not your enemy," he tells me. "So why are you treating me like one?"

"I hadn't had a drink in years," I reply. "Years."

He looks out into the hall then at me once more. "Let me take you to lunch," he says. "Whatever misunderstanding that has occurred here, I am sure we can resolve it in a mature manner."

"A mature manner." I scoff.

Now I am making him a little nervous. He closes the door, save for a one inch crack.

"I am sorry if you have regrets, Delilah, but there is no call for this kind of behavior," he says too close to me.

"My husband asked for your name," I tell him.

"You told your husband about us?"

"Of course I told him," I say. "He is my husband."

Nathaniel shakes his head. "What would make you do something like that? You do know it could put us both in jeopardy? With all the scandals in the news, there are policies about office relationships and outside conduct here. And the cuts are not over, Delilah?"

"I am sure you'll be alright," I say, acerbically, even though I am fully aware the threat is directed at me.

"What is wrong with you?" he says.

"What is wrong with me?"

I don't know.

Something.

"I thought we understood each other," he says. "You're acting like what happened was something it wasn't. And if you remember correctly, I had more than a few drinks myself."

"Yes, but you clearly can handle your liquor. I, on the other hand, couldn't stand on my own. Do you want to see the scar on my knee?"

"You're exaggerating," he tells me. And when I do not respond, he adds, "You could have asked someone else to take you home, Delilah. You and I both know why you stayed."

The glass window shakes so violently, the walls tremble and, as they do so, my pink-eared bunny enters the picture. He walks behind Nathaniel to stand two feet to the rear of my enemy on the left; this is a defensive, aggressive position.

I hiss, "Let. Me. Go."

Releasing me slowly from his grip, as though only now realizing he had taken hold of my arm in the first place, Nathaniel says in a much calmer tone, "What happened shouldn't have happened, Delilah. I think we are both in agreement about that. But if you expect me to stand here while you point a finger at me, then you are sorely mistaken. It is not my fault you have regrets."

He sounds like Lillian. The fault is mine. It is all mine. No one else's.

Take some responsibility for your life.

Straightening his clothes, Nathaniel prepares to rejoin the others. Before he does so, he says, "Now, if you would like to finish this conversation, I would be more than happy to take you to lunch or dinner or what-have-you, discuss the matter like mature adults. Otherwise, I think we are finished here."

Yes, finished.

When I do not respond for an extended beat, Nathaniel narrows his eyes. He shakes his head before he exits the room, all the while muttering something under his breath, something I cannot quite hear.

It is lunchtime, so I grab my bag and make my way to the parking garage to eat alone in my car. Everything feels different now, like I am a species once removed. I was born and my bones fused together. Then I became less and less malleable over the years. Society went about chiseling away my edges, whittling me into something resembling the norm, but never the norm because my edges would not smooth. It is like I am entangled, caught in the snare outside the Paper Nickel. And the fires of hell are burning inside me in response.

And still I question: *Maybe it is all my fault.*

The ground beneath Westgrove, Gardner, and Jones has become less secure. A parade of eyes stares at me wherever I go. I cannot help but wonder if it is Nathaniel's doing. Although I have worked for the company longer, although I have saved the owners an immense amount of money, Nathaniel is in a position of greater power and control. He has the ear of those who could cause me harm. He wasn't wrong about me being in jeopardy. And I wouldn't put it past him to go on the offensive. Yvonne was a guess that proved my suspicions. And she worked for the company much longer than me.

After finishing out the day quietly in my office, I climb into my car and sit for a moment, staring ahead at the massive structure of water stained concrete. There is an emptiness inside me that consumes all.

To get home, I must exit the parking garage and head through the outdoor parking lot to the main road. There are three stops along the path that I usually take. As I come to a halt at the second stop, I look left and see Nathaniel standing next to his SUV, engaged in conversation with a man from the eighth floor, one from the upper echelon. A vehicle pulls up behind me and I have to decide between turning into the parking lot or pressing forward toward the main road. I turn back, park in an empty spot, wait, watch.

Nathaniel and the man go their separate ways. Then Nathaniel climbs into his SUV, and a few minutes later he is heading north on the main road.

I follow at a distance.

He stops at the gas station four minutes away. Because I don't want him to see me, I pull around to the building across the street and watch from my bird's eye view.

Nathaniel pumps gas into his vehicle, all the while chatting up a girl I recognize from the local grocery mart. She is only seventeen, thin, long shapely legs. Then he enters the convenient store and comes out a few minutes later with a case of beer and a small brown bag.

Nathaniel continues north.

Again, I follow.

Approximately twenty three minutes from Westgrove, Gardner, and Jones, there is a high-end apartment complex that our company uses to put people up from time to time. The Butchers, for example, stayed there while making their original cuts. But the other butchers have since gone home. Only Nathaniel remained on board permanently. It is strange that he should still be in this complex. I wonder if it is on the company's dime.

Typing a code into the keypad, Nathaniel waits only a moment before the metal bars of the security gate swing open. I cannot follow without him seeing me; nor can I piggyback on another vehicle because there is no one else around. Plus, I know the place is equipped with video cameras. They are visible from the street.

So, after a few minutes of lingering, I decide to drive home. But the closer and closer I get to my dark empty house, the worse the gnawing sensation in the pit of my stomach grows.

Somehow, and I am not sure how, I wind up outside Nathaniel's gate again, this time in the middle of the night when the crescent moon marks a coal black sky. I sit in wait, rubbing my hands together, scroll of lighted pictures flashing through my brain: Ian in the kitchen, the trees outside the Paper Nickel, the glass behind Mr. F's desk, my pink-eared bunny, the quivering green door, Ian's old truck, a mysterious woman slicing up my father's buttocks, my

mother's funeral, my sisters laughing, color, color, color...
You have to stop.

I start thinking about the last conversation I had with Father O'Neil. It was after my appointment at the gynecologist. He was sitting in his office eating an onion bagel, smudge of cream cheese on his lip. I went to him in the hope that maybe, just maybe, there was something he could do. After hearing my story from end to end, Father O'Neil sat quietly for a moment then placed his hand on my hand, assigned some prayers, and suggested I join his support group on Thursday nights.

"Act of contrition?" I replied. "And a support group?"

I declined.

Then I stood up and, without additional remark, left the room. Whatever bridge existed was broken, irreparably.

So, here I am, sitting in the cold dead night outside Nathaniel's apartment complex, waiting, because it doesn't feel right that I am the only one who has to pay for our sin. Why should I have to be the only one?

It doesn't fucking feel right!

CHAPTER FOURTEEN

Light is a form of electromagnetic radiation. It is energy that illuminates the world around us.

As I lay in bed, blinking slowly, the last light of the day pushes through the slats of the blinds in my master bedroom to burnish the floor and create a soft buttery glow. Particles dance in the stream. They drift and float.

My eyes turn to the bedside table, where a mud yellow spider, perhaps the same spider that has been leaving a trail of webs around my house, crawls in front of the broken green lights of the alarm clock then suddenly stops, almost as though recognizing my eyes upon it, and scurries away to disappear in the darkness between the small stack of books and the wall.

I throw my legs over the side of the bed and take a moment to steady myself. Then I walk to the window and yank the curtains shut, blocking the daylight from entering the room.

Pressing the heels of my palms against my eyes, I see splashes of color in uneven alternating rings. The color changes shades before finally fading to black. What little sleep I have been getting has been marred by strange and disturbing nightmares.

What is happening to me?

It is a good thing that Westgrove, Gardner, and

Jones sent Nathaniel to an out of town training for the last two days. Otherwise, I don't know what I would have done.

A headache pounds behind my eyes with violent force. Lying in bed all day did nothing to help. In fact, I merely lost time.

"You need to get healthy," I say, faintly. "That's what you need to do. You need to forget about him and get healthy. Get your head straight."

After changing into athletic wear, I step outside to go for a three mile run around my neighborhood. It is a quiet place populated with quiet people, one of the main reasons Ian and I decided to settle here. But for the occasional child playing basketball or person walking his or her dog, the subdivision appears deserted. The paths are smooth, the vegetation plentiful, and there is a floating fountain in the center of the pond that expels sprays of water. In the right light, the water glistens. The weather has been manic of late, but today it is nice. It is perfect. I place my earphones over my ears and turn up the music, find my stride. Usually, when I do this it lessens the wild thoughts in my head, but right now my mind is buzzing. I see Ian looking at me the way he looked at me in that old pickup truck and Nathaniel smiling as he offered me my favorite coffee. I see my father bursting through the scraped green door and my mother gnashing her teeth. I see Lillian cackling like a hyena in Mr. F's office and a razor sharp blade slicing through my father's skin. Then there are the trees outside the Paper Nickel, the darkness, pages and pages of sexually transmitted diseases, my pink-eared bunny, the glass turtle ashtray, and blood. There is so much blood.

I stop to catch my breath.

Sweating profusely, I return home to peel my clothes

off and jump into the shower. The ringing in my head disappears the minute the water begins to flow; however, the fix is only temporary and I know it. For the umpteenth time, I lean forward and perform an examination of my private area. Everything looks pink and healthy. It doesn't matter that there are no obvious signs of a problem. It doesn't matter that my gynecologist called to say I am clean. I know my body. I KNOW there is something infecting me. It is why I scheduled for a second opinion. The tests are wrong.

They're fucking wrong.

A wall of cold air hits me the moment I step out of the shower. Wrapping myself in a towel, I wipe the fog off the mirror with the palm of my hand then suck air in through my teeth. My eyes are the same glacial green, my bones in their usual locations, but I am different now. The youthful padding in my face is all but gone. And the purple pools under my eyes are deeper, darker than they have ever been. I step on the scale to learn that I am ten pounds lighter than my ideal weight, the weight my doctor said was too light in the first place. And when I open the towel and examine my image in the mirror, I do not see a skeleton shrink wrapped in skin but something very, very close. It is like I am a couple missed meals away from anorexia nervosa. Like I am someone else.

Dahlia instead of Delilah.

After drying my hair with a towel and rubbing a bit of product through my curls for moisture, I slip on a satin trim scoop neck cotton camisole with built-in bra as well as a pair of panties. Then I reach into my makeup bag and dig out what I need to fix my face. The purple pools under my eyes are the greatest problem, so I hide them with carefully applied cover up, avoiding the shellac method. Then I add color with a little mascara, tinted lip gloss, and blush. The goal is to reduce remarks about my appearance, not garner more attention.

Even though I am ahead of schedule, I throw on my favorite jeans, a baggy white shirt, and the retro jacket Ian bought me when we first married, when he did not have a clue about women's sizes. It is a light jacket, perfect for air conditioned rooms. I remember how proud he was of finding the item and how ashamed I felt because it did not fit. So, I packed it away in the closet with the hope that I could wear it one day. Now there is room inside to spare.

Stop thinking about Ian.

My stomach starts to growl. I head to the kitchen to search for something edible in the refrigerator. There isn't much. The yogurt is expired, so I toss it in the trash along with an opened can of tuna fish. There are noodles in a Tupperware bowl that stink of rot. I reclose the top and shove the bowl to the side with a plan to clean later. Then I pull open the crisper drawer and find a single Red Delicious apple, which I give a quick whiff and scan.

Slamming the refrigerator shut, I take my first bite of the day, juice dribbling out the side of my mouth in the process, like I don't know how to eat. I swipe the juice away with the top of my hand.

In the living room, I notice a photo of us, a photo of Ian and me. It is in a silver frame with the word LOVE engraved at the bottom. There is no scenery in the background of the picture. Rather it is a close-up of our faces; we are smiling. I set the photo facedown then sit in the quiet, nibbling away at my apple until it is nothing but core encased in thin random clumps of mesocarp.

There is an unpleasant stillness in the air.

What now?

I should not have made plans with Jane. I should not have made period. *What am I doing?*

The delicate segue between afternoon and night has already begun. Pulling the curtains to the side, I watch the change, but it is different somehow. The house feels as though it is swelling; it is swallowing me whole. I wonder if I will know pleasure again, or comfort.

Please, God, make it stop.

A stack of mail sits on the counter in wait to be opened. With a long deep sigh, I cross the room to sift through flyers and postcards, faux notices and bills. As I am about to give up the effort, I catch sight of a handwritten envelope near the bottom of the pile. It has my uncle's name and address scrolled across the top left corner in blue ink. I set everything else aside and hold the letter in my hand for an extended period.

In the kitchen, I lean with my spine against the stove. I did not learn of my uncle's existence until I overhead Bailey talking about him with my brother. When I asked who they were talking about, they informed me of the family members on my mother's side, who I had assumed were dead. I was almost thirty years old at the time. That would make it two years prior to my mother's passing.

The letter makes my hands tremble; though, I do not know why exactly. He is probably just writing in response to the message I sent him after my mother's body was found. Strangely enough, Bailey had my uncle's address. Or maybe it is not strange at all because I am the only outsider.

I take a deep breath and read.

Dear Delilah,

I am writing to ask that you refrain from inquiring further about our family's history. My sister, your mother, was an extremely troubled woman who brought nothing but pain and suffering to those around her. Although it was not Joanne's fault entirely, there were actions she could have taken to improve her circumstances. She made her choices. At this time my family strongly believes opening up lines of communication with Joanne's children would be a mistake, especially now that you and your siblings are grown. Please understand that I am not writing this to hurt you or anyone else but to protect my mother, who has been through more than enough on account Joanne's issues. I implore you to respect our wishes and refrain from contacting us again.

Deepest Condolences,
Uncle (Dickey) Dickson

P.S. I am sorry to disappoint you, but you will not find the answers you are seeking here!

My hand drops with the letter in it.
Fuck Dickey Dickson!
Fuck the whole lot of them!
Blood drains from my skull to force me to the floor. Sitting on the cold, hard tile, I stare at my reflection in the stainless steel appliance in front of me, the image distorted like that in a funhouse mirror. Although I can no longer remember my mother's face, I know that I look like her. I have been told a million times. It is my cap of dark hair, as well as my full pomegranate lips and almond shaped eyes. Digging up the past is a foolish thing to do. I should have known better. After all, I am the unwanted. I am the unloved. My uncle's letter is just another in a long line of confirmations.

I. Am. The. Rejected.

At once I cannot stand the stench of the garbage in the room. The rancid smell is so thick it makes it near impossible for me to take in air. I yank the trash bag out of its container and take it to the receptacle outside; however, the receptacle is packed to the brim. Only now do I realize that I have not placed the garbage at the curb for weeks. The flies are buzzing.

I try to jam the garbage into the receptacle anyway. Trash spills out of the side; it crashes on the ground with a bang and a splash. The stench overwhelms me.

Throwing my arm up over my nose, I turn and press my hand against the corner of the exterior of my house for support. That is when I see them. My neighbors. They are outside. Everyone within my line of sight anyway. A single neighbor in front of each visible house, right down the line, and they are all focused on me.

What the hell is this?

"What are you doing?" I yell after an extended beat, but no one answers.

Then, one after the next, my neighbors disappear behind the front doors of their respective homes, slamming those doors behind them like dominoes in the process.

The golden orange light from the lamppost must be playing tricks on me because there isn't a door that doesn't look green.

And everything is vibrating.

The whole goddamn world.

The green from my neighbors' doors drips down onto steps then into the street, collecting to form the makings of a river.

As quickly as possible, I return to my kitchen and crumble up Uncle Dickie's letter. I don't want to see it anymore. I don't want to touch it, so I throw it on the ground. Now it looks like a coiled snake ready to strike.

No, no, no, no, no.

I pick the letter up and smooth it out with my hand then fold it neatly and place it in a kitchen drawer. I don't know why, but it means something.

What does it mean?

My mother was fifty-seven years old when she died. Aside from her children, she left behind a mother, two brothers, and a sister, none of whom attended her funeral. Her body was found by a stranger on account of the stench.

My head throbs, so I curl up on the couch and close my eyes. Eventually I drift away into a nightmare.

It is the sound of the doorbell that wakes me.

Jane is twenty minutes late, tardiness her modus operandi. Of course, given my track record at work, I have no right to complain. She greets me with a smile from the open doorway. Jane has on distressed blue jeans paired with a v-neck charcoal heather tee and stark white blazer. It is a simple, sassy look that suits her figure well. Her mom hair is pulled up off her neck, bangs swept to the side.

As we climb into her vehicle, I say, "Jane, you look fantastic." But my voice sounds bland, like I am exhausted.

Although my headache has been downgraded to a dull pulsation, there is a feeling in my chest that I cannot shake.

"I'm glad you suggested this," Jane says before examining me more closely. She knits her brows. "You okay?"

Am I okay?

A picture of Nathaniel flashes before my eyes, accompanied by a reemergence of the prickling sensation between my legs. "Yes, Jane, I'm fine. Why do you ask?"

She bites her bottom lip. It is one of her quirks. "No reason. For a moment I thought maybe—I don't know what I thought, Delilah. Don't listen to me. I'm half crazed from motherhood."

There is a full moon outside casting a purplish-silver

glow over the land. The roads are slick and muddy, the smell of rain in the air.

"Can I ask you something?" Jane says. She does not wait for my reply before continuing. "Did something happen at the Paper Nickel?"

We are heading north on Oak Street now, fifteen minutes from my house. The traffic is heavy. A small group of bicyclists with reflectors are taking up too much of the road. At the intersection where Jane stops, a black cat crosses our path. I want to spit three times, but I can't because Jane is waiting for my answer. Now the bicyclists are everywhere. They are all around. And she is staring at me.

My voice sounds dry. It even cracks a little. "No, Jane." After a pause, I add, "And what do you even mean?"

Splitting her attention between me and the road, Jane shakes her head slowly. "Nothing," she says. "Forget I asked."

I stare at her but do not otherwise respond.

Then Jane says, "I thought I noticed something."

"You thought you noticed something at the Paper Nickel?" I reply, coolly. "You were there all of twenty minutes, Jane."

The volume of Jane's voice elevates. "I'm so sorry about that, Delilah. I wouldn't have left if it wasn't necessary."

I hear Bailey telling me how necessary it was for my mother to abandon me into the hands of violence. I even see Bailey in my head. But now she is with Lillian. And the two have judged me irresponsible, unworthy of support.

"It's fine," I say. "How much longer do you think?"

"Nelly's is right up the road," Jane replies.

The dimly lit sports bar is seated in the center of a rundown plaza. Its parking lot is littered with potholes and windblown trash. There is a man in ragged clothes on the corner by the bus stop. He is pushing a shopping cart of what I can only assume are his belongings up and down the street.

Are those sores on his neck or is that just the light?

I squeeze my thighs together tightly.

"This is Nelly's?" I say with an air of judgment.

Jane extracts the key from the ignition of her vehicle. "You mean you have never been here before, Delilah? You're the one who suggested this place."

"Yes, Jane, I know I suggested it," I hiss.

We exit her car.

"On the recommendation of others."

"Whose recommendation?" Jane says.

I do not respond.

She enters the sports bar first, whipping the glass door open. I follow a moment later, the door closing by its own momentum behind me.

Nelly's is the opposite of the Paper Nickel. It is a small, quiet place with a dark, pub-like atmosphere. Everything is made of wood. The chairs are wood. The table is wood. The bar is wood. There are sports memorabilia and flat screen televisions on the walls. At the center of the establishment is the owner's crown jewel, a massive nicked and scratched bar approximately twenty-eight inches in depth. The bar extends across most of the room. It takes up space. Behind it is an impressive stock of liquor, lit from many angles. Colored glass gleams in the light.

Jane cocks her head. "Well, isn't this a coincidence?"

I follow Jane's line of sight to the table of Westgrove, Gardner, and Jones employees. There is only one person I do not recognize, and that is the redhead sitting next to Nathaniel.

He's back.

I knew he would be.

"I didn't expect them to be here, Jane," I say, defensively.

She sharpens her tone only enough to express what she is thinking. "Are you telling me the truth, Delilah?"

"Why would you ask me something like that?" I reply.

Even though Jane's suspicions are warranted, I feel offended. After all, she is saying she doesn't believe me.

The group is seated beyond the breezeway in clear view of where Jane and I are standing. What catches my attention the most is that the intern from our office is markedly absent.

I perform a scan of the rest of the place. It's mainly sports memorabilia and old video game machines. A few of the regulars are perched on barstools in front of the bar. And a couple is seated in the far corner, where it is dark, private.

Then I turn my attention to Nathaniel, who has been watching us since Jane and I entered the building. I don't like the look on his face.

Take that fucking look off your face.

The door opens behind me, and I feel a breeze on my skin. It sweeps through my hair. The next thing I know, Jacob Wallace's hand is on my spine and he is saying, "Nothing but surprises today. Who told you about Nelly's, Delilah?"

The rapidity in which my lies form sends a chill through my bones. "A few of us were talking, so I figured I would see what all of the fuss is about."

Jane's hot stare burns a hole through the side of my head.

"I hear the wings are fantastic here," she tells

Wallace after a beat. Then she smiles at me.

Wallace says, "Don't let the décor fool you, Jane. There is no better in town. Isn't that right, Nelly?"

The old guy behind the counter gives a nod. "And don't you forget it. Tell your friends."

Wallace steps around to my other side. "Come join us. There is plenty of room."

"We don't want to intrude," Jane says, but this is her way of being polite and everyone knows it.

At the table where Nathaniel and the others are seated, I gather that the redhead invited Wallace without Nathaniel's knowledge. And the other Westgrove, Gardner, and Jones employees showed up of their own accord, unexpectedly.

The redhead gives Jane and me the once over. It is the classic size-up, which adds another degree of tension to an already tension filled room.

"We're not planning on staying long," Jane says in response to the redhead's glare. "Isn't that right, Delilah?"

A parade of eyes stares back at me.

I remain silent.

The bartender brings Wallace a drink. The two seem to know each other well. They chit-chat for a good minute.

Then Wallace, Jane, and I review the menus, and as we do so, I feel the pressure of Nathaniel's glower. He knocks down the last of his drink then slams his glass on the table and storms off to play video games on the other side of the bar.

Ha.

Again, Jane looks my way.

The redhead asks, "What's that about?"

Before Wallace takes another sip of his drink, he says, "You never can tell, so who cares."

Although I have no appetite, I order a burger and

fries to keep up the pretenses. Wallace and Jane go for the hot wings, while the redhead waves food off all together, and the other Westgrove, Gardner, and Jones employees finish their meals.

After the food arrives, Nathaniel makes his way to the semi-secluded area of the bar. It is on the rear right side of the building where the second set of game machines is located. A soft electric blue glow highlights the section. The restrooms are down the hall, one on each side with the women's on the right.

Claiming I need to use the restroom, I stand and excuse myself from the table.

"We'll save your seat for you," Wallace tells me.

I nod.

But as I head to the ladies room, Nathaniel grabs hold of my arm, as expected, his fingers burning with the heat of having been stoked in a fire. "Exactly what do you think you are doing here, Delilah?"

The smell of liquor is hot on his breath—scotch or bourbon, something strong, a man's drink, a drinker's drink, something that belongs in a crystal decanter by a leather couch.

Suddenly, the lights seem brighter yet farther away.

The throbbing in my head increases exponentially.

"I don't know what you are talking about," I reply in a faint voice.

"Oh, I think you do," he says. And he squeezes my arm tighter, too tight in fact, fingernails digging fresh marks.

Thick green acrylic polish begins to drip southward on the walls as copies of my uncle's letter carpet the floor.

I look down the hallway, which opens slowly at the end. It becomes slightly wider as well.

What is happening to me?

Through the tunnels of my eyes, I see the darkness between the trees outside the Paper Nickel. I hear the sound of nocturnal creatures and man's breathing. Standing in front of those trees is my pink-eared bunny, watching, waiting. I left him behind next to the glass turtle ashtray on the table and everything changed.

Nathaniel wrenches me closer. In a demanding voice, he says, "Explain yourself."

Explain myself.

You explain yourself.

"Let go of my arm," I tell him calmly.

"I want to know what you think you are doing," he says.

"You should really let go of my arm."

He nearly cracks a bone with his grip.

The whole world wants me to bend. But I've bending my whole life. And I'm sick of it.

So, nodding at the table, I say, "What if they see you, Nathaniel? What then, huh?"

He yanks me deeper into the hall and, in so doing, removes us from the other's line of sight. In a low, furious voice, he says, "Why are you here? Do you think this is a game?"

Isn't it?

I feel the sensation of a slow smile slide across my face. It is not purposeful, not something I mean to do. Otherwise, I do not respond.

The vein on the side of Nathaniel's neck pulsates. He is angry, but not nearly as angry as me.

CHAPTER FIFTEEN

There is the cursing, and the lying and the murder, the stealing and the adultery; they break bounds, and bloodshed follows bloodshed—Hosea 4:2.

Nathaniel pushes me up against the wall, his forearm an inch from my head, blocking my peripheral vision on the right. As his body presses against mine, I feel the heat and moisture of his breath on my skin. His scent is different now, musky rather than citrusy. The fermented stench of liquor is in his mouth, so heavy I can practically taste it.

With a look in his eye that reminds me of the Paper Nickel, he runs his middle finger over my lips, gently tracing the border. "What is it about you, Delilah" he says.

My lack of consent?

Nathaniel is a tall man, dominating in the manner, like an officer of the law. His build is slender and muscular, strong. He has what some refer to as a *presence*, which draws the attention of those around him. Whenever he is in a room, he commands it with an air of superiority.

Slipping his fingers around the back of my neck, he takes hold of me forcefully and, with a vigorous jerk, yanks me slightly closer. My mouth opens in response. Then he shoves his tongue through the space between my lips and slides his hand to the small of my back, fingers firm against my spine, pressing his body against mine, grinding.

The voice inside my head screams for me to stop him, but I don't. Instead, I wait. I stand there like a vacant structure, taking all of this the way I have taken everything else in my life—with little to no response. His hands over my body. Mouth against my mouth. Breath on my skin. I take it as I took what happened outside the Paper Nickel. And the abandonment. And the rejection. And the abuse.

Do something, you useless piece of shit!

I take it with my fingernails deep in my palms, digging for blood, every inch of my body cold, numb. I take it because, from the time I entered this world until this very moment, it is all I have been conditioned to do. And to be honest, I am not sure I have a choice anymore.

Goddamn it, don't just stand there!

There is no doubt in my mind that Nathaniel is capable of reading the signs. He is a smart, cunning man, and from what I have witnessed quite calculating. So, why he chooses not to, I do not know.

Breathily, he says, "Is this what you want, Delilah?" His fingers sink into my hair at the base of my skull. "You don't have to be ashamed," he adds in a whisper. "It's natural. How we are made. Do you hear me, Delilah? You don't need to feel regret. It's alright."

It's anything but alright.

Suddenly I am whisked into the darkness between the trees outside the Paper Nickel, my skin smarting from the attack of razor sharp rocks and twigs, slices of debris. Nathaniel's breathy voice is in my ear. *You're alright, Delilah. You're alright.* My blood goes cold. And there is a raking sensation inside my stomach that causes me to shiver. It feels an awful lot like a bastard child encased in its placenta sac, kicking violently while in wait to be born. Prickles light up between my thighs. And my bones feel as though they are going to snap from the pressure of weight.

I look past Nathaniel to the wood paneled wall, the knots and the imperfections, the grain. My pink-eared bunny moves behind Nathaniel in measured steps, from one side to the other, to land in an aggressive, defensive position in the hallway. Now it is the three of us.

Hello again, my friend.

"You're so beautiful," Nathaniel tells me as his hand moves up under my baggy shirt. He presses his fingers against my spine, while my head throbs. The pain slams against my temples with the force of a hammer. And all the while, I cannot take my eyes off my pink-eared bunny. I should not have left him next to the glass turtle ashtray on the table behind the dirty green door. Why did I leave him there?

What the fuck is wrong with me?

But then again, maybe it's okay now. Maybe this is how it is supposed to be, my path.

I hear music from the main room and beeping and laser sounds from the video game machines nearby. There is an electric buzz creeping out of the light fixture above the ladies room door. Combined, the noise is deafening, so much so I want to throw my hands up over my ears. But I do not move.

Nathaniel pulls me deeper into the recess off the hallway. It is a dimly lit, relatively private space. And there is no one around, at least not in the vicinity.

I recognize the look in Nathaniel's eyes as one of wantonness. "Is it, Delilah?" he says. His lips move over my neck then up to my ear. "Is this what you want?"

No.

He leans away to study my face and his expression turns dark. "If not this, then what?" he growls.

A stretch of silence fills the space between us.

Nathaniel cocks his head and holds me in his stare.

Then he smiles and cups my face with his hand, sucks on my bottom lip. "You're a strange bird, Delilah," he says as he slides the top of his index finger over my right breast then squeezes. He shoves his tongue into my mouth and adds in a whisper, "All you have to do is say the word. We can go out back. No regrets or remorse. Just say the word."

My pink-eared bunny stands to my left, large black eyes fixed on what is happening. I turn my head to look at him. He does not blink because he cannot blink. His eyes are always open. Always dark. Always watching.

Meanwhile, Nathaniel slides his hand down my stomach to the space between my thighs.

I stiffen like a corpse in automatic response.

He laughs.

In my ear, he breathes, "Let's not pretend anymore, Delilah. We both know why you are here."

Wrong.

This is a man who takes whatever he wants whenever he wants it, no matter the wreckage he leaves behind. He is the wanted. He is the loved. He is the accepted. The world has opened its arms to him, for his satisfaction, and embraced him warmly, while I have spent a lifetime in the cold pit with the swinging pendulum, alone.

With his eyes fixed on mine, Nathaniel shoves his hand down the front of my pants. Even though I clutch him by the wrist, he pushes deeper, until finally his fingers are but a microscopic fraction of an inch away from my clitoris.

With his erection hard against my leg, he says in a breathy voice, "Let me."

I cannot deny the aching between my thighs or how

much I miss being wanted in this fashion.

But I don't want him.

I don't want him!

After an extended beat, he repeats, "Let me, Delilah."

He kisses my neck and, for a reason I cannot explain, I release my grip. Then Nathaniel reaches under to massage my clitoris, slowly, steadily at first, then faster and faster, with increasing intensity. And all the while, I study him with cold, empty eyes.

Not a man.

A piece of human trash.

Nothing like Ian.

Sinking his finger into my vagina, he kisses me once more.

When finally he realizes that my body is not responding, a troubled look flashes across his face; he tries harder and harder, watching, expecting. And when I still fail to writhe and moan, give in to his seductions, the vein on the side of his neck pulsates and protrudes. He loses his temper and yanks me forward, toward him, harshly, almost violently, with his hand still in my pants, finger inside me. The muscles in his jaw tighten. They shift as his teeth clench. "If not this, then what?" he says, ripping his hand out from between my thighs.

A lengthy silence ensues. We hold eye contact. It feels strange now, like looking into the eyes of an enemy. My enemy.

Why didn't I see this before?

He is nothing.

Nathaniel's expression grows softer and softer, as though he has come to a decision unrelated to the circumstances at hand. He runs his fingers down one of my ringlets, tugs it like a bell. It is the same way he tugged my hair outside the Paper Nickel. Then he says, more to himself than to me, "You really are a crazy bitch, aren't you?"

Maybe I am.

I do not respond.

He tastes my bottom lip and runs the top of his index fingers softly over my sternum. "It's only because you feel bad," he says.

Wrong.

"There is no point in giving in to your regrets, Delilah." He grinds his erection against me. "You came here for a reason. We both know that you came here for a reason. All you have to do is say the word."

Nathaniel smiles. And it is a good smile, the kind of smile that makes others want to do the same, infectious. But I am not in the smiling mood.

He kisses me with his eyes open.

Both our eyes are open.

"Tell me what is going on in that beautiful head of yours," he says as he brushes a soft finger across my hairline. "I am sure we can come to a mature understanding."

Never in my life have I met someone so utterly narcissistic. It is like an undiscovered species unveiled right before my eyes.

Nathaniel brushes his thumb over my bottom lip. "You have the perfect mouth," he says. He kisses me gently. "The size. The shape." He pauses briefly before adding, "Perfect for sucking my cock."

I want him to die. But my pink-eared bunny is gone. I don't know where he went. Left in his place is a lifetime of shame and regret, sorrow, weakness. I don't know who I am anymore.

Dahlia instead of Delilah.

Nathaniel clutches me by my arm as I try to leave. He swings me around to face him, our bodies crashing into one another. We hold eye contact for an extended beat. Then he releases his grip and raises his hands into the air as if everything that just happened was all one big joke.

"Your choice," he says, practically laughing.

I walk away slowly, pushing past him for the ladies room in the process. Once inside, I stand with my shoulder blades against the door, my body trembling profusely.

If only I could scrape that smile out of his eyes with a serrated knife.

Nelly's is a surprisingly clean place. There is not a single mark on the wall or tissue on the floor. Jasmine with a hint of vanilla laces the air. Everything is gleaming.

I head over to the sink and drink water from the faucet. With my hands bolted to the counter, I stare at myself in the mirror. I HATE what I see.

Weakling.

My eyes are the same glacial green they have always been. My bones are in their usual locations. But I am different now. Something has changed inside of me.

A click that set off a spark...

Only Wallace, Jane, and the redhead are at the table upon my return. The other two employees from Westgrove, Gardner, and Jones have gone home. And Nathaniel is on the other side of the bar chatting up a young woman with short blond hair and tight jeans that show off her assets. Glancing over his shoulder at me, Nathaniel smiles.

"Were you sick again?" Jane asks, her mouth full hot wings. After I sit, she adds, "You were gone a while."

I do not respond. Instead, I push my fries around on the plate in front of me and study the ketchup bottle.

Wallace nudges a basket of onion rings my way. "Try

them. You'll like them," he says. "Nelly's specialty."

The redhead flashes me a dirty look. She's jealous. She thinks I am encroaching on her territory.

What are you doing here?

I should go home.

A moment later, Nathaniel returns with a fresh drink in his hand. He makes himself comfortable in the seat across from mine, the one situated between the redhead and Jane. Pushing a coin between his fingers, he holds me in his stare.

Wallace notices, so I turn my attention elsewhere in an attempt to diffuse suspicions.

"You're not eating," Jane says in her motherly voice. "Is there something wrong with your burger, Delilah?"

"I guess I'm not that hungry," I reply.

Her eyes move from me to Nathaniel to the redhead to Wallace then to me again.

I know what she is thinking, so I say, "The bug isn't a hundred percent gone, Jane," to put her off track. "I mean it has come back."

Knitting her brows, she cleans herself up with a moist towelette. "Maybe we should call it a night then?"

Sickness rises into my throat. The thought of returning to that dark, empty house sends a lash through my stomach. I want to go home. I need to go home. But I hate that empty house.

Wallace wipes his mouth with a napkin. "I think I will call it a night as well," he says, still chewing. "Give me a minute. I'll walk you ladies to your car."

The redhead sinks in her seat. She is clearly disappointed.

Sorry, hon.

As Wallace finishes the last of his beer, Jane and I collect our belonging in preparation to leave. Then Wallace sets his bottle on the table and takes care of the bill.

Outside, Wallace says, "Delilah, I just want to say..." He looks at Jane then flashes me a sad smile, "I'm glad you made it tonight. See you on Monday."

"Monday, sure, yeah."

Once Jane and I are in her vehicle again and the key is in the ignition, she sets her attention firmly on me and says in her less than motherly voice, "Are you having an affair with Wallace?"

"What? No," I reply, exasperatedly. "He's married."

"Everyone knows he and his wife split up over a month ago."

They split up?

"I am not having an affair with Jacob Wallace, Jane," I say. "And I don't know why you would ask me something like that in the first place. Can you take me home now, please?"

"Of course," she says. "Are you having an affair with Nathaniel then?"

I feel my eyes widen.

"My God, Jane, are you serious?"

She starts the motor. "I saw the two of you in there, Delilah. You were giving each other the evil eye. And in my experience, when a man and a woman give each other the evil eye, sex is usually involved."

My cheeks burn hot from the rush of blood. "I am not going to justify that with a response, Jane. It's absurd."

"You can trust me, Delilah," she says. "If you need someone to listen or—"

"Jane, please. I'm tired. Take me home."

We pull out of Nelly's parking lot and onto Oak Street in a southbound direction. As we proceed on the road, it begins to drizzle, not enough for Jane to flick on the wipers but enough to notice. There is moisture in the air and a chill that permeates the bone like tiny razor sharp slivers.

"Your husband wasn't at your house when I picked you up," Jane says after she turns down the music. "Is he still away on business? It's been a while."

"Jane..."

"I don't mean to pry."

It kind of seems like you do.

"Oh, no?"

She shakes her head, frustrated by my unwillingness to share my personal life with her. "Why are you like this, Delilah," she asks.

It's a common question.

Instead of trying to answer, I look out the window at the sky, which is a deep shade of black with tacked up stars and a purple-silver moon.

Jane pulls into my driveway and shoves the gear handle into park. With the engine still running, she says, "I think we should press pause on our weekend excursions for a while."

Excursions? We've been out twice.

"You can't be serious, Jane. What did I do?"

She fails to give me an answer.

After climbing out of the vehicle, I slam the passenger's door shut behind me and stand in front of my garage with my arms folded over my chest.

Jane drives away. The wheels of her vehicle spin and squeal on the wet pavement in the process.

Once again I am the unwanted.

I am the unloved.

I am the jettisoned.

There is a throw blanket hanging off of the chair in the living room. I grab it and curl up on the couch, stare at the picture frame I set facedown. Meanwhile, the letter

from my Uncle Dickson is sitting in the drawer.
    I am the rejected.
    My lashes grow wet.
    The house swells to double its size.
    I am alone.

CHAPTER SIXTEEN

There is a theory that says obsessive compulsive disorder and romantic affairs are nearly the same when taken from a biochemical perspective. When I think about that—how love and illness go hand in hand—it makes sense. After all, Ian promised.
He said he would never let me self-destruct. Standing before family and friends, before God Himself, he vowed to love me for better or for worse. But when the worse came, he disappeared. I might understand it if I did not warn him of my problematic tendencies. I might not hold a grudge. But I told Ian from the start that I had the bad habit of burning everything good in my life to the ground. He laughed at first, thought it was a joke; then his expression changed as realization began to register. Coated in sweat from our vigorous sexual activity, he pulled me into an embrace and promised he would keep us from imploding. I did not have to worry, he said, and for the first time in my life, I didn't. I felt safe. Of course he lied.

Flicking on the lamp, I see a quick flash of burning light followed by a startling burst and a popping sound, then darkness. The light sticks in my eyes for an extra few seconds before finally fading to black. I blink slowly as the wires of my brain clear their paths in an effort to make the adjustment. There is still some illumination in the room streaming in from the window, pale silver moonlight that extends to less than the halfway point. Given the other lamp is a few feet away and there is enough illumination in the room for me to get around, I do not bother trying for another light source. I am too tired to put in the effort. And there doesn't seem to be a point.

What is the point of anything?

The blinking causes the grit in my eyes to scrape against my corneas. It is not uncommon after waking, as I am prone to dry sleepers, so I attempt to swipe them away. Instead of removing the sleepers, I end up pushing the granules deeper beneath my lids. Now it feels like I am blinking against sandpaper. My eyes swell with tears in response.

The clock on the wall tells me that I managed to obtain several hours of sleep, and yet I do not feel rested. In fact, the exhaustion seems to extend all the way to the cellular level. It is because of the dreams, the awful nightmares, bizarre images, color. As my mind replays some of the worst moments, an aching sensation fills the pit of my stomach and the urge to scream rises inside me. Of course I restrain myself from committing the act. I am not a crazy person.

I am not like her.

Proceeding up the stairs to the master bedroom, I notice that the hairs on my neck stand at attention while the ones on my arms light up with gooseflesh. It almost feels as though I have been struck by an electrical wire, the nerves on the inside of my body now on the outside, exposed and raw.

I look past the staircase rail and into the living room in search of the reason. From my current location, I can see almost all of the space, save for the darkest of the black corners and part of the kitchen. Anything beyond the wall separating one area from the other remains a mystery.

My mouth goes dry as I say, "Ian, is that you?"

Please be you, Ian.

There is nothing but the sound of clicking and hissing of appliances and the soft hum of electricity.

My pupils grow wide to take in more of the scene. I can practically feel them expand.

"Ian, if that is you, say something."

The silence is worse than the dark. And I have always hated the dark, especially the danger it brings. But that is not what bothers me most. It is the fact that I felt this sensation when I first woke on the couch, the sensation of someone being in the room. I reasoned myself out of the suspicion, brushed it off as part of my last dream, paranoia. The feel of unwelcomed hands on my body took a little longer to squash, but I brushed that off as well. Now I am not so sure I wasn't being hasty.

"Ian, if that is you, please stop messing around. Say something."

The truth is I already know it isn't Ian. He understands my fears of the dark and would never be so cruel, no matter how angry or disappointed he was in me. He would give me some kind of indication of his presence, grudge or no grudge.

Gripping the staircase rail, I remind myself that we live in a quiet neighborhood where there is virtually no crime save for a few car break-ins committed by rebellious teenagers. Moreover, I am positive that I locked the door behind me upon my return home.

I did lock the door, right?

The fear is irrational. I know it is irrational. I need to remind myself and strike it out as the result of loneliness.

But am I lonely or just sick of the shit?

The refrigerator makes a loud click then shifts into

its usual hum in the kitchen, ice clinking as it fills the bin. I listen for another minute to allow the rational side of my brain to catch up to its counterpart. Then I proceed up the stairs to my master bedroom, where I throw open the curtains and flood the space with a mixture of street- and moonlight. The silvery orange gold combination is strangely eerie, almost otherworldly, but I lump the thought in with the paranoid ones and drop onto the mattress, folding in on myself like origami.

With a sigh, I roll over onto my back, stare up at the knockdown plaster ceiling. I blink slowly at the shapes and the imperfections. Memories of my latest dreams slither around my brain like restless snakes set upon moving prey. I try to push the thoughts from my head, but they keep returning.

My attention settles on the far corner of the room, where there is a dark irregularity that causes me to prop my upper body higher onto my elbows. There appears to be a stain slightly larger than a baseball on the ceiling near the corner. It is the type of mark that indicates mold, so I throw my legs over the side of the bed, pause briefly to stop my head from swimming, and proceed across the floor to the corner for a closer look.

He can't get away with it.

It is hard to tell if the irregularity is really a stain or if it is merely a lack of illumination in the room, so I slap some books off the reading chair and drag the chair over to the corner to climb up onto the arm rails. My balance is precarious at best. And still I cannot determine if the irregularity is a stain or something else.

My belly burns with a sensation I do not fully comprehend.

Hopping down, I switch on the closest lamp, which was a gift from Ian's mother. My eyes immediately shift into a squinting position in response to the adjustment of light. As soon as everything comes into focus again, I return to the arm rails of the chair, teetering slightly as I find my balance once more. Then I extend my hand to brush my fingers over the area in question, press my hand against it. It is cool to the touch; however, I cannot tell for certain if it is damp. Whether it is the exhaustion or something else, the irregularity suddenly seems to move and change. It spreads onto the wall directly across from my bed. And all the while, there is a gnawing sensation in the pit of my stomach that makes me think of barbed wire racking across flesh. I almost grab the hunting knife hidden in Ian's bottom drawer.

Why does he even have that thing? He doesn't hunt.

I collapse into a sitting position with my hands dangling between my knees. My home is filled with infectious spores, the unseen probably floating around in the air right now, blooming behind the sheetrock. I am breathing it in. It is coursing through my veins, blackening my lungs. My throat grows scratchy and constricts. I cough in response then cough again. The space between my thighs lights up with tiny prickles. There is nothing but corruption and filth. It is everywhere.

Why didn't you do something?
What's wrong with you?
Everyone just takes.

From the supply closet downstairs, I retrieve the blue bucket and cleaning supplies then haul the items up the stairs and fill the bucket with scalding hot water from the faucet of the garden tub. Once I am squarely in position on the arm rails, I begin to clean the corner of the ceiling with an antibacterial, antifungal solution.

I scrub.

And I scrub.

And I scrub.

But the problem only grows worse. In fact the irregularity spreads like a weed in mid-summertime heat. Knowing I have to get rid of the filth, I retrieve a scouring pad from under the cabinet and use that, pressing harder and harder with each passing second. Sweat moistens my hair. Droplets form along my brows. My joints stiffen to the point of sticking. And the skin on the top of my fingers, especially my knuckles, begins to crack, bleed. I proceed with the process around half the room.

How could you let it happen?

How could you let any of it happen?

When finally I can do no more, I give up and toss the scouring pad into the bucket. It causes the water to splash across the floor, but I do not bother to clean it up because I am exhausted, every inch of my body aching. I collapse into the chair with my fingers digging at my scalp.

A long while passes before I look up to assess the damage to my home. There are piles and piles of paint scrapings all around the room, some of which tracked across the floor, pieces in my hair, pieces on my clothes, pieces all over my bed, everywhere. The scrapings under my fingernails are so deeply embedded I feel pain. I should have put on gloves. I don't know what I was thinking. My hands are burning raw.

I have to make him take responsibility.

After hauling the bucket downstairs, I head into the kitchen, where I wash my hands in the sink. It feels like someone pouring battery acid all over my skin. My eyes tear up in response.

I find my uncle's letter on the floor. After some hesitation, I pick it up slowly. Although it is strange that I do not recall having taken it out of the drawer in the first place, I am sure I did because now it is in my hand, folded neatly. I reread the letter, the sensation in my chest snapping like a cord on a two ton elevator, causing me to plunge toward the earth.

Uncle Dickson thinks he can shut me up with a piece of paper and ink. He thinks he can write me off.

Nathaniel thinks he can shut me up by shoving his tongue down my throat. He thinks he can use me whenever he wants.

My husband thinks he can shut me up by ignoring my calls. He thinks he can get rid of me so easily.

Well, fuck them.

Fuck them all!

Bile ascends my throat as I fold up the letter, head upstairs, and place it on the table next to my bed. The walls in my bedroom remind me of a painting called Madness by TLM, scraped and littered with gouges from end to end.

I think about the pills in the medicine cabinet in the next room, how easily they could take the emptiness and the pain away, but then why should I be the one to resort to such methods?

Why just me?!

My bedroom reeks of strong chemicals and latex. I have mold behind the walls, spores in the air. The space between my legs tingles. And I am completely and utterly alone.

Sitting on the floor with my knees bent and my arms on my knees, hands pointed toward the ceiling but at a diagonal, fingers weaved together in a knot, I close my eyes and count backwards from ten to clear my thoughts.

"Ten."

Ian has not tried to call me in the last week.

"Nine."

He hasn't called and probably never will again.

"Eight."

My family wants nothing to do with me.

"Seven."

They want nothing to do with me even though they have their own dirty little secrets.

"Six."

The scars from my father's belt buckle still pulsate.

"Five."

The scars still pulsate and there is no cure for the pain.

"Four."

Nathaniel takes whatever he wants whenever he wants it.

"Three."

He takes whatever he wants and the world embraces and loves him all the same.

"Two."

My mother forgot the name she gave me on the day of my birth.

"One."

She forgot the name she gave me and put Dahlia instead of Delilah as though I never existed at all.

The last part repeats itself in my head as a mantra: *Dahlia instead of Delilah. Dahlia instead of Delilah. Dahlia instead of Delilah.*

Whether it is the mixture of chemicals or something else, the smell of death is in the air. I feel my pink-eared bunny sitting beside me on the floor. I do not have to turn my head to know that he is present. It is like a weight in the room, an extra layer of thickness.

"I understand," I say, faintly.

The next thing I know, it is morning and bright golden sunlight is streaming in through the windows to burnish the floor. Dust particles dance in the light in celebration of the return of day. I tear open my closet doors and search for the perfect outfit, iron it as well. Then I perform my normal morning routine, the one I used to perform before everything got off track, and cover the purple pools under my eyes with some well blended concealer, add blush and a bit of gloss. The loss of fat enhances my cheekbones. I look and feel great—or as much as can, given the state of my life.

My uncle's letter goes neatly into the kitchen drawer.

Arriving before most of my coworkers, I find an open parking space in the outdoor lot of Westgrove, Gardner, and Jones. It seems like a sign, the marker of change. I take the elevator up to my floor and make sure I am seen by those in the vicinity. The compliments rain as the birds chirp outside.

By mid-afternoon, Nathaniel finds me alone in the copy room and takes position beside me. He does not utter a word but stares at the copy machine as it spits out sheet after sheet. Then he glances over his shoulder to check if there are others close by in the hall before finally turning my way. Although I keep my attention fixed on the copier, I can see him through my peripherals. The same wanton look is in his eye as at the Paper Nickel and at Nelly's. He studies me for a beat before he says, "You look different, Delilah. I am not sure what it is, but something has changed."

Yes, it has.

I do not answer directly. Instead I take my time. "Where is your little play thing today?" I ask him. "I haven't seen her roaming the halls this morning."

Nathaniel laughs. He waits for me to give him my full undivided attention and smiles. It is a good smile, the kind of smile that makes others want to do the same, infectious. But I am not in a smiling mood.

"Did you take your lunch in the park by the river today?" he says after closing the gap between us by a single short step.

"I don't eat there anymore."

"Why is that?"

"Why do you want to know?"

"Because maybe I want to join you next time."

"Do you?"

"Is that something you would like?"

"Does it matter?"

"How come you would ask me that? It seems a little odd."

I do not respond.

Nathaniel pivots on his heel so that we face opposite directions, shoulder to shoulder. I am facing the copier, while he is facing the door. He whispers in my ear, "I can't stop thinking about the other night, Delilah. Do you have any idea how much I want to throw you on that table right now, rip those legs apart, and have my way with you? You smell amazing."

What brazenness.

Does he have no sense of fear?

Of course, it did seem like I followed him to Nelly's.

The mantra in my head is far more powerful than any of his predictable words. *Dahlia instead of Delilah. Dahlia instead of Delilah. Dahlia instead of Delilah.*

Maybe my mother knew something I didn't.

Nathaniel slips his hand up under my skirt to slide his fingers softly, slowly up my thigh. When his fingertips reach the lace band that encircles my leg, they pause briefly then attempt to slide their way up underneath to his favorite location of my body. Meanwhile, my teeth grind together with violent force.

Not here. But soon.

"Just say the word," he says.

Only, we are interrupted by Sebastian Walker's approach from down the hall. Sebastian is Suzanne Kline's executive assistant, a small man with dark keen eyes and mousy brown hair.

Nathaniel quickly withdrawals his hand from under my skirt then turns to watch the copier spit out additional sheets. It is work as usual.

When Sebastian first enters the room, there is an extended awkward silence before he finally lifts a brow and says with a sigh, "How long do you think it's going to be? I am in a rush."

Grabbing my copies off the tray, I reply, "All yours."

Nathaniel forgoes his place in line with a hesitant wave of his hand, but it is clear he is frustrated.

Good.

In my office, I sit in quiet anticipation as the workday draws to a close. The door is left open so that I can watch others pass in the hall. As expected, Nathaniel materializes in my doorway before the end of day rush. He says nothing, just stands there, stares at me. And right as he is about to step foot into the room, the hall begins to swell with people wanting to go home. He gives a quick nod then disappears behind the other side of the wall. It is no matter.

His day is coming.

The building clears. I shut off my computer, slowly, calmly, and lock my office door. Then I perform a visual sweep to make sure no one else is around. Aside from the occasional straggler, the place is empty.

It is a two minute walk to Nathaniel's office, which is located at the center of the 'L' on the left hand side of the building, close to the break room. Standing outside the door, I listen for a good minute to ensure he is gone.

Silence.

Nathaniel's office is exactly as expected, a beautifully maintained space with Asian accents, book lined walls, and pleasant view of the city, the kind of space that makes others believe he is something he is not. And this is his doing, not Tamaka's. In fact, Tamaka Americanized his workspace, except for a few special family keepsakes. No, this Eastern beauty belongs fully to its new inhabitant.

The fraud.

There is the sound of rain playing in the background from a white noise machine, which tells me he is still in the building. I look around anyway, running my fingers over knick-knacks, snooping in his drawers, sifting through paperwork. Nathaniel is in the process of buying a house. I read through the documents to learn which house and when the transaction is set to close.

This is it.

To my surprise, his computer is unlocked. A flashback of Ian enters my head, and the room begins to glow.

I click around to see what I can find, but there is nothing but work files on Nathaniel's computer. He is a careful man.

On the shelf in the farthest corner, there is a framed photograph of a blue-eyed woman. I study the image for an extended beat. Nathaniel clearly has a type.

Hearing Nathaniel's deep voice resonating from down the hall, a panic rises inside me. I drop the framed photograph, pick it up, set it as closely as possible in its original location then make a mad dash for the room next door.

Wallace looks up from behind a stack of paperwork that makes the stack on my desk pale in comparison. With a curious expression on his face, he says, "Delilah," nothing else.

I do not know what to say because I had no intention of entering his office, so I remain silent.

He places the document in his hand on his desk and

eyes me for an extended beat. "So, what can I do for you?"

It is like crossed wires. I cannot formulate an answer. *What the hell am I doing here?*

"Delilah, are you alright?"

Finally, I come up with something, though my response is still delayed by a good two seconds. "I am trying to avoid Suzanne. Do you mind if I wait here for a minute?"

He waves for me to take a seat, but I choose to stand.

"Are you sure you're alright?" he says. "You're sweating."

"Am I? I guess I didn't notice."

Wallace looks at his computer monitor. "You ever wish you could pack it all in and move to one of those countries where fifty cents lets you live like a king? I mean this is so fucked." He turns his attention to me and holds me in his stare. "You look especially nice today," he adds.

My cheeks burn hot from the rush of blood.

There is a knock at the door. The pretty young intern sticks half her body into the room. She looks from Wallace to me then to Wallace again. "They are ready for you, sir," she says.

"Tell them I'll be there in a minute," Wallace replies.

The intern leaves, closing the door behind her.

Even though she looks as though she hasn't slept for days, I say, "She really is a beautiful girl, isn't she?"

Wallace's jacket is hanging off of his chair. As he puts it on, he replies, "Not my type, if I'm to be honest."

He closes the gap between us and holds me in his gaze once more. "May I walk you out?"

There is nothing I can do now. I have to leave. The cleaners are here, Nathaniel is in his office, and Wallace is hovering. But I cannot go home. The walls are closing in around me there. Ian is gone.

He's gone.

So, I head to the gym for a workout. By the time I am done on the nautilus machines and the indoor track, my muscles throb and I can barely feel my fingers and toes. Sweat drenches my hair. It drips from pores.

There is a sauna located in the far end of the women's locker room. The sign on the door reads: *No clothes. No shoes. No electronics.* I take my shoes off but leave on my clothes and enter the steam room. With my earphones still over my ears, I turn the volume way up, almost as high as it can go. It is the only thing that drowns out the mantra. *Dahlia instead of Delilah. Dahlia instead of Delilah. Dahlia instead of Delilah.*

One way or another, the fucker will get his due.

Sitting with my elbows on my knees, I stare blankly out the glass door and listen to In Life's Wake, a hard metal core band, pink-eared bunny beside me. I do not have to say a word because my pink-eared bunny already knows what is in my head. We are in complete and total agreement.

I turn up the sound.

CHAPTER SEVENTEEN

It is the difference in atmospheric pressure that creates forceful winds. And temperature has a great deal to do with it.

As the evening picks up speed, I turn the corner to my street and notice the front door of my house halfway open. It gives me pause. Of course it gives me pause. But then I realize I am in the middle of the road with another vehicle behind me, so I pull forward into my driveway and look around the vicinity. My car begins to roll as I focus my attention on the door. I shift the car into park and sit in the quiet with my eyes locked on my house. It is a strange feeling to come home to something so unusual. A sneaking suspicion takes up residency in the pit of my stomach. I perform a visual sweep of the neighborhood but do not find anything out of the ordinary. Ian's car is nowhere to be found. It is neither in the driveway nor at the curb, and if my eyes are working correctly, which I believe that they are, it is not within visible distance either. Because we use our garage for storage, I know his car is not behind the rolling door. Putting the pieces together with the fact that Ian has been refusing to return my calls, it goes to figure that he is not the one inside the house. But then again, from my current position, I cannot see any reason to believe there has been a break-in. There is neither destruction on the doorframe from jimmying nor broken glass around the exterior. In fact there is no hint of a crime at all.

I am certain I locked up on my way out to work this morning, or at least I think that I did.

Did I lock up?

Like always there is a lingering sliver of doubt to make me question my own mind. Sometimes I get a little distracted, if not outright foggy of the brain. Sometimes there are gaps.

A strong gust of wind slams against my vehicle with a sudden force. The windows on both sides shudder in response. The weather forecast calls for heavy winds and rain later this evening with a high probability for major thunder storms after midnight. The day is only now starting to fade.

I step out into the gale and my hair is immediately lifted off my shoulders. It blows in every direction, whipping wildly at my face. Although I do my best to constrain it, I fail at the task. The wind is too strong. It causes me to lose my grip on the door handle. The driver's side door slams shut with a metallic crashing, an echoing sound. There is electricity in the air that digs deep into my bones. I battle my way up the pavers as sickness rises into my throat.

What if it is him?

Nathaniel.

What if he is waiting for me?

I'm not ready.

A receptacle blows over nearby. Now debris is flying loose across the grass, tumbling from one yard to the next. A piece of paper sticks against the post holding my mailbox, while a plastic bag floats in the air. I am nearly bowled over by the force of the wind. Fatigue is heavy on my bones. But this is my house. I need to know who is inside it. I need to be strong.

Be strong.

In my mind's eye, I see Nathaniel sitting on the couch in my living room, a wickedly infectious smile snaked across his face. I would not put it past him to enter my home without an invitation. He is a pompous man who takes whatever he wants whenever he wants it. And I am on his radar once more. I see him smelling the finger he shoved inside me at the Paper Nickel and at Nelly's Tavern. I see him licking that finger, taking pleasure in making me stiffen like a corpse.

Suddenly, a cold chill runs the length of my spine. What if Nathaniel saw me leaving his office or heard me rummaging through his things? That would make his presence at my house less of a stretch of imagination. What if I did not put the picture of his woman in the right place or if I accidently left his computer open on the wrong electronic file? Nathaniel is not stupid. He'd figure it out, confront me at a place where others could not or would not go. There is something in his eyes that I find disturbing, a glint beyond the color and charisma. He has nothing to fear from the likes of me, and he knows it.

I am the unwanted.

I am the unloved.

I am the rejected.

And he can do whatever he wants to me whenever he wants to do it; he can get away with it without repercussion.

No. Not anymore.

The pavers are hard under my feet, almost as though the rubbers of my soles are missing. I proceed with measured steps, while gooseflesh forms and spreads across my arms. The hairs on my neck stand erect. It reminds me of when I woke on the couch, when I felt the sensation of unwanted hands on my body but squashed the thought as paranoia.

Stopping two feet from the front door, which is now open wider on account of the forceful wind, I listen for everything and anything that might let me know what to expect. But I cannot hear a thing. In fact, I cannot even hear the appliances over the heavy *whooshing* sound. My hair whips wildly about, lashing at my face with violence. There is a sensation of hot coals in my throat, and my mouth is dry.

A noise draws my attention left. I catch sight of my next door neighbor shoving a bagful of trash into the garbage receptacle on the outside of his house. He raises his hand in greeting, but I do not respond. For a moment I consider asking him to help me check out my property, but we are not the type of neighbors who assist one another. And I do not want to come off as weird. So, I wait for him to fall out of my line of sight.

The sky is an ugly shade of washed out gray, cloudless and dead set on rain. There is the smell of grilled food in the air, a light burning of animal fat and flesh, and the sound of traffic beyond the wall. A couple of birds create a ruckus in the trees then fly away to a new location. The effect is eerie.

Pushing the front door to my house as wide as it can go, I say, "Hello," but my voice sounds strained. I clear my throat and try again, this time louder. When no one answers, I take a step into the foyer, my chest rising and falling quickly as a result of trepidation. "Ian, is that you? Hello? You left the door open."

Only now do I realize that my gym bag is in my hand. I do not recall grabbing it before exiting the vehicle, but I must have done so because I am gripping the straps tightly, my fingernails digging fresh trenches in the pits of my palms.

I drop the bag onto the floor in the middle of the foyer then slowly inch my way through the rooms. Looking left, I notice a set of suitcases next to the dining table. They are the same ones Ian used when he went away. In the kitchen, there is stack of mail on the counter that looks as though someone has been shuffling through it. Envelops to a few overdue bills have been torn open and left with their flaps pointed outward. Ian's cellphone is resting next to one of the bills. I breathe a sigh of relief.

Thank God.

After a brief pause at the bottom of the staircase, I proceed up to my master bedroom. My guess is that Ian is in the shower. That is why he did not respond when I called.

I push the door to the master bedroom open slowly with the tips of my fingers. The hinges creak and strain. To my surprise, I find my husband sitting on the edge of our bed, waiting. From the looks of it, he has been waiting for a while. The expression on his face is dark and unfriendly, almost disturbing. As he fixes me in his blue steel glare, I feel the full weight of my guilt and shame. I feel hollowed.

Am I hollowed?

With measured steps, I enter the room. Lowering my head then lifting it again, I say in a soft voice, "When did you get home?" It seems like a fair, neutral question and a good place to start, but Ian does not respond. "Are you planning to stay or have you only come to collect your things?" After an extended beat, I add, "Why are you just sitting there, Ian? Say something."

Next to the television on the dresser is an open bottle of beer. Its sweat pools to form a harmful ring at the bottom where the bottle meets the furniture. There is also a bottle on the bedside table, which I can only assume is empty. And I think I saw one by the refrigerator downstairs. The fermented stench of alcohol is in the air. For some reason, it reminds me of the glass turtle ashtray next to my pink-eared bunny on the table behind the dirty green door. In my mind's eye, I see flashes of color, movement, the gnashing of teeth. I force the images from my head and say, "How long have you been drinking?"

Only now does Ian open his mouth. "Is that really where you want to start, Delilah?"

My throat is so dry it hurts to swallow. He has a right to be angry with me. It's fair. But then again there is enough guilt to go around ten times over. And the fact that I am the only one being pointed at does not escape my attention.

"I understand you are angry, Ian," I say, calmly, clearly. "I really do."

"You understand," he mumbles and scoffs. "That's rich."

Yes, it is.

There is nothing more I want than to peel away Ian's veneer and return us to a happier time; however, the look in his eye is so ugly, so aggressively combative, I cannot even think.

His attention shifts to the bedroom walls, to the piles of paint scrapings on the floor and chips weaved into the area rug. I must admit, under the flood of incandescent light, the room looks worse than it did previously. It looks like the madder version of Madness. The paint scrapings are everywhere—tracked across the floor, spread out over the dresser, scattered into bits on our bed. They are even in the master bathroom. And I still haven't been able to scratch them out from under my fingernails, at least not completely.

"What the fuck, Delilah?" Ian says. Though his voice

is calm and steady, almost soft, his eyes are full of anger and confusion. "Do you mind telling me what the hell happened here?"

The muscles in my jaw tighten of their own accord. "Where have you been, Ian?" I reply, coolly. "And why haven't you been returning my calls?"

"I have only been gone a few weeks, and you destroyed our fucking house," he says. "Not to mention the fact that you haven't paid a bill."

"Where have you been?"

Shaking his head, he says, "This is...I don't even know what this is, Delilah. I don't know where to start." After a lengthy pause, he adds, "I didn't call because I needed time to think."

To think?

"And?"

"And what?"

"Have you come to a decision?"

Ian does not respond.

Based on his red rimmed eyes and slouched posture, he is exhausted. But of course he has always worked too hard. It is one of the many things I respect about him.

Only now do I realize my car keys are still in my hand. I am holding them like a weapon. I set the keys on the dresser next to the beer and walk over to my husband, careful not to breach his space. "So, why have you come then, Ian?"

"Honestly, I don't know," he says. "I thought I could come here and..." He waves his hand to indicate that he is referring to the room. "I didn't expect this."

There is a part of me that wants to touch him, that wants him to touch me. Instead I say, icily, "You couldn't have called to tell me where you were staying? You couldn't have had the courtesy? What if there was an accident, Ian?

What if someone broke into the house? Do you even care what happens to me anymore? Where were you?"

Do you even care?!

He stares me down with his blue, blue eyes. "Do you honestly believe you have the right to ask questions at this point, Delilah? I mean look around this place. Look what you've done to our home."

"Put that aside for a minute."

"Put it aside," he mumbles. "I don't even know what to fucking say."

"You're still my husband."

"Yeah, well, maybe you should've thought of that before you went ahead and fucked some other guy."

Suddenly, I am a whipped dog again. I hold back my tears.

Ian's hard exterior slowly begins to melt, and he says, "I'm sorry. I didn't come here to fight."

"How many times do I have to apologize?" I reply. "Ten? Twenty? You know I would take it back if I could."

"Only you can't take it back, Delilah. Neither of us can," he says. "And therein lies the rub."

Yes, there it lies.

A long silence ensues.

I walk over to stand against the wall next to the master bathroom, my arms folded over my chest as if to create a protective shield.

Ian and I hold eye contact.

"You've lost a lot of weight," he says, softly, sadly. Then he motions at his face. "You're different. The way you look. I can hardly recognize you."

"Is that a bad thing?"

"It's not a thing either way, Delilah," he says. "It's an observation. That's all."

"So, what now then? Are you done with me?" I ask

directly. "Is that why you are here? To collect your things?"

Is it over?

Ian crosses the floor to stare out the window. I can almost feel the thoughts racing through his brain.

"What happened to never letting us implode?" I say, coolly.

Though he turns to face me, the gap between us remains considerable.

"I could have kept what I did a secret, Ian," I tell him. "You would have never known. But I was honest. Honest, Ian. I did the right thing."

"The right thing," he mumbles, scoffs. "The right thing, Delilah! Are you serious? Do you even hear the words coming out of your mouth?" He sweeps the room with his eyes before adding, "I mean goddamn it."

I do not respond.

Ian begins to pace the floor. He stops to take in the mess. "I will tell you what I see. You've lost your fucking mind, Delilah. That's what's happened here. You've lost your mind."

Have I?

"I really wish you wouldn't say that, Ian."

"Well, I don't know what to make of all this, Delilah. It would be nice if you would explain it to me."

Another lengthy silence ensues.

Then Ian closes the gap between us with long, rushed strides. He takes hold of me. "How could you do it? How could you sleep with another man?" Lowering his voice, he adds, "I don't know if I can ever trust you again."

"I'm sorry."

"I fucking loved you, Delilah." He shakes his head.

Loved. Past tense.

The next thing I know, Ian lifts the office chair slightly off the ground and slams it down against the floor.

Then he drops his face before lifting it to look me in the eye. Something happens. It is like a shift in the atmosphere, a change in the pressure. Ian's warm, moist breath is on my skin, as comfortable as a blanket freshly extracted from the dryer. The space between my thighs aches for his touch. He has me pinned against the wall, his body pressed against mine, our chests rising and falling with quickened breaths. For a second, I think he is going to forget about the pain and the suffering, the wrongs we have inflicted on each other and kiss me the way he used to kiss me when we were in love, or lust. But then his expression changes and he turns away instead.

Before Ian can take another step backwards, I grab hold of his hand and guide it slowly down my pants. He watches me do this with a surprised look in his eye. There is a brief moment when he considers how to respond. He studies me. Then he gives in and slides his fingers deep into my vagina while brushing my clitoris with his thumb. No one knows my body like Ian. He knows me better than I know myself. He slips his tongue into my mouth, kissing me passionately, while I squeeze his shirt from the pleasure. Then he runs his lips across my neck and up to my ear to suck on my earlobe. I sink my fingernails into his forearms as I close in on an orgasm.

I am close.

Incredibly close.

I am right there.

But then everything stops.

When I open my eyes again, I find Ian collapsed on my collar bone. The moment is over. Perhaps we are as well.

"You have to forgive me," I say. "We were separated."

Ian rips his hand out of my pants. He points a finger

204

in my face and says, "Fuck you, Delilah. Fuck you for ruining everything."

"Yeah, well, fuck you too, Ian," I snap back. After all, he started us on this path.

Pushing his fingers through his hair, he crosses the floor and releases a deep sigh. Slowly, he says, "How the hell did we get like this?"

I sit on the bed across from him.

I do not know.

A long silence ensues.

After a while Ian says, "You want to know what bothers me the most, Delilah? That you won't tell me his name. I mean if it really is over, like you said."

Is it over?

When I do not respond, Ian stands up. He gives me one last long look; then he exits the bedroom to collect his bags downstairs, the ones packed and ready to go.

I follow him into the foyer. "But you don't have your car."

"It's in the shop," he says. "Justin will be here any minute. I can't do this anymore, Delilah."

Ian heads toward the front door.

Stop him.

"Nathaniel," I yell. "His name is Nathaniel."

Although Ian holds before leaving, he does not turn around. His suitcases are still in his hands, the muscles in his forearms popping.

"I would take it back if I could." There is more I should say. I should tell him everything from beginning to end. It is right there, waiting on my lips. It wants to come out. But for some reason, it doesn't.

"Delilah—"

"Don't leave me alone right now, Ian. Stay for dinner. Stay for an hour. That's all I ask."

But Justin is here, the radio in his vehicle playing loudly outside. We are out of time.

"I'm sorry," Ian says. "I can't."

A minute later and Ian is gone. I stand alone in the middle of our driveway, arms crossed over my chest, the sky well on its way to oil black.

In the house, I shut the front door behind me and lock it up tight. Then I sit on the bottom step of the stairs, the voice in my head so loud I can barely think. It is like a scratching at my brain. *Dahlia instead of Delilah. Dahlia instead of Delilah. Dahlia instead of Delilah.*

Ian is gone.

And I am the unwanted.

He is gone.

And I am the unloved.

But why should I be the only one paying for my mistakes?

As I remember the unspoken conversation I had with my pink-eared bunny, my fingernails dig new tracks in my palms. They draw blood, the sticky wetness a familiar sensation.

There is only one thing I know for certain now. It may be the only thing I know at all: Keeping oneself sane is tedious work.

CHAPTER EIGHTEEN

It is said that when a person dies, he or she loses twenty-one grams. Although some have speculated that the loss represents the soul leaving the body, others do not agree. Either way, death remains.

Sitting behind my desk at Westgrove, Gardner, and Jones, I barely have the energy to think about death or loss or anything else. In fact, all I can do is watch the colors in the room change from golden yellow to pale pink and finally to muted gray. I have not done an ounce of work since my late arrival. In fact, I have not done an ounce of work in days. Ian is gone. He has not contacted me since driving out of our neighborhood in Justin's 1969 Mustang. I am beginning to think that I may never hear from Ian again. The feeling in my chest is how I imagine parents must feel after losing a child. Twenty-one grams and the wounds sting like torn staples.

With the hour growing late then later, the end of day rush fills the halls with the sound of footsteps and shuffling, cacophony. There is a smell in the air that reminds me of death, of wet graveyards and moldy damp tombs. It also reminds me of the old people at my church, or the church I used to attend when I actually attended church, people one breath away from the end, decay already set in their bones. I want nothing more than to close my eyes, but every time I do, all I see is the space between the trees outside the Paper Nickel. Now, Ian is standing in that space, waiting, watching; he is turning his back on me.

He is gone.

I glance at the notice on my screen. Suzanne Kline, my superior, sent it to me via email. Apparently, my boss is not happy with my productivity or lack thereof and now wants me to schedule a meeting with her through her assistant. But if Suzanne Kline wants to meet with me, she is going to have to schedule it herself.

The cleaners are in the building. They are unloading their supplies. A minute later, vacuums roar to life, and there is the sound of debris being sucked up through plastic tubes.

I lift a hand in greeting to Mr. Campbell, the head of our maintenance department. He is a tall, thin man, lanky with bad posture. Campbell has a little less hair every time I see him. At this point all he has left is on the sides of his head, right above his ears, and a track across his skull. Although he lifts a hand in return, he does not come over to chat. Introversion is one of his better qualities. Campbell does not waste other people's time.

Another second clicks by on the clock, then another and another. The cleaners begin to disappear. Although I have not eaten in days, my body feels heavier than it has ever felt. I can barely lift it out of my seat much less lug it across the floor. Somehow I collect my belongings, spider mites scurrying across my brain, and lumber my way to the elevators, where I take the first one that arrives down to the bottom floor. Westgrove, Gardner, and Jones is eerie in its near empty state.

Despite the fact that I did not make it to work on time this morning, I somehow managed to snag a parking spot in the outdoor lot. With slow heavy steps, a pace equivalent to a condemned man's guillotine march, I head to my car. Then I drop my handbag on the hood of my vehicle and ransack my bag for my keys. They are nowhere to be found. I rummage around some more before finally losing my temper and dumping the contents of my bag out onto the hood of my car. I pick through unusable pens, receipts, tampons, change, sticky notes....

No keys.

Fuck.

Sinking my fingernails deep into the palms of my hand, I release what sounds like a muted scream. It is as though what my vocal chords produce catches in my sinus cavity and must permeate the barrier in order to hit the atmosphere.

I look around, partially expecting Nathaniel to materialize out of thin air, but then I remember the reason he missed work. Today is the day he closes on his new home. After all, Nathaniel gets whatever he wants whenever he wants it. The world belongs to him.

Not me.

"Delilah," Jacob Wallace says, and I feel the pressure of his hand on my arm. "Is everything alright?"

A rush of blood fills my cheeks, as evidenced by the warmth.

I look at Wallace's hand on my arm and follow it up to his concerned eyes. Except when it comes to the movement of electronic work files, he really is a kind man. "I can't find my keys," I tell him.

Wallace offers to help, but I say, "That's alright." It is an automatic response. "I probably left them in the drawer upstairs anyway."

He sparks up a one-sided conversation, and as his mouth continues to move, I understand less and less of what he is saying. It is as though my brain is disconnected. It is not functioning. Nothing registers. Wallace's muted voice dissipates in the air. I watch his lips change shape. And I stare at him with what I can only imagine as a look of vacancy.

Then, without reason, I say in a faint voice, "I'm hungry."

Only, I'm not.

Wallace stops talking to study my face. My random announcement has clearly caught him off guard.

There is a look in his eyes that reminds me of the look I have seen in the eyes of other men. It makes me imagine my spine pressed up against the car and a hand sliding its way up the back of my dress. But then I shake the thought from my head and add, "Do you want to get something to eat?"

Wallace does not answer right away. He takes his time. "With you?" he says.

"Yes, Jacob," I reply. "With me."

The look in his eye deepens.

The next thing I know I am in his four door sedan with 80s rock softly playing on the radio and the scent of artificial raspberries lacing the air. Wallace knows a lot about 80s musicians, and he is deadest on sharing his knowledge, every last bit of it, with me.

What are you doing?

I blink and am sitting across from Wallace at a table at a fine dining restaurant. What strikes me the most is that I do not fully remember getting from point A to point B or exactly when we arrived, nor do I remember being seated at the table. But the crystal and the silverware are shining. And the thread count on the linen is high. From nearly every direction, I hear the sound of conversation and the scraping of forks and spoons, knives. The crystal chandeliers are twinkling.

I should not be here.

Wallace waves his hand to attract our waitress's attention. When the young woman arrives at our table, he asks her to bring us their very best wine. If I did not know any better, I would say that Wallace believes we are on a date and means to impress me.

Does he mean to impress me?

"How is your steak?" he says shortly after we begin to consume our meals.

For some reason, there is a dreamlike quality to the moment, like everything exists behind a filter of fog. I respond without thought. "Bloody," I reply, faintly. But then I take another bite.

"I can have them send it to the kitchen to fix," Wallace says.

Even though I have not eaten much over the last two days and I find the blood in the meat sickening, I say, "No, it's fine. You don't have to do that."

Wallace waves our waitress over to take the steak back to be heated a little longer anyway. Then he pulls what I think he believes is a romantic gesture by shoving a forkful of food into my mouth. "Try this," he says. "Veal scaloppini with mushroom sauce. It's made with dry vermouth and a touch of, well, I'll let you figure it out." He watches me chew. "What do you think?"

I think I am not the only one who needs to take responsibility for my life.

Though I am not a fan, I smile and nod because it seems to make him happy.

Although he is less attractive than Ian and Nathaniel, there is something about Wallace that women find appealing. I believe it is the way he communicates, how he holds himself with surety while using humor to make those around him feel a little more comfortable. He is also extremely intelligent and does well financially, which is like icing a cake to females.

"How about you?" he says, which causes me to realize I have not been listening at all.

"How about me what?"

"Do you have any anecdotes you'd like to share?"

Oh, I have anecdotes.

The tables in the room are too close together, the air too thick with the odor of food. It makes it hard for me to concentrate. "None that you would be interested in," I tell him.

I feel a sad smile slide across my face.

Wallace studies me for an extended beat. Placing his hand on mine, he says, "I know what you are going through, Delilah."

"Do you?"

"I've been there," he tells me. "When Sarah and I split."

Dear Lord, am I really that obvious?

My head lowers of its own volition. When I lift it again, Wallace and I hold eye contact.

Then we hold eye contact again in the parking lot outside Westgrove, Gardner, and Jones.

How we moved from point A to point B is absent from my memory. I don't even recall getting into Wallace's car.

Twisting at the waist, I drop my handbag onto the hood of my vehicle and search for my keys once more.

Wallace walks around to my right and stands close enough for me to detect the scent of his spicy deodorant but not so close as to breach my personal space.

"I must have left them in my office," I tell him.

We face each other. There is no one else around.

A long awkward beat passes before I say, "Good night, Jacob. Thank you for dinner."

He does not respond.

There is another awkward moment before I turn to head into the building. Although it is not yet dark, the sky is fading fast, and again, the smell of rain is in the air. Sometimes I think that is all it ever does. Rain.

Typically, there are two security guards who work the evening shift at Westgrove, Gardner, and Jones. Oliver Hamlin called out sick, which means Eduardo Martinez is the only guard on duty tonight. Martinez is around fifty years old. He has a strong rolling accent that sometimes makes his words impossible to understand. He is a gentle man, more a place setter than a true deterrent to crime, not well suited to the job. Oliver, conversely, is monstrous in size and personality, capable of encouraging even the fiercest of individuals to behave as they should. But Oliver is out.

As I make my way to the elevators, I lift a hand in greeting to Eduardo. He is starting his rounds and will be locking everything down very soon.

"Forgot my keys," I call out to him while pressing the elevator button several times. "I'll only be a minute."

Eduardo nods and waves in return.

In my office, I search for my missing keys, checking the top of my desk and the draws, as well as other random locations. It does not take long for me to notice the glint of metal on the floor. In my vacant stupor, I must have dropped my keys on the way out of the room previously.

I pick them up.

Here you are.

The cleaners have moved on to another floor. The stench of disinfectant laces the air. All of the lights are off, except the ones on the vending machines in the break room and those for the emergency exits. Because there is enough natural light in my office for me to get around, I do not bother to flip the switch on for the overheads.

After retrieving my keys from the floor, I turn around slowly and am surprised to find Jacob Wallace standing in the doorway, staring back at me. His presence startles me for only a second. But then he looks at me, and I look at him, and the next thing I know, Wallace is kicking the door shut and we are ripping off each other's clothes.

A chair gets knocked over in front of my desk.

Our bodies slam against the bookcase.

There is a strong sense of urgency in the moment, like if we do not do this now, we may never have the opportunity again.

Wallace cups my breast in his hand then fondles it with his tongue, takes it into his mouth.

The way we go at it causes the bookcase to shake violently. Some of the books and knick-knacks tumble off the shelves, one of which catches the corner of my eye. The sting is sharp and immediate, followed by a heavy trickle of blood. I dip my finger into the red and look at it. There will be considerable swelling, of that I am sure.

Everything stops.

"Shit," Wallace says. "Shit, are you alright?"

That's what I am.

Shit.

I do not respond to his question. Instead, I shove my tongue into his mouth and yank his shirt off then dig my fingernails deep into his flesh.

Wallace hisses but plays along.

His body is much better than his clothes indicate. It is as though he has been keeping his best feature a secret. I brush my fingers over his rippling muscles then unbuckle his belt and unzip his pants. Grinning all the while, Wallace watches me do this.

Without removing my panties, he pulls the crotch aside and thrusts himself into me. Because Wallace is well endowed, he fills me completely. I am in a loose dress, which makes the whole process easier. He pulls down the top of my dress as he works my neck with his mouth.

With one of my hands on the back of Wallace's neck, I drop the other to his buttocks and encourage him to go deeper and deeper still.

"Harder," I pant. I want Wallace to hurt me. I want pain to take away the pain. "Harder."

Wallace is quick to oblige.

We slide across the front of the bookcase, where the boards dig into my spine and create fresh bruises. As Wallace increases the speed of his rhythm, my spine takes a beating.

Then, to my surprise, he lifts me off the ground and throws me onto the desk, where he slips my panties over my ankles and drops to his knees, kissing my upper thigh and tonguing the space between my legs. I shiver in response and knock the keyboard onto the office chair.

Wallace takes hold of my legs. He yanks me forward, thrusts himself inside me, grinds. I lie on the desk, writhing, moaning with pleasure.

He pulls my bra down and runs his hand over my breast, then uses his mouth.

The paperwork goes everywhere.

"You don't know how long I've wanted this," he says. His voice is soft as a whisper, his mouth close to my ear. There is the faint scent of artificial raspberries on his skin and the taste of expensive wine on his lips.

Wallace unhooks the front of my bra to study me in the failing light, and everything slows. It is an intimate moment.

No.

Not like this.

I drop my hands to his buttocks and pressure him to change the pace.

"Pin me down," I say, softly, faintly.

An unsure look flashes across Wallace's face, but I soothe his worries by adding, "Trust me, I won't break."

He spins me around to take me from behind, cramming himself deep inside me, pumping so hard my legs crash against the corner of the desk. Now there is nothing but the sounds of heavy breathing and the slapping of skin, pulsating blood.

"Harder," I say, even though my legs are stinging from the pain. "Harder."

Wallace slams me against the wall. I accidentally yank the blinds off their track. My legs wrap around him for support as he picks up the rhythm. I throw my head back, moan, fingernails embedded in the flesh of his neck, draw blood.

Wallace throws me against the desk, but this time on the other side, where there is more room. Taking his hand in my own, I wrap his fingers around my neck for him to choke me. At first he resists, but when I refuse to give up on the idea, he slowly tightens his grip around my throat.

The tighter Wallace squeezes, the more I moan. And the more I moan, the tighter he squeezes. Soon a strange sensation envelops my body. I begin to lose oxygen.

Yes.

On the verge of dizziness, I sink my fingernails into the side of Wallace's hand. He tears his hand away quickly and shakes out the pain. Then he throws me onto the floor and rips my legs open to jam himself up inside me, harder and harder still. My wrists are pinned together in his hands.

Wallace grazes me with his razor sharp stubble as his

rhythm picks up speed. I turn my head in response. The blood from the wound I received by the bookcase has not yet coagulated. It slides into the soft curve under my eye to pool.

Breaking free of Wallace's grip, I lead his hand up to my throat then wrap my fingers tightly around his wrist.

With his body heavy on mine and his grip tight about my trachea, Wallace releases one last long moan. His spine curves upward. Then he deflates on top of me as though empty of air.

He falls to the side to lie next to me on the floor and, after a brief pause, begins to laugh. "I never thought in a million years," he says.

Neither did I.

The room grows dark, and as it does so, Wallace caresses my hair gently with his fingertips. My breasts are fully exposed, as are his genitals.

Silence ensues as we recover from the vigorous activity.

What the hell is wrong with you?

But Wallace's refractory period is short, shorter than most, perhaps the shortest I have ever seen. Before long he grows hard again, runs his hand up my thigh for another round. He wants more. The room reeks of sex, wine, and artificial raspberries. There are books and knick-knacks all over the floor, along with other debris. The keyboard is hanging off the edge of the chair, looking as though it might crash to the ground at any second, and there are loose papers and files everywhere, along with pens and highlighters.

I blink and Wallace is on top of me. He is sweating all over my chest. Grunting like an animal. Panting his wine and vermouth breath in my face. His body is crushing me. I cannot inhale or exhale or escape.

No.

My head drops to the side. Even though the room is almost black, I see my pink-eared bunny lying next to me on the floor. It is as though he is glowing in the dark. My pink-eared bunny and I hold each other's stare. Then my eyes begin to swell with tears and everything blurs.

Wallace jams himself inside me, again and again.

No.

What happens next is beyond my understanding. Somehow, and I am not sure how, I find the stone award I received for exceptional work in my hand. I have no recollection of ever having picked it up. The taste of liquor is strong in my mouth. It is unbearable. And the fermented stench of alcohol is equally unbearable in my nostrils.

Wallace is shoving himself inside me, rocking, pumping. He is sweating all over me, ramming, jamming. He is breathing his putrid breath in my face, crushing me with his body. I cannot breathe. I am in the space between the trees outside the Paper Nickel. Sharp twigs and debris are slashing like razors at my flesh. It is too dark for me to see beyond the faint shapes and silhouettes.

Wallace pins me to the ground. He crams his tongue into my mouth and chokes me with his hand. I want to scream, but I cannot. And all the while I hear a man's voice saying, "You're so beautiful, Delilah. You're so beautiful."

Stop.

Something strange rises up inside me. It is like something that has always been there yet never known. My fingers tighten around the stone award I received for exceptional work. The award feels heavy in my hand. It is far heavier than it looks.

And now it is in the air, above my head, coming around and then down as though moved by an invisible force.

There is a terrible *thunk* as the stone award makes contact, crashing into the side of Wallace's skull.

I swing again.

And again.

And again.

Like a woman possessed, I slide out from under the man on top of me, take a straddled position over him, and continue to bash in his brains, screaming madly all the while. Over and over and over, I strike Wallace with the stone award until my hands give out and the achievement drips with blood. Wallace's face feels like spaghetti smothered in tomato sauce. And when it is finally done, when I cannot lift the award a second longer, I collapse on top of him and fall into a hysterical weep.

After the last of my tears are shed, my fingers unlock and the stone award I received for exceptional work rolls out of my hand onto the floor to create a soft *thudding* sound.

Then I pull myself onto my knees beside Wallace's limp body. At this point, I am trembling, confused. I am not even sure I know where I am. It is dark in the room. And the fog is only now beginning to lift.

Slowly I realize what I have done. With panic in my voice, I cry, "Jacob, oh my God, Jacob, I'm sorry!"

I shake him, but he does not respond.

Sheer terror fills my veins.

"Jacob, please, get up! You need to get up, please!"
Please.

Nothing.

"Do not do this to me, Jacob. I need you to wake."

With a trembling hand, I press my fingers against the vein on Wallace's neck to check for a pulse. There is none. And it is hard to find under the mess in the first place.

Oh, God, what have I done?

Still on the floor, I kick at his body with my bare feet, hoping to jolt him alive. "Goddamn it, get up, Jacob! Get up!"

Of course he doesn't.

At some point, and I am not exactly sure when, my pink-eared bunny flicks on the overhead light.

I shield my eyes with my hand as I look over my shoulder at him, my breasts still exposed, hair matted, my body covered in a thick, sticky substance. The light reminds me of the light outside the Paper Nickel, far away yet bright from a pumped up charge. Pushing myself up onto a set of unsteady legs, I follow my pink-eared bunny out of my office and into the dark, leaving a trail of blood and debris behind me.

No, I am still in the room.

And Jacob Wallace is dead.

He is dead.

I killed him.

And it is all Nathaniel Martin's fault.

CHAPTER NINETEEN

A powerful surge of adrenaline is a common marker of shock. Shock can make a person feel separated from a situation, disconnected, or create an out of body experience. It can fill a person with overwhelming emotion, cause physical sickness and clear away rational thought.

Sitting alone in the hallway with what feels like an anvil on my chest, leaning against the wall, I cannot concentrate. I pull at the sleeves of my dress, try to cover myself up, but the sleeves keep falling down again. With my left hand clamped against my right shoulder, I hold up one side of my dress. I do not know how long I have been sitting here. It could be an hour or it could be ten minutes. My pink-eared bunny is gone. He disappeared shortly after I stepped into the hall. It may be because he knew I was too weak to go after him.

Wallace is dead.

My God, he is dead.

I killed him.

As soon as I can talk myself into it, I crawl on my hands and knees to the door. My mind feels as though it has been fractured, my thoughts chaotic, drifting. They are strewn about like shattered glass. At first I wait by the door, if only because I am too afraid to do anything else. The metallic stench of blood is in the air, and something I do not understand.

With slow, disjointed movements, I slide my hand up the wall to the light switch, flick it on once more. I don't remember ever shutting it off. I need to know what I have done. Unnatural light blasts through the space like activated gunpowder, causing me to have a physical response. My eyes need a moment to adjust. Once they do, though, I have a sudden intake of air. Then I slide down the wall to the ground and sit with my hands on my knees, palms facing upward. The weight on my chest doubles. My mouth goes dry.

There is a pool of blood around Wallace's head, soaking its way through the commercial grade carpet. Through the tunnels of my eyes, the scene appears distant, like it has been twice removed or separated from me by a thick violet-gray sheet of impenetrable cellophane.

My cheeks grow hot and wet. I swipe at them with my wrist then crawl over to Wallace's limp body, sit by his side.

My God, he is really dead.

What have I done?

I can smell the final release of his bodily fluids.

Placing my hand on Wallace's chest, I close my eyes and squeeze my eyelids tightly together. Then I lift a trembling, bloody hand to my raw and swollen mouth to feel where Wallace's mouth had been. The image of Wallace kissing me passionately against the bookshelves flashes across my mind. There is no way he thought it would end like this, of that I am sure.

"I'm so sorry," I say, but the words are not so much words as broken sounds. Lowering my voice to barely a whisper, I add a cracked, "I did not want this. I did not want it."

I didn't.

Wallace's face is barely recognizable now. I am
certain there are many who would not be able to tell it is
him.

And all the while, the same four words keep playing
in my head: *Dahlia instead of Delilah. Dahlia instead of Delilah.
Dahlia instead of Delilah.*

The wound at the corner of my brow is swollen. It
feels as though it is the size of a golf ball. I press my fingers
against the lump, and a small trickle of blood oozes out to
slide down the side of my face. My hair feels matted and
sticky with a substance similar in viscosity to maple syrup.
The amount of blood on me pales in comparison to the
pool surrounding Wallace's head. As I stare at his limp
body, I slowly begin to go numb.

The stone award for exceptional work is on the floor
two feet from Wallace's battered skull. Clumps of hair and
flesh stick to the achievement, along with dried blood.
Wallace's face reminds me of canned tomatoes.

Please, God, help me.

I drop to the side, onto my hands, and vomit up the
raw steak I had eaten, as well as the veal scaloppini with dry
vermouth and cut of mushroom. It tastes worse coming up
than it did descending.

Wiping the vomit away with my arm, I cover
Wallace's genitals with his shirt and place my hand on his
chest. Then I rock back and forth, praying in my head to
God to make it stop, make everything stop.

Please.

The stench of sex and death overwhelms me. Feeling
as though I am going to be sick once more, I push myself
up onto my feet. My legs feel queer now, like they have
never been used. I cling to the doorframe for support and
puke in the hall, right outside the room. Then the dry
heaves start.

On my knees in the poorly lit space beyond my office, I lift my face toward the ceiling and sit in the quiet for a good long minute before forcing myself into the ladies room. The lights come on automatically, flickering two or three times before settling into a steady yellow-white glow.

I rush to the sink and drink straight from the tap, my mouth dry as the desert, my throat burning raw. The water chokes in my throat. I spit a little up.

Feeling a tacky sensation all over my fingers, I shove my hands under the faucet to wash them. It is like pouring acid on flesh. And the water runs red.

What have I done?

The exhaustion I feel is greater than I have ever known. I collapse onto the floor, onto the cold hard tile, and sit under the unforgiving restroom lights breathing in the sour odor of chemicals, sweat, sex, and blood. As the water continues to rush from the faucet, I stare at it blankly. After a while I feel a strange sense of calm envelope me, warm as a blanket. My mind begins to clear of all thought. There is comfort in the nothingness, in the silence.

Then Eduardo Martinez bursts through the door of the ladies room. The look on his face shifts from shock to terror to fear to concern, all in a minute with everything in between.

I do not react at all.

Martinez remains stock still in the open doorway for a heavy beat, staring at me. Then he squats in front of me and says in his rolling accent, which now sounds strangely far away, "Ms. Delilah, Ms. Delilah, are you alright?"

Am I alright?

The way he calls me Ms. Delilah reminds me of first grade, when all of the teachers went by their first names and prefixes.

I do not respond.

"Ms. Delilah, I am going to call for help," Martinez says; however, he does not leave directly. He stays with me an extra few seconds before rushing out the door.

I do not know how much time passes before Martinez returns. Not long, I believe. In his hand he has a cellphone, which he apparently left on his desk downstairs, and under his arm, rolled in half once, is a thin army green blanket.

"Can you tell me what happened, Ms. Delilah?" he says as he throws the blanket over my shoulders. "Was it Mr. Jacob? I saw him in your office. Did he do this to you?"

Jacob.

My God, Jacob is dead.

An extended silence ensues.

Martinez scans the ladies room with his eyes before he says, softly, "I am so sorry, Ms. Delilah. Please forgive me. I should not have left you alone."

Only now do I look at him, the parent I never had, the one I deserved. It strikes me, what he must be thinking, especially after stumbling into my office and facing such a sight. Even now, in this room. The sticky wet blood on my hands. Torn dress. Bruises. Lacerations. I saw my reflection in the mirror after drinking from the tap. The swollen knot is impossible to miss, as is the ring of black and blue finger sized marks about my throat. Of course I have always bruised easily on account of low iron, but that is something I do not need to share.

Martinez shuts the faucet off after he wets a paper towel with water. Then he attempts to clean the blood off my face. The wound above my eyebrow smarts wickedly. I hiss.

"Everything will be alright, Ms. Delilah," Martinez says. Though I know he means to reassure me, it sounds as though he is really trying to convince himself. "The police are coming. They'll be here soon."

The police.

Ian.

The urge to explain the course of events that transpired rises up inside me. But when I open my mouth, nothing comes out. The words stick in my throat. Wallace did NOT deserve what happened to him. He did NOT deserve to die at my hands. He was a kind man, a good man, and now he is gone.

Gone.

I want to do the right thing. I want to tell the truth. But my voice is destroyed from dry heaving and compression. It feels as though someone poured gasoline down my throat and lit a match.

"You'll be alright, Ms. Delilah," Martinez says, and for whatever reason, the words prick sharp as pins.

Green acrylic paint begins to slowly make its way across the floor, like a quarter-sized leak in a boat, spreading as gradually as the blood that encircled Wallace's head. I shift positions to keep the paint from touching my legs and feet.

No.

Martinez thinks it would be best if we wait downstairs, so he helps me to the elevator then sits with me in the reception area until the police arrive. Now we are by the green bio-friendly indoor retaining wall. He tries to make conversation but gives up quickly when I fail to respond.

As soon the flashing lights become visible, Martinez picks through his keys for the one that opens the front door to the building and lets the officers inside.

I do not move an inch.

It's over.

Everything is over.

I am done.

To my surprise, Martinez goes into a long, drawn out explanation of what he believes transpired. He directs the police to my office, where they find Jacob Wallace's dead body along with the weapon that killed him.

"Self-defense," I hear Martinez say at one point. I also hear, "...nice young lady."

Blinking slowly, I stare at the flashing lights, the images they cast on the wall. Overall, the place is still dimly lit. Only later do they turn on all of the lights.

One of the officers in charge is Ronald Forester, a forty-some year old man with sandy brown hair, mud brown eyes, and a narrow pinched nose. There is something feminine in his build, but he presents as a manly type of man. Forester drops to a knee in front of me. I recognize the move as one designed to be nonthreatening, yet I feel threatened.

"Ma'am," he says, and even though he tries to hide it, there is a slight southern drawl. "Can you tell me your name, ma'am?" When I do not reply directly, he says, "Ma'am," once more, "can you tell me your name, please?"

"Delilah," I say. It is difficult for me to speak, painful. "Maconwood. Delilah Maconwood."

"Ms. Maconwood, are you severely hurt anywhere? Do you need immediate medical attention?"

Do I?

I shake my head no, slowly.

"Would you please tell me what happened?" Forester says. But there is movement all around, people coming and going, so I cannot focus. "Ma'am," he says, impatiently, "please tell me what happened here. Take your time."

I wonder about the training program at his precinct because his approach is for shit.

The elevator opens. Philip Landon, Forester's partner, equal in position and authority, if not slightly higher, steps out after having been to my office. Forester joins Landon by the security desk, and the two engage in a private conversation, taking turns to glance at me every once in a while. Landon looks as though he is mixed race, maybe part Native American. Then Forester disappears inside the elevator, and Landon moves off to speak to someone else.

It is right around now that Maria Rodriguez arrives. She is the foremost victim's advocate in the area.

While an EMT flashes a penlight in my eyes, Rodriguez provides me with her professional information. She explains that she is there to help me through every step of the process. I don't want her around.

Go away.

"No signs of a concussion," the EMT says. He has light green eyes and brownish red hair. "But you may need a stitch or two. We should get you to the hospital."

Martinez notifies me that he has been trying to reach my emergency contact but has been unable to get through. "Is there anyone else I should call?" he asks. "Another family member or friend maybe? Someone else?"

Someone else.

"No," I reply. Then I grab my neck in response to the pain.

"Your throat is extremely swollen," the EMT says. "I think it would be best if you try not to talk for a while."

But the police want to continue their line of questioning.

"It can wait until after she's been seen by the

doctor," Rodriguez snaps.

If I did not know any better, I would say there is history between Rodriguez and Forester, a history that is not pleasant.

A flurry of activity makes my head spin. I lean forward to put my head between my knees, but that only makes it worse.

The next thing I know, I am being carted off to the hospital, and everything is moving around me quickly.

As I look out the window, cars and buildings flash by. I think about the night Ian told me he would do anything to protect me from harm. We had just finished watching a movie about a set of parents who met to discuss whether or not to hide their children's crimes. When the movie ended, Ian looked at me sideways and said, "It would not even be a question, Delilah. You know that, right? I mean if you killed someone. I'd hide the body, bury it somewhere or dump it in the river and lie."

"Would you?" I said.

"In a heartbeat."

At the time, I am sure that he meant it.

Ian.

What is Ian going to think of me now?

The trip to the hospital allows me a moment to think, to come up with a plan. I should confess. I know I should confess. In fact, there is nothing more I want to do. But at the same time, why should I spend the rest of my life in jail for what amounts to an innocent mistake? After all, I did not mean to kill Wallace. It was an accident. And if the tables were turned, I would not want him to go to jail for me. Why should both of our lives be ruined? And who is really at fault here?

No, the best course of action would be to hold as closely to the truth as possible and leave out the rest. So, I make a plan to tell the police about my missing keys and everything that occurred during my dinner with Wallace. I will tell them how Wallace followed me to my office and describe what it felt like to have his fingers tight about my throat, cutting off my air supply. I will tell the police how he was crushing me with the weight of his body, sweating all over me, and how I could not scream because he shoved his tongue into my mouth. I will even tell them how I found the award for exceptional work on the floor and how I have no idea how it ended in my hand or when I swung it around to bash Wallace's brains in, or at least I will tell them something to that end.

It is best not to overthink it, I decide. I don't want my story to sound scripted. It needs to be natural.

You can do this.

But then, when it comes time to answer the police officers' questions, my plan disintegrates to a degree. I neglect to respond to half of what they want to know, rattle on about nothing important, scramble my words, my lips trembling all the while. And by the time I am done, I am hysterical, crying, "Maybe it's my fault, I don't know, I don't know."

Only the others in the room disagree with me. Except for Forester, who is not so sure.

Forester continues to press for answers. He asks the same questions over and over again but in different ways, focusing mainly on the shirt I placed over Wallace's genital region to cover up his shame.

"Let's go through this one more time," he says. "Why did you cover him again? I don't understand."

My temper flares, but it doesn't matter because the vast majority of evidence corroborates my story—the fingernail marks on Wallace's wrists, arms, and neck; the destroyed state of my office; every bruise, cut, and lump;

the point that I did not flee the scene. The lead detective can suspect something is awry all he wants, but the plain fact of the matter is the others are on my side. The evidence is on my side. And Wallace used force.

For the next three hours, I am poked and prodded, violated in ways I never thought imaginable after a supposed trauma. A small framed young African American woman enters the room. She puts on her blue latex gloves and begins to take scrapings from under my fingernails and swab samples from inside my mouth. Bodily fluids are collected from my vagina, and multiple rounds of pictures are taken of my wounds. The whole process steals my dignity. It takes what strength I have left.

No more.

And when it is done, when it is finally over, I am handed some pills to take to reduce my risk for pregnancy and sexually transmitted diseases, which only cracks my mind open to a greater degree.

"Can I have another panel run?" I say. "Just to be certain. I want another panel run."

When everyone is gone but the last person in the room besides me, I dry my tears with my arm and say faintly, "What about my clothes? Where are my clothes? I want to go home." Of course I already know the answer. I've seen it a million times in movies and television shows.

"The police need to keep them as evidence," Rodriguez tells me. "We will find you something else to wear, though. Don't you worry about a thing."

Don't worry.

They give me ill-fitting jogging pants and an oversized t-shirt with a breast cancer awareness sign on it. Now I look like a drug addict who got caught in something rough.

Then Ian enters the room. He stops rather suddenly

the moment he sees me. "I only received word thirty minutes ago, and there was traffic," he says, faintly. Closing the gap between us, he lowers his voice even more before adding, "Are you alright, Delilah?"

Am I alright?

I hardly know.

Overwhelmed with exhaustion and brimming with emotion, I begin to cry. And I keep crying for days. It is like a pressure valve has been opened. Hot steam is pouring out.

Ian stays at our house to take care of me over the coming week. He cooks and he cleans and he puts on my favorite shows.

I am also visited by a slew of people—my sisters, who make no secret of their suspicions; Jane, who needs to be comforted more than I do; and not one but two company lawyers, who are only concerned about the possibility of a lawsuit.

Losing his Irish temper, Ian physically forces the tall attorney out of our house, yelling, "She's been through enough! What the fuck is the matter with you?!"

As Jane and I sit in the lawn chairs outside, she informs me that Eduardo Martinez has been suspended from his job pending a review. I have Ian go to Westgrove, Gardner, and Jones to argue the matter, but it doesn't do any good. Martinez is a terrible guard. At the same time, he is the reason I am not sitting in a jail cell right now. But for Martinez, I would have come clean. He gave me my solution.

"Ian," I say one night when everything is quiet and we are lying next to each other in bed. "What happened...What happened was my fault."

He brushes his fingers gently down my cheek and replies, "You don't know what you are saying right now,

Delilah. It's the pills. Get some sleep. We'll talk in the morning."

Only, we don't talk. And the morning passes.

Ian makes me my favorite macaroni and cheese, the kind with the crumbs, while I try to keep Wallace's crushed skull out of my head. I can still feel the sensation of the stone award in my hand, its weight, its texture. I can hear the sound it made as I swung it around to bash in a man's brains.

Night after night, I wake in terror, coated in perspiration, my dreams plagued with the memories of what I have done and the threat of the police learning the truth.

God, forgive me.

"I shouldn't have left," Ian tells me after I experience a particularly nasty nightmare. His eyes swell with tears. "I'm sorry, babe. It's my fault."

But the true culprit is still out there. And he gets whatever he wants whenever he wants it.

Ian does not sleep under the covers with me. He sleeps over them. With his arm about my waist, I slide up into his nook and close my eyes, listening to the sound of his heartbeat and respiration. I should not be allowed to be happy. Wallace is gone. I do not have the right. I killed the man. But Ian is home. And I cannot help but feel the comfort he brings.

In a panic, I open my eyes to see my husband in front of me, cupping my face between his hands. "Look at me, Delilah," he says. "Look at me." But I am confused. "I'm right here," he tells me. "Breathe." As I begin to calm, Ian lets go of my face. "It is only a nightmare," he says. "I'm not going to let anything else happen to you. Do you hear me, Delilah? Never again. I promise."

Never again.

The moment cools.

Ian and I head downstairs to the kitchen for some chamomile tea. He puts on the kettle before taking a seat across from me at the table in the moonlit room. Then he reaches across the table to hold my hand.

"Do you remember that movie about the parents who had to decide whether or not to turn their children in for murdering a homeless person?" I ask him.

"You mean when I told you I would bury the body," Ian replies and sort of chuckles. "Of course."

"And now?"

"Now?"

"Would you still?"

He studies me for a prolonged beat, and as he does so, silence fills the room. Then Ian says, "Always."

"I love you," I tell him.

"I love you, too," he says in return. "Now drink your tea."

When I close my eyes to sleep again, I do not dream of Wallace's caved in face or the space between the trees, pink-eared bunnies or dirty green doors, but of my husband's touch. And I feel fine.

What the fuck does that say about me?

CHAPTER TWENTY

The thing about feeling fine is the same thing about forgiveness: It rarely lasts long.

So, when Detective Forester contacts me to come down to the station, I am not the least bit surprised. If anything, I am amazed that he waited so long, what with his mind most likely running through the scenarios, the different possibilities, extracting the pieces that don't quite add up correctly, don't fit neatly in his predetermined puzzle. My guess is he has come up with a theory, one that, if proven accurate, will boost his career to the next level. I am merely a means to an end. But, of course, I have been worse.

Stepping into my closet, I begin to search for my most conservative outfit. It needs to scream *I am not a slut* or *the type of person who would point a finger falsely.* As I slip into my clothes, one garment at a time, I catch sight of Ian staring at me from the other room. There is something about the way he is watching me that I do not like. Once the mind gets to clicking and the nasty thoughts creep in— and those nasty thoughts always creep in—forgiveness goes right out the door. Then the hope that you have mustered, dissipates, along with any spark you have left.

I join my husband in front of the mirror by the double sinks in our bathroom. The reflection I see today is better than it was yesterday, the dark purple fading to a soft greenish-yellow and the swelling gone. As Ian finishes brushing his teeth, I touch up my face with a bit of concealer and powder and say, "I think I should go alone."

He shuts off the water. "Delilah—"

"It's okay," I tell him. "It's what I want. Really."

Ian and I finish getting ready in silence then exit the house at the same time. After he kisses me on the forehead the way a father would kiss his child, we climb into separate cars and head off in different directions.

Right now I cannot think about anyone or anything except Detective Forester. It's the vibe he gives me, like he doesn't believe a word out of my mouth. He is, at this time, the most dangerous person in my life.

Self-defense.

By the time I arrive at the police station, my mind is in a twist and my brow beaded with perspiration. I feel a panic attack waiting under the surface. My conservative clothes are squeezing too tightly. What if I hang myself on my words? I need to get my shit together.

Choking the steering wheel, I close my eyes and breathe then count backward from ten to clear my head.

Calm down.

Inside the station, I give my name to the woman behind the bulletproof glass and am directed to take a seat in the waiting area. There are several magazines on the table next to the faux leather loveseat and more in the wooden rack by the door. I sift through the reading material only to learn that it is all outdated, most by more than a year. The majority of the covers are well-worn, if not outright torn. On the television, the stock market channel is playing with the volume on low. You would have to be able to read lips to know what the hell is being said. I wonder why the person in charge puts it on at all.

I need to get out of here.

The woman from behind the bulletproof glass calls me up to the front. She is a middle aged lady with short dark hair and a forgettable face. If I saw her on the street in ten minutes, I probably would not put her together with the station. After informing me that the detectives are ready to see me now, she points to the door and hits a button. A buzzer goes off and I am allowed to open the door to proceed deeper inside the building. The woman then steps out from behind the bulletproof glass to lead me past a series of busy desks. She leads me all the way to a private room on the left hand side, half way to the rear. Forester and Landon are already waiting for me. Although both of the officers stand when I enter the room, it is Landon who says, "Thank you for coming on such short notice, Ms. Maconwood."

Landon has been kind to me since the day we met. He eyes me the way so many men have eyed me before.

Without verbally responding, I take a seat in an empty chair and rest my hands neatly on the table, weaving my fingers together to prevent them from digging new tracks in my palms. That is all I would need right now, a fistful of blood.

Calm down.

The female officer exits the room, closing the door behind her. Then the detectives take their respective seats across from me at the table. A short silence ensues, in which time Landon reviews the file in his hand and Forester studies me.

Finally, Forester says, "There are a few things we need to clear up, ma'am." His drawl sounds slightly thicker than it did the night of Wallace's demise.

"Can you run us through everything that happened the night of Jacob Wallace's death?" Forester asks; though, he is not really asking. "And try not to leave anything out."

I look from Forester to Landon then to Forester again. Although I agreed to answer their questions of my own free will, I feel annoyed. They have not brought me here for something specific, something new, but for another fishing expedition. "Are you serious?" I ask them. "How many times do I have to go through this with you? When you called me in this morning, you said you needed me to stop by to clear up a few minor details. That is what you said on the phone, Detective Landon."

"I understand your frustration, Ms. Maconwood," Landon says. "Please, just one more time."

One more time.

Whenever my temper flares, my mind races with incredible speed, and suddenly it comes to a halt on the idea that if I had truly been a victim of Wallace, then this meeting, this whole affair, would be a case of re-victimization. And I find that offensive, if not outright deplorable.

"A man is dead," Forester reminds me. "I am sure a woman of your intelligence can understand why we are asking this of you."

Yes, I'm sure you're sure.

"You already have the medical reports, as well as everything else," I reply.

Landon flashes Forester a hot look. If I am not mistaken, Landon likes me—he is possibly even attracted to me—which means that I am here for Forester.

"Alright," I say, "where *exactly* would you like me to start?"

Forester is quick to give answer. "Start with why you took the time to cover the genitals of the man who *allegedly* attacked you?" He REALLY emphasizes the word *allegedly*. And he moves forward slightly in his seat when he says it, as if to drive his disbelief home. "Because that is what I don't get, Ms. Maconwood. If the relation between the two of you was not consensual."

"I am going be honest with you, Detective Forester," I say.

"Please do."

"I don't know."

"You don't know?"

"I can't explain it."

Forester studies me for an extended beat. "That is your response? You can't explain it?"

I scan the room with my eyes. There is a camera in the upper right corner behind Landon's head. I can only assume it is recording. It makes me uncomfortable, what it might see.

I nod.

"Please answer aloud for the tape," Landon says.

A beat passes before I respond. "The truth is I am not certain that I am the one who covered him. Everything happened quickly. And there are pieces I don't remember. Maybe because of my injuries. I don't know."

Detective Forester's eyes sharpen, as does his tongue. "Why would Mr. Martinez say you covered him then? He said it was you. Unless someone else was there that we don't know about."

My pink-eared bunny.

"I am not saying I didn't do it. I am saying I don't remember, Detective. I think I was in shock."

Landon looks over at Forester.

"There are things I remember and things that are bleary," I add. "So, yeah, I don't remember covering the man. In fact, I don't remember every single detail of that night with complete clarity. But show me someone who would after such a trauma and I will tell you that person is stronger than me."

"I see," Detective Forester says, incredulously.

"Detectives," I say, coolly. "I have told you everything at this point. So, if there is nothing more..."

I start to get up from my seat.

When Forester opens his mouth to respond, Landon shoots him down with a look. Then Landon turns his attention to me and says, "Thank you for taking the time to come in today, Ms. Maconwood. We appreciate your cooperation."

"Actually, I have one more question," Forester says before I make it out the door.

"Can you tell me about your relationship with Nathaniel Martin, Ms. Maconwood?"

I sit back down. "Excuse me?"

"It has come to our attention that Mr. Wallace and Mr. Martin were overheard at your workplace discussing you," Forester tells me.

Sickness rises in my throat. "What?"

Landon loses patience with Forester. It is written in Landon's body language. "There was a bet on you," Landon says.

"A bet?" I say more to myself than anyone else. "I don't know anything about any bet."

Those fuckers.

"Only Mr. Wallace wasn't interested in participating," Forester says. "Which begs the question: Why would a man like that, a man who basically attempted to defend your honor, turn around and do what you say he did to you?"

I do not respond.

"Have you ever engaged in any extra-marital affairs?" Forester adds.

"I am not sure what you are getting at."

Of course, I know what he is getting at, so it makes no sense why I said what I said.

"Have you ever cheated on your husband?"

"Not while we've been together, no. Now, I have answered all of your questions. There is nothing else I can tell you. So, the next time we talk, it will be my lawyer present."

"Please be sure to make yourself available in case we need to discuss more," Forester tells me.

"Of course."

"I'll walk you to your car," Landon tells me.

Once I am safe and sound in my vehicle and Landon has disappeared inside the municipal building, I shove my key into the ignition and head down the road in a northbound direction. Tears fill my eyes. They cloud my vision. What I have done is now clawing its way through my insides.

He knows.

Forester knows.

Time disappears.

Then Ian is placing me in the passenger's seat of his car. Forced air is blowing in my face. As he slides his body in behind the steering wheel, I throw open the passenger door, lean out, and puke what little I have in my stomach out onto the asphalt. Actually, I puke it out into my hand. The vomit drips through my fingers to land on the ground. Then I turn my hand over to dump the rest and shake to knock off the remainder.

Ian pops out of the vehicle to grab a towel from the trunk. He then uses the towel to wipe the puke off my face and hands. Some of the vomit made its way into my hair. Ian folds the towel in half, turns it over, and wipes down my curls as well.

"Look at me," he says. "Look at me, Delilah. Listen to the sound of my voice."

I vaguely remember dipping my hand in the holy water and entering the empty congregation room.

"You passed out at the church," Ian tells me.

But I don't remember driving to there in the first place.

What's wrong with me?

I don't know who I am anymore.

Dahlia instead of Delilah.

My fingers crawl up my face to my hairline, where I feel a small knot. Thankfully, there is no blood.

Ian gently nudges me back into his car. Then he closes the passenger's door and slides into the driver's seat once again. He drives out of the parking lot, leaving my car behind under the shade of trees.

As I stare out the window at the flashing colors, I say, "I didn't tell them the truth, Ian."

"What? What do you mean?"

Silence fills the vehicle. It is the only thing I hear aside from the hum of the road.

CHAPTER TWENTY-ONE

When a person experiences trauma, there is a certain expectation with regard to how that person is supposed to behave. And apparently I am not acting the part.

The questions and the comments come, constant and unrelenting. *Are you sure you're alright? You can talk to me. You don't have to put on a brave face. Why are you trying to handle this all by yourself? Don't you know it is fine to be vulnerable?* Then there are my sisters' questions and comments, while my brother takes no interest at all. *Can you explain that part one more time? So, you went to dinner with him? You were alone with him in the car? But nothing happened until—what?—the two of you were back at work? It seems a little strange, don't you think? What did the police say? Is the investigation still ongoing or is it done?*

A rush of rage consumes me with each and every remark. It is like they want me to be broken or flawed. I am either the victim or the villain, perhaps a little of both. Most wish me to be a poor pathetic little girl who others need to save, pick up, brush off, set neatly on a shelf. It is all okay as long as I am not a threat to the delicate balance, as long as I am nothing at all. My sisters want me to be her, my mother, if only so that it gives them someone to judge, makes them feel superior. But I have played their games. I have played them masterfully. And I will never play them again.

Dahlia instead of Delilah.

The one outlier in all of this is the only person in the world I actually care about—Ian. Instead of questioning or commenting, he has chosen to remain silent, at least of late. Although he still cooks for me, watches television with me, there is something in the quiet that screams more about what is going on in his head than any words. The only questions Ian has asked since wiping puke off my face in the middle of the parking lot outside the church is if I want pasta or eggs for dinner and what I meant when I said I did not tell the truth.

"Can we talk about this later?" I replied to this last one, hoping he might forget about it and fail to bring the subject up again. Fortunately for me, it worked. Ian has not asked since.

But something is off now. The dynamic between us is different. Maybe it has been there for a while. In fact, I know that it has. Every night Ian returns later and later from work. He doesn't hold me in bed quite so tight anymore. And sometimes, not all the time, but sometimes, he looks at me like I am a complete stranger, like I am someone he doesn't even know.

I have to fix this.

Fix us.

Damp with perspiration, I throw the blankets off my legs and step into the bathroom to splash cold water on my face. From the doorway, I can see Ian sleeping peacefully. There is zero chance that I will get any shuteye, so I see no point in trying. Rather than spend the rest of the night staring at the knockdown plaster ceiling, tossing and turning under the sheets, I walk softly across the floor to my closet, where I put on my trainers and head out for a run to clear my head.

There is a special kind of sound to the night. It is

like an echo of an echo or a whisper far from the ear. If you listen closely, you can hear the sound of scurrying, scratching, nocturnal creatures, and the breath of danger with everything in between.

Slipping my earphones into place, I set off down the road, slowly at first but then with increasing speed.

I do not want to return to the confinement of my bedroom anytime soon, so I continue on toward the park, which is approximately two miles away. Though the music blasts through my eardrums, I do not turn it down. Instead, my head matches the sound to a flurry of memories. I see flashes like pages in a book that remind me of a montage.

It is well past midnight. The sky is leaden and starless. A silver moon, crescent in form, offers little illumination; however, there are enough well-spaced streetlights for me to make my way around. I am no longer afraid of the dark. I cannot say why, but the fear is gone.

After a few laps around the pond, my planter fasciitis kicks in to force an early return home. Before long my run becomes a walk and my walk becomes a limp.

About a quarter mile out from my house, three young men in a Jeep speed past with their windows open. They look about college age and intoxicated. They disappear around the corner, only to drive by again, this time in the opposite direction. The ones on the passengers' side whistle and shout obscenities. One of them slaps his hand on the outer part of the Jeep door and says filthy, disgusting things, such vile things. Then they drive up the road.

A few minutes later, I see the vehicle once more. It comes around when I turn the corner. The driver stops a few hundred feet in front of me then shifts into reverse until they are at my side.

What is this?

I do not like it one bit.

Only one of the men in the vehicle has strawberry blond hair. He has a thick, masculine nose and deep set eyes. The strawberry blond is sitting on the passenger's side in the front. Leaning with his head out of the window, he says, "Pretty lady, what are you doing all by yourself?"

What am I doing?

I do not respond. Instead, I keep walking, my pace consistent with that before they arrived.

They drop back and follow me, slowly, then pull up beside me once more. "What's your name?" the strawberry blond asks. When I do not reply, he adds, "Don't be rude now. We're simply trying to make conversation."

I stop and look him in the eye. He is a child in a young man's body.

"What do you want?" I ask, coolly.

"We want to help you out," the one with the military cut in the backseat of the vehicle replies. "It looks like you hurt your foot. Get in. We'll take you wherever you want to go."

All the fucking same.

Everywhere, they are all the fucking same.

"No thanks," I tell them. And I start walking again. They follow.

The strawberry blond says, "C'mon now, pretty lady, we're trying to be good Samaritans here. Let us give you a ride." He slaps the driver as if to indicate what kind of ride he means.

Isn't he funny?

The comedian.

Although the driver laughs, he is less inclined to participate than the others. In fact, the driver says, "She's not interested, George. Let's go."

"Nah, she's interested," the strawberry blond insists.

He looks at me the way so many men have looked at me before, and my intestines twist.

There is a voice in my head screaming. The red flag is in the air. There are three of them and one of me. I am alone. Yet for some reason, I feel calm, utterly calm. Like no one and nothing can touch me anymore.

"Go home, children," I say without looking at them, my pace unaltered.

The boy in the back laughs, while the driver says, "She's not interested, George. And Frank is waiting."

But George isn't convinced. So, I stop and turn my attention his way. We stare at each other.

Slowly, like the light of the sun spreading over the land, George's expression gives. We communicate with one another without breathing a word. Then George slaps the outside portion of his door and says, "Maybe another time."

I don't think so.

The Jeep speeds away, kicking up small rocks and dust in the process. I am sprayed with a rush of sand, while tires squeal loudly as they spin down the road.

Forcing myself into a run, I ignore the pain in my foot and return home. My skin is coated in a thin layer of sweat, my hair damp. I walk through the front door, and the first thing I do is stop off at the kitchen for a bottle of water.

With my hand on the knob of the drawer holding the letter from my uncle, I take the first sip of my drink. My hand holds steady on the knob, but I do not pull the drawer open. Instead, I drop my hand to my side and walk upstairs.

No one can touch me.

Ian is awake and waiting for me in the bedroom. As soon as he sees me, his jaw tightens, and I know he is mad.

The only illumination in the room is that streaming in through the windows and from the light I left on in the master bathroom before I set out for my run.

"Where the fuck have you been, Delilah?!" Ian snaps. It is not so much a yell he delivers as a forceful tone. "Do you have any idea what time it is? It's the middle of the night."

He was worried about me.

The broken green lines on the alarm clock are visible from where I am standing. It is actually after 2:00 AM.

"I needed to clear my head," I tell him before I walk into the bathroom to grab a towel off the rack. Then, wiping the sweat off my brow, I return and ask, "What's the matter? Why are you acting like this? I just went for a run."

"You went for a run," Ian mumbles. He distorts the features of his face. "You went for a run in the middle of the night? Alone no less? After everything that has happened?"

Yeah.

"I don't understand what the problem is," I say.

"The problem!" he says, heatedly. "The problem, Delilah!" Lowing his voice, he adds through gritted teeth, "There are so many problems—so many fucking problems—I don't even know where to begin."

Confused, I shake my head. Ian's animosity is coming from nowhere. It almost seems as though he has been waiting to unload it for quite a while.

With his hand in the air, last two fingers bent more than the rest, he says in a calmer voice, "Let's look at this, shall we? Take a seat."

I remain standing.

"You've let our bills go delinquent," he says, coolly. "And you've destroyed our house."

"I am planning on painting," I tell him. In fact, I have already selected the color. It is called Storm.

But Ian keeps going without pause. He talks over me. "You had an affair, Delilah, and wound up attacked."

I feel a gulf form between my brows.

"Hell," he says, "a man is dead now. I know it was in self-defense, but you're running around in the middle of the night two seconds after it happened. You refuse to see a therapist. And you're saying things, so many fucking things."

"What are you talking about, Ian?" I ask him.

"And now you're standing here in front of me telling me you don't get it."

I don't.

He drops into a sitting position on the end of our bed and, after an extended pause, adds, "What the hell is going on here, Delilah? Because I need you to explain it to me."

My mind sifts through the possible explanations. All I can come up with is that I have not slept in days. The nightmares have been constant, unrelenting, and many remain even after I wake. Every time I close my eyes, I see the stone award for exceptional work in my hand and feel its weight, its grittiness, the sensation of flesh and hair, blood. I see the award rise and come down with a whoosh, wildly, crashing through a man's skull. I see brains on the floor surrounded by a puddle of blood and a face that reminds me of canned tomatoes. But the part that bothers me most, that makes it so that I never want to sleep again, is that when I see these things, I do not feel remorse. Not as I should, anyway. It feels more like a warm embrace. And at the end of my nightmare, my pink-eared bunny is waiting for me in the space between the trees.

Wallace is on top of me, panting, sweating, ramming,

jamming. Nathaniel is on top of me doing the same. That is when the warmth heats to a rage. I see the lights on the Paper Nickel, astonishingly bright yet far away and Nathaniel Martin's infections smile as it snakes across his face. And it is only when the blood begins to drip and flow, when it spreads out like slow motion acrylic paint making its way across the floor, all the way to the space between the trees, where my pink eared-bunny is waiting, that I wake with a start.

And then—then!—odd as it may seem, the area between my thighs tingles. I ache not for sex but for *violent* sex, the kind that brings pain. And a part of me feels ashamed. But only a part. The other half no longer cares.

Ian sinks his fingers deep into his hair and sighs. He is growing sick of me. I wonder if I am losing him for good.

Am I losing him?

He drops his hand to his side and lifts his head to hold me in his sight. I am sure he means to say something but cannot find the words. Either way, there is no need for us to talk.

The interesting thing about my sweat is that it rarely exudes harsh odor. Covered in perspiration from my run, sticky and wet, I climb on top of my husband, straddle position. Almost immediately his expression turns to surprise. Then I slip my tongue into his mouth and kiss him the way I should have kissed him a thousand times during our years together.

I wait for Ian's response. For a second, it appears as though he is going to reject me. My body goes tight.

But then Ian wraps his arms around my waist and, with his hand firmly pressed against my spine, returns my kiss with equal passion, force.

A few seconds later and he is already hard.

Slipping my hand under the elastic of Ian's boxers, I shape my fingers into an O, run them up and down his penis, the way he did when he was watching porn. Ian begins to breathe heavily. He whispers in my ear, "Are you sure about this?"

But I have never liked talking about sex. I am more of a doer. So, I drop to my knees and take him into my mouth.

He closes his eyes as he leans back with his hand on my head. The tension in his frame quickly begins to melt away.

Then Ian drops his hand to my shoulder, squeezes and says, "Oh God, Delilah, oh God."

God has nothing to do with it.

I crawl onto my husband, straddle position once more, pull off his shirt, run my fingers over his firm rippling body.

Ian flips me around to lie me flat on the bed. He helps me kick off my running shoes then slips my pants over my ankles, tosses them against the wall, removes my shirt and bra.

Kissing my thighs, he proceeds to the space between my legs and works my clitoris as an expert with his tongue. I grab hold of Ian's hair in response. "Get up here," I say as I claw at his shoulders. I want him inside me.

Ian takes hold of my buttocks. Applying pressure, he pulls me in close. Now we are one, and my breath catches in my throat.

Somewhere in the middle of all this, I close my eyes and feel the sensation of the stone award for exceptional work in my hand. The stone award comes swinging around to crack open Wallace's skull like a coconut, his insides spilling out all over the floor. And all the while I breathe, "Harder. Ian, harder. Yes."

My husband follows my every command.

The stone award descends again, and my legs tremble.

And again.

I moan.

Over.

And over.

And over.

Now I am on top, as I was on the day of Wallace's untimely demise. Ian is in a semi-slouched sitting position with his legs stretched out beneath me and his spine against the upholstered headboard, which beats against the wall like a drum. I drop my hands to each side of our legs, throw my head back, and arch my spine. Behind my eyelids, I see color.

Ian rests one hand on my hip while the other runs over my breast to cup the bottom. He takes my breast into his mouth.

I am close.

So close.

Harder.

He slips his arm around my ribcage and turns me forty-five degrees to lie me flat on the bed. My head hangs off the edge, my long hair dangling loosely.

Squeezing, pumping, his hands clamp around my thighs. Ian pulls me in as he pushes. My toes begin to curl. Then he slaps his hands onto the bed, one on each side of my body. His spine arches upward. And he thrusts himself into me deep and deeper still.

The stone award for exceptional work swings around to crash violently against Wallace's skull, shattering bone.

Ian thrusts.

We both release one last long inarticulate sound.

And the stone award for exceptional work drops to

the floor with a *thud*.

Lying in bed in the dimly lit room, the bedcovers wet from our lovemaking, Ian slides a sheet over us and says, "I don't know what to say." There is a brief moment when it seems as though he means to add more but opts not to do so. Communication is a cactus for us both.

A few minutes later, I climb out of bed to clean myself up in the bathroom. With the faucet running, I sit on the floor, my spine against the vanity for support. I feel strange, shaky, not fully myself.

What was that?

Dear God, what was that?

And what the hell does it say about me as a person?

All the while I keep hearing those four little words in my head: *Dahlia instead of Delilah. Dahlia instead of Delilah. Dahlia instead of Delilah.*

Ian enters the room to towel himself off. Upon finding me on the floor with my knees to my chest and my arms wrapped around my knees, he says, "What is going on, Delilah? Is everything alright?"

I do not respond.

He studies me for a beat before turning on the shower. A plume of steam rises above the shower door. It soon begins to fog the mirror.

Then Ian takes hold of my hands and pulls me up into his arms. He brushes his thumb gently across my chin and kisses me softly on the lips. "When you are ready," he tells me. "I am right here."

But I cannot share the truth with my husband. How can I tell him about the stone award for exceptional work or what happened the night of Wallace's demise? There is no way.

Cactus.

We enter the shower together and wash each other

with almond scented body soap. It is a sensual experience.

I run my hand up Ian's thigh, massage his scrotum region then drop to my knees and take him into my mouth yet again, water raining on top of me.

He braces himself with his hand and forearm against the wall, panting heavily. His other hand he uses to serve as a guide. Then he yanks me to my feet, spins me around, and takes me from behind.

The water feels hot on my skin.

The steam rises.

I close my eyes.

Ian pins me against the shower wall. With his forearm flat against the tile, he repeatedly thrusts himself into me. Soon his muscles go tight. He injects me with his semen then slips his hand between my legs to finish me off.

But when I turn around to look into my husband's eyes, I find that the shower is raining blood. It is pouring out over us, circling the drain, dripping off the tiles. Ian is covered in it. He looks as though he emerged from a bloody pool.

In a panic, I fall into the corner. My entire body trembles with fright.

"What is it?" Ian says, pawing at me. "Delilah, what's happening? What the hell is going on?"

The blood is saturating his hair. It is painting the shower door red.

I close my eyes and count backwards from ten.

Please God, make it stop.

When I open my eyes again, the blood is gone. Ian is fine. The water is clear. It was all in my head.

He pulls me into an embrace and kisses my temple before he shuts off the water. Then we step out into the cold and wrap ourselves in our respective towels.

"Are you sure you're alright?" he asks as he studies

me queerly. He also helps me dry off.

Am I alright?

The answer comes to me slowly.

I don't know.

However, I do not respond.

Ian tucks me into bed. "Are you hungry? I am going to make us something to eat," he says.

As best as I can, I muster a smile.

A few seconds later, there is the clinking of pots and pans and the whirring of the juicer downstairs.

Ian's cellphone is on the nightstand by his side of the bed. It lights up but does not make a sound because the ringer is off. When I lean over to investigate, I see that it is after five o'clock in the morning. The message is from Ian's coworker Tom. It is about the upcoming business trip he and Ian have planned. I look over my shoulder at the open doorway. Ian never mentioned anything about going on any trips. In fact, he promised he would put those on hold for the time being.

I slap his phone on the nightstand in its original position before he returns.

Then Ian enters the room with two plates of food. The one with eggs and pork bacon is for him, while the one with eggs and turkey bacon is for me. He hands me my plate and kisses me on the cheek before he walks around to the other side of the bed. There, he picks up the remote, turns on the television, flips through some channels, and slides in next to me, our legs touching.

"Still doing alright?" he says after a while.

Fucking sonuvabitch.

When I do not respond, Ian turns his attention to the television. He laughs at some stupid jokes as he continues to shovel forkfuls of food into his mouth. I watch him with a blooming hatred—that ridiculous laugh, the food in his teeth, his fucking lies. It takes all that I have not to slap the fork straight down his throat.

Outside, the sky shifts from charcoal gray to pale gold, well on its way to cornflower blue. Soon the soft gilded clouds will be hanging high in the atmosphere, relieved of the pressure that had been holding them down. It is set to be a beautiful day. But like with most other things, beauty does not last long.

CHAPTER TWENTY-TWO

Psalm 58:10 says, "The righteous will rejoice in vengeance; he will bathe his feet in the blood of the wicked."

How comforting a thought.

It has been two days since Ian left. Two long days. The sky has shifted from cornflower blue to pale purple to charcoal gray. The clouds have spread out like a blanket over the earth, gauzy and layered, dead set on eclipsing the sun, while the ground is now covered in pools of rainwater, mud, and muck. It is thundering outside. The lightning is well on its way. But I am in a decent mood because the phone conversation with the head of the HR Department at Westgrove, Gardner, and Jones went well. Now it will not be long until Nathaniel gets what he deserves.

And it is about damn time.

Sitting on the couch by the window, I watch the inclement weather and listen to the rain as it beats against wood, metal, and asphalt. The sound reminds me of that Easter Sunday so long ago, the dirty green door and the stench of exotic food, the cigarette smoke heavy in my nostrils. If only I had not left my pink-eared bunny next to the glass turtle ashtray on the table. Then maybe my mother would not have opened the door to call after me. Maybe my father would not have ascended those stairs.

And all the rest.

I see the gnashing of my mother's teeth as my father's hands squeeze tighter and tighter about her throat, the green door quivering, the broken glass, and of course the color.

My cellphone is on the counter next to the bills in front of the barstools. Its vibration draws my attention. I know I should get up and answer the phone, but I do not want to spend the energy to cross the room. Plus, there is the fear of who might be on the other end of the line. What if it is Detective Forester again? He just so happened to run into me at the grocery store the other day. Forester loves his little interrogations. From the look he wore on his face, he will never stop. Only now he doesn't have the right. The case is closed. I acted in self-defense.

Ha.

Because there is a small chance that the call might be from Ian, I decide I have to know either way. There is a single voice message waiting for me on my cell. I hit play and hear the sound of the HR Director's voice.

"Mrs. Maconwood, this is Dan Torrington again," he says. "I was wondering if you would come into the office to sign some forms, maybe answer a few more questions about the complaint you filed. Also, we need to set up a date for your return to work. Please call me as soon as you get this. Then I'll have my secretary arrange a good time for us to meet."

Apparently, the free ride is over. Sexual assault on company grounds only gets you four weeks.

Setting the phone where I found it on the counter, I drop into the occasional chair, slouch style, and imagine what it will be like to return to the job—all those eyeballs and whispers, questions and false support. The thought is like fire ants under my skin, crawling, burrowing, injecting me with their poison. But what choice do I have? A girl has got to work. There are bills to pay. Otherwise, Ian would be home.

I suppose I could get a lawyer, seek some kind of settlement, something that would buy me more time and give Ian a break, but then again what if it opens a can of worms I need to keep closed? The thought gets pushed straight out of my head and buried under a pile of lye. None of that matters now. What matters is that a man is dead, and Nathaniel needs to take responsibility for what he has done.

He needs to take responsibility.

After a quick shower and change of clothes, I hop into my car and head over to Westgrove, Gardner, and Jones to do some paperwork. I don't bother calling to schedule because I want it over with and enough time has already been wasted. Although the sky seems to be lightening, the sun hard at work to push through the clouds, the rain has not yet let up. I flip on my windshield wipers and lean forward in my seat.

All of the outdoor parking spaces have been claimed, so I park in the dank, dark parking garage and make my way inside Westgrove, Gardner, and Jones to take the elevator to the seventh floor. Stepping into the hustle-and-bustle, my shoulders lift with tension. I need a moment to calm. My nerves feel as though they are on the outside of my body, exposed to the elements. It is the building, being inside it once more. The physical reaction is one I did not predict. I take a deep breath before pushing forward.

Through the tunnels of my eyes, I see people I hardly know busy at work. Employees on different floors do not typically interact with one another. It is like a caste system here. But everyone is staring at me now. They know who I am.

Of course, there has been talk.

I make my way down the corridor to the HR Department, which resides in the back, and at the half way point see Nathaniel Martin exiting through HR's main door. Other than turn around and head the way that I had come, there is nowhere for me to go. So, I keep to my course. Now we have no choice but to pass each other in the hall. The expression on Nathaniel's face is that of pure rage, his features distorted, his eyes bitterly sharp. I half expect him to clamp his hand around my arm and drag me off me into some dark empty room, but Nathaniel merely flashes me a dangerous look as we continue in opposite directions.

I glance at him, while he does the same to me. Then Nathaniel disappears around the corner, and I stop in front of the main door to the HR Department, breathe a sigh of relief.

The meeting with Dan takes all of an hour. To my surprise, it was another who started the claim against Nathaniel. I just finished it off, the final nail as they say.

"In any case, you can verify all of this with the police," I tell him and the older Asian woman joining us before I stand up to leave. "Or better yet ask Sebastian directly, since he was the primary source."

"Don't you worry about a thing," the woman tells me. "We've already started to look into the matter. Rest assured we will take care of this."

Now the butcher is on the chopping block, while I am set to get whatever I want. The only downside is that I have to return to work in a week.

Imagining Nathaniel's face as he is escorted from the building by Oliver Hamlin, the monster security guard, is the highlight of my day. I can barely hold back a smile as I make my way to my car. The sky is pouring rain at this point. It is one of the worst storms I have ever seen, outside of a hurricane. Water is literally hammering the earth. The sun has disappeared without reason in the span of an hour.

As soon as I hit the button on the remote to unlock my vehicle, I feel pressure around my arm. Looking down, I see a hand then follow it up to Nathaniel's face.

He drags me into the shadows of the dank, dark garage. And an odd emotion rises in my chest.

Who the fuck does he—

"What do you think you are doing, Delilah?" he says, heatedly.

Yanking my arm from his grip, I reply in my iciest tone, "Let go of me right now."

We hold eye contact for an extended beat.

Nathaniel drops his voice low. "You went to them, didn't you? You filed a complaint against me." His voice elevates here. "Didn't you, Delilah?!" Then he slaps the concrete wall with the palm of his hand as he adds, "You fucking bitch!" The sound reminds me of the stone award for exceptional work as it fell from my hand to the floor in my office the night of Wallace's demise. "You insane cunt."

"Let me pass," I say, coolly.

He grabs hold of my arm once more, breaching my space. "You may have gotten everyone else to buy your bullshit, Delilah," he snarls, "but I am not an idiot. I see you for what you are. Exactly what you are."

And what am I?

"If you don't let me pass," I reply but do not finish my thought.

The rain is especially loud. No one would hear me if I screamed. Nathaniel's pupils remind me of the space between the trees, and my fingernails dig fresh tracks in my palms.

Then Nathaniel shakes me violently. "Now you're going to listen to me," he says. "Because I'm telling you—"

"Telling me?"

Warning me.

"Yes, I'm telling you—"

But before he can finish his thought, the elevator dings and voices play in the air.

I rip my arm out of Nathaniel's grip, scramble for the right key to my vehicle, and climb inside the car before he can stop me. With the others there, chatting, laughing, piling into the SUV four cars away from my own, Nathaniel has no choice but to watch as I drive away.

And I keep driving.

I drive for a long time, until finally I end up in front of his house. His new house. The one he closed on recently.

Nathaniel lives in a four thousand square foot contemporary craftsman with a three car garage on three and a half acres of land in the middle of nowhere on a dead-end road. His nearest neighbor is a long walk away. The place is secluded.

Behind Nathaniel's property line resides a state park with a nature trail that abuts his backyard. After performing a slow drive-by of his house, I swing around and pull into the parking lot of the state park, taking the farthest spot from the entrance, right under the canopy of trees. The willows make it so that you can barely see my car unless you are practically on top of it. Although the rain has finally stopped, the ground is soaked several layers deep and everything is dripping.

There are multiple paths along the trail. Because I am not outdoor inclined, it takes me a while to figure out which way to go. Sloshing through the mud and the muck, getting whipped in the face with wet branches and sliding down small hills, I nearly give up. But then I take a spill and rip a dirty hole through my jeans, scraping my knee in the process, only to look up and catch a glimpse of bright white trim beyond the trees. The trim tells me I am close.

Even though Nathaniel's nearest neighbor is a fair distance up the road, I decide I cannot walk directly through Nathaniel's backyard. It's too risky. So, I follow the trees to the far edge of his house, my feet sinking into the earth, my hands covered in bits of bark, everything wet.

Then I emerge from the woods and look around. It is quiet here, peaceful. The only sounds are coming from the creatures in the forest, and even they are not stirring much on account of the inclement weather.

With swift steps, I make my way to the south side of Nathaniel's house and peek through his windows to see what I can learn. There are no blinds, no black-out curtains, or anything else to obstruct my view. The place appears unoccupied and absent of electric light, but I wait a few minutes longer to be sure.

There is a voice in my head screaming for me to turn around, leave, but I need to know more about the man who threatened me. I need to understand him because this is not over. So, I check the doors to see if they are locked. Of course they are. Then I try the windows, one after the next, until finally I come to an open one off the small room at the end. The room is located between the kitchen and the garage. Nathaniel apparently uses it for storage, as evidence by the boxes and supplies. A mere half inch separates the bottom of the window from its sill, but it is enough for me to make my way inside his home.

Scanning the area, I find a pile of wood scraps in a large wooden container several feet away. I fill my arms with as many long scraps as I can carry and drop them in from of the window to give me extra height. Then I push the window upward as hard as I possibly can. It doesn't budge. I try again, and again the window goes nowhere. It is now that I notice the towel on the ledge of the interior side soaking up water. The window is stuck. And when I try to force it open once more, I slice my finger on something slimy and sharp. Then I remove my sweater to wipe off the signs of my blood.

You have to know.

Several metal retention rods lie next to the pile of wood on the left hand side of the yard. I grab the one with the sharpest edge and use it as leverage to pry the window open. It takes some doing. In fact it takes all of my strength. But eventually the window begins to move, slowly at first, like a zipper caught, then smoothly until it sticks again. There is just enough space now for me to slide my way through the opening to enter his home.

Tossing the metal bar to the side, I clap the grit and the grime off my hands. Then, holding my body weight as my feet slip and slide down the wet exterior of the house, I pull myself up, struggling, straining, only to fall on my shoulder on the other side, landing on the sodden towel I knocked off the ledge in the process. The floor is wet with rainwater released from the towel as a result of pressure from my arm.

With my hand clamped over my injured shoulder, I check the garage to make sure Nathaniel's pristine SUV is not there. It isn't. Then I search the house for an alarm and find one in the room off the garage. Thankfully, it is not yet operational. I relax some.

He is a fool.

Proceeding deeper into the house, I run my hands over Nathaniel's electronics and page through a couple of his books. It isn't until now that I realize I have been tracking mud and debris through the rooms. I take off my shoes and clean up the mess with a wad of paper towels then shove the lot deep into the garbage bin, where it won't be noticed. Then I continue to explore the place with only damp socks on my feet. My shoes I leave in the living room.

Nathaniel is a collector of fine art and items from around the world. His style is basically minimalistic. He favors negative space.

I walk through his kitchen and his living room quickly then enter his master bedroom, where the lamp is still on in the corner. It is an interesting piece, urban industrial in design.

Flipping the light on in the closet, I finger my way through his clothes, which are organized by color. He has an extensive array of expensive suits and Turnbull & Asser ties. There is next to nothing in his closet that isn't high-end.

Gradiose bastard.

I shove one of his ties into my pocket then switch off the closet light and knock the door closed with my elbow.

Right above Nathaniel's bed is an abstract piece of art made of rich, bold pigments. I stand still as I study it. Slowly, I begin to realize what it reminds me of—a woman's vagina. And I hate him all the more.

Next I enter his master bathroom and examine his moisturizes and colognes. Some of the moisturizers I try on my skin. Then I pick up the first bottle of cologne that I see and turn it over in my hands, giving it a spray. This is the source of Nathaniel's preferred citrusy bergamot scent. I choke on the smell and have to cough several times to clear my throat. My stomach twists into a knot.

Clicking off the light, I re-enter Nathaniel's master bedroom. On the chair in the corner is a single box, the only box Nathaniel has not yet unpacked. Sitting on top of it is a Canon EOS Rebel T7i, similar to the camera up and coming photographer S.S. uses to shoot professional models. I tinker around with the camera for a while, adjusting the settings and looking through the lens. Nathaniel probably uses the damn thing to film unsuspecting women during sex. A part of me wants to destroy it, but instead I set it on the box exactly where I found it and move to another location in the room.

Although Nathaniel's master bedroom is designed for substantial pieces of furniture, the massive California king that serves as the focal point takes up considerable space. Behind the bed is a tufted upholstered headboard, and beneath it is what appears to be a Persian hand woven rug.

I fall onto the bed and rest with my hands on my chest, staring up at the coffered ceiling. The panels are painted in a shade lighter than the side walls, the beams stark white. I have the urge to crawl under the covers, if only because the thread count is so high, double-ply, and the feel of the material against my skin luxurious. The faint scent of detergent is detectable on the sheets. Nathaniel must have washed them recently.

I close my eyes and imagine what it must be like to be able to afford such things, but I guess it is the butchers who get whatever they want whenever they want it, not people like me.

At least that was how it used to work.

When my eyes reopen, it takes a moment for me to soak up the scene. Blinking slowly, an open condom wrapper gradually comes into focus. The wrapper is sitting on the nightstand along with two books, one by Dean Koontz and the other by Bret Easton Ellis. I pick up the one by Koontz then notice Nathaniel's laptop on the dresser and put the book where I found it. Of course, the computer is password protected.

My stomach begins to growl, and I feel intense pangs of hunger. I need to eat, so I set Nathaniel's laptop on his living room chair and return to the kitchen to see if I can find something small to tie me over until I get home. It is darker in the house now. I have to switch on the light in the kitchen. Aside from the case of beer on the bottom shelf, Nathaniel's refrigerator is jam packed with healthy food. Basically, it is the exact opposite of mine. I grab a celery stick and start munching on it before I elbow the refrigerator door closed.

The clock on the stove says it is slightly after 8:00 PM. Only now do I realize that I have been here for hours and Nathaniel is probably well on his way. I must have fallen asleep on his bed; though, I don't know how that is possible given the fact that my mind never seems to shut off.

"Shit," I say in a semi-panic. Then I toss the celery stick into the garbage bin, reopen the top, shove the stick deeper where it cannot be seen, and shut the lid once more.

Stopping in the middle of the room, I say, "Okay, think, think." I need to remember everything that I touched so that I can wipe it clean.

But the key is already in the lock. I hear it along with the sound of Nathaniel's voice.

Now I am in a state of full panic.

By some miracle, I manage to think clearly enough to switch off the light before Nathaniel makes it inside. Then I hide in pantry, my heart slamming against my ribcage and blood pulsating in my ear like a drum.

Two different voices overlap each other. Nathaniel has a woman with him. They are loud.

"Do you want something to drink?" Nathaniel asks

her as his voice moves toward the kitchen. "Beer? Soda? Wine?"

No, no, no, no, no. Please, God, no. I bite my bottom lip.

"Water would be nice," the woman replies.

Shit.

The next thing I know, Nathaniel is in the same room with me, not fifteen feet away. I can see him through the slats in the door. Instead of grabbing bottled spring water from the refrigerator, he fills a clear glass with tap from the sink. For a second it almost seems as though he is looking over his shoulder by way of his peripherals, as if he senses me here.

Oh, God, did he see my shoes?

The woman enters the room. She looks vaguely familiar, but I cannot place her. She is tall and thin with short dark hair and clear creamy skin. Running a finger softly, slowly, over Nathaniel's ear then down the back of his neck, she kisses him.

At this point, my eyes drop to my feet.

You have to get out of here.

I stare at my toes.

Nathaniel shuts off the faucet and sets the glass of water on the counter before he takes the woman into his arms. Then everything heats up quickly.

The next thing I know, he has the short haired woman on the table in the corner. Her heels are off, and he is sliding her panties over her ankles. Then Nathaniel unbuttons and unzips his pants and rams himself inside her, unprotected.

All the while, I am stuck in the pantry forced to watch, the space between my legs tingling from the disease he may have given me. My stomach in knots from his bastard child encased its placenta sac.

The woman says, "Not so hard, Nathaniel. Slow

down, slow down."

But Nathaniel does not comply.

Instead, he looks up, straight at the pantry door. For an extended beat it seems as though he can see through the door and directly at me, like he knows that I am here.

Oh, God, does he know?

He is putting on this show for me.

I step as far back as I can go with my spine firmly against the shelves, nearly knocking over a can of corn in the process.

"Nathaniel," the woman says, loudly, "not so hard. We have time."

He shoves his tongue into her mouth to shut her up.

I know who she is now, one the powers at Westgrove, Gardner, and Jones. He is trying to undo the damage he's done.

He rams himself into her harder, and harder, all the while eyeing the pantry door.

Then he lifts her off the table and carries her into the next room, where I can no longer see.

Only now do I release the air I've been holding in my lungs since they entered the kitchen.

"You're so beautiful," I hear Nathaniel say in the next room. And the woman moans.

There is no way I can risk grabbing my shoes without being caught, so I decide to leave them behind. Between the kitchen and the garage is the room Nathaniel uses for storage, the same one I used to gain entry to his home. I cut across the kitchen and exit through the way I entered as quietly as possible, making sure to set the sodden towel into place on the ledge. It falls to the floor, so I pick it up and reset it.

The window sticks about an inch from the sill as I try to pull it closed. I try again and again, but the damn thing won't budge. I have to leave it and hope that Nathaniel doesn't notice the half inch change.

Though it is dark outside, there is enough moonlight for me to carefully make my way around. I return the scraps of wood to their container in the yard and the retention rod where I found it then quickly make my way into the woods.

Once I am a far enough distance from Nathaniel's house, I click on the flashlight on my keychain and follow the nature trail to my car. It is a miracle I do not get lost. I am not great with remembering directions.

With trembling hands, I shove the key into the ignition and turn on the heat. My socks are soaked. I am coated in mud and covered with slimy debris, freezing. The rain has cooled everything down.

"What the fuck is wrong with you?" I say, softly.

All I can do is hope that Nathaniel will think one of his conquests accidently left shoes behind at his house. Even if he suspects something is awry, I seriously doubt he will tie it to me because he has never taken me to his home. As far as he knows, I have no idea where he lives.

Did I put his computer back in his room?

With my heartbeat settling into its normal pace, I head down the road, careful not to speed. The light at the four-way turns red before I can make it through the crossing. I stop and strangle the steering wheel, close my eyes and count backwards from ten. All the while, Nathaniel's voice keeps playing in my ear. *You're so beautiful. You're so beautiful. You're so beautiful.*

When my eyes reopen, I slowly look to my right. Sitting next to me in the car is my pink-eared bunny. He remains face forward. My car is the only one at the intersection. The light stays red for a long, long time. In fact, it feels like forever.

Then it turns green.

CHAPTER TWENTY-THREE

After I untangle myself from the covers, I slip out of bed, walk downstairs, and step out onto the patio. It takes a moment for my bare feet to adjust to the cold concrete, my toes wiggling their way to warmth. With my arms wrapped about my chest, I inhale the morning air, which is chilly from the storm that passed the night before. A sense of calm washes over me. The sky is on the verge of transformation. It is seguing into a lovely pinkish gold. Ian will be home soon. Then we can get to being what we were meant to be all along. There will peace.

As I think about this, my mind drifts and the calm dissipates like scented molecules over time. I do not want Nathaniel to be in my head, but here he is. He believes he sees me for what I am.

He doesn't.

If anything, it is the other way around. When we first met, I thought Nathaniel was a kind and decent person. The Paper Nickel showed me the truth—the moment he touched me, the way he behaved afterward, and something else, something more, something I will never be able to explain. If not for the fact that he burrowed his way under my skin like a tic set for the bloodstream, dead bent on clawing its way to the brain to cause harm, I would push him from my thoughts all together. I have a bad feeling about Nathaniel Martin. A terrible, sick feeling. He is under my skin. And I don't know what that means.

The more reasonable part of my mind tries to bring sense to the matter. It is easy to believe that I am overreacting, especially after Jane's call. She contacted me last night before I closed my eyes to sleep. I was so tired, my body weak from lack of sustenance and rest, I almost did not pick up the phone. But then I did and heard Jane's voice.

"Just thought I would check in on you," she said. "Are you doing alright?" My relationship with Jane has not been the same since it fractured. There was always a wall of ill connection between us. Now the wall seems thicker than ever. "Did you hear the news about Nathaniel Martin?"

"Jane, I haven't exactly been keeping up on what's going on down there," I replied, coolly. "Why? What's happened?"

"They are saying he is on his way out," she said with a touch of excitement in her voice.

On his way out.

"And I have to tell you, Delilah, the look on his face—the look on his face scared me."

"Wait, back up a minute, Jane. I'm not sure I understand. What happened?"

"They're letting him go," she said. "Or at least it looks that way. I think it is a dot-all-your-i's kind of situation."

"Go as in fired?"

"Yeah, yes, fired. Can you believe it? The golden boy. The Butcher of Westgrove. They are giving him the proverbial ax."

It took a moment for me to process the information. Jane did not wait for me to think. She went right into her next statement. "Not that this has much to do with you,

Delilah, or anything to do with you at all. The rumor has it that the intern is the one who did him in. Something inappropriate on the grounds, I guess."

Inappropriate.

Is that what they call it now?

"Jane," I said, my mind spinning, "I need you to rewind for a second. What exactly have you heard?"

"The intern, the intern," she said, impatiently, "the tall one, the blond, annoyingly sweet. I can't think of her name right now. What is it again? It's right there. Don't you hate when that happens? What is it?" Jane clicked her tongue as if rummaging through her mind for a name.

"Focus, Jane!" I replied. "Please."

"Sorry," she said. "I don't know for sure, Delilah. It is all very hush-hush around here. But there has been talk."

"What kind of talk?"

"Misuse of power and position for one thing. I'll let you put the pieces together. Beyond that, your guess is as good as mine." After a beat, she added, "I always knew there was something wrong with the man."

My fingers were touching my lips when I felt the onset of a smile. Westgrove, Gardner, and Jones is letting Nathaniel go.

Well, alright.

"Jane?"

"Yes?"

"Has there been talk about me?" I asked her.

She did not want to answer, as evidenced by her hesitation, but I pressured her into it. "Everyone knows about the bet," she said softly. "I'm sorry, Delilah. I'm so sorry. I should have been there for you. I haven't been a very good friend."

Neither have I.

A brief silence ensued before I thanked Jane for

calling and hung up the phone.

Now I can't stop thinking about the conversation. Nathaniel's removal from his position at Westgrove, Gardner, and Jones serves as a win—it should feel like a win—but it doesn't. The raking across my skull, scratching at my brain, creates more anxiety than anything else. Maybe it is because I left my tennis shoes behind at his house and the computer on the sofa, as well as the window cracked a half inch higher than when I found it. But then again, there is no way Nathaniel could tie any of those things to me. I probably am low on his register. He is out of my life. I should be happy, rejoicing. So, why is the voice in the corner of my mind still screaming it isn't over?

It isn't over!

After my morning juice, I turn on the shower and sit on the edge of the garden tub while steam fills the room. I run my hand across the condensation and stare at my watery image in the mirror. The person I was before the Paper Nickel, before I met Nathaniel Martin, is not the person standing in front of me. I am different now. A skeleton shrink wrapped in skin and something else.

I step into the shower, lather, rinse, repeat, all the while running through the laundry list of things I need to get done before my husband gets home. Taking the car drive from the airport to our house into account, Ian should return sometime between 1:45 and 2:15 AM, depending on traffic. Everything needs to be perfect. I want it to be perfect, like regrowth after a burn. It is time to replant.

There is a bathrobe hanging off the hook by the shower door. I slip on the robe and go downstairs to have some ice tea outside on the porch. As I am standing there under the warmth of the sun, a glint of metal catches my eye. It looks like a black SUV heading south down the road toward my house. Suddenly I am filled with an incredible sense of dread. I rush deeper into the backyard and strain my eyes for a better look. But the vehicle has already driven past. I cut through my house and tear open the front door to check from the other side. There is only one car on the road that I can see. It is a silver sedan with a fin on top. I stand in the open doorway for another minute or two before finally chalking the whole thing up to an overactive imagination. Laughing softly, I close the door.

Maybe I really am losing my mind.

Still, something is off, the sensation in the pit of my stomach like churning acid. I check every room in the house to make sure all of the windows and doors are locked. I would set the alarm but can't because I neglected to pay the bill and the company shut off our service.

The scratching at my brain intensifies.

You're being ridiculous.

Am I being ridiculous?

Because I cannot walk around all day in my robe, I change into some comfortable clothes.

Then I start preparations for painting the walls in my master bedroom. First, I drag the furniture out of the way. Some of the pieces are too heavy to pull, so I sit on the floor with my back braced against the wall for support and push off with my feet. It takes some doing; however, the furniture slowly begins to move away from the walls.

Second, I lay out the plastic sheets to protect the hardwood floors from spillage.

But when I go to open the can with the metal opening tool, I find that the device is not in the bag. I do not feel like walking all the way down the stairs to rummage through the garage for something to use, so I grab my husband's hunting knife from under his clothes in the bottom drawer. The knife was a gift from his uncle even though Ian has never hunted a day in his life and never needed it. The blade is two and half inch serrated steel with three mm thickness. I use it to pop the top on the can then turn the knife over in my hands, staring at it, before I set it aside.

Why?

A second later, I am shoving the thing under the mattress for a reason I cannot explain.

With a wooden stir, I mix the binders and the pigments in the paint to ensure consistency of color and coverage. The color is called Storm. It is similar to a soft French gray with cool blue undertones. Despite the name, I find it calming.

Ian will love this.

He has to love this.

I am about to pour the paint into the tray when I realize that I purchased the wrong rollers. The ones I have are too small. It would take me twenty years to complete the project. Now I have to go to the home improvement store again to purchase the right ones before I can start the job.

The strange feeling in my chest strengthens as I put on my shoes. I have a wicked migraine as well.

From my house to the home improvement store is approximately thirty-five minutes, slightly longer if you take the scenic route, which I do. The sun is shining and I am not in a hurry. Maybe the warmth has finally decided to stay for good.

If we are lucky.

I pass the church with the colossal wooden doors then swing around and find myself sitting in its parking lot. Mass is releasing. People are funneling through the doorway and down the concrete steps for their cars.

Not seven but seventy-seven sticks in my head. It is the

number of times we can screw up and still find forgiveness. And that is what I need. Right?

Forgive me, Father.

Slowly, I open the driver's side door and climb out of the vehicle. With a measured pace, I cross the parking lot for the concrete steps but come to a stop. What happened to Wallace was a mistake. It was a terrible accident. However, it was not my fault. Or at least it wasn't all my fault. It was more Nathaniel than anything else.

Nathaniel.

Nathaniel.

Nathaniel.

Why is he still in my life?

I want him gone.

The last time I tried to confess my sins, I passed out and had to be driven home by my husband. Was that because of my own guilt or because that sonuvabitch Nathaniel is still walking around out there, his bastard child encased its placenta sac kicking violently while in wait to be born?

No, that's not right. No bastard here.

It feels as though every single person in the parking lot is now staring at me. A circle of eyes. The judgment is unbearable. My fingernails sink into my palms, break the skin.

I run back to my vehicle.

Shoving the key into the ignition and the car into gear, I slam my foot against the accelerator and speed down the road. The next thing I know I am pulling into the rearmost spot of the parking lot outside the home improvement store. For I don't know how long, I sit there with my hands on the wheel and tears in my eyes. I am NOT guilty. It was an accident. I did nothing wrong. He is the one to blame. Nathaniel. Not me.

HE. IS. TO. BLAME.

The sun is out, the gilded white clouds, and the sky is a backdrop of serene blue.

I wipe the tears from my eyes with my hand, take a deep breath, and pull myself together before entering the store. With my head as high as I can hold it, I find an older gentleman to help me select the right roller for the type of job I intend to do. He has long white hippie hair and a bright yellow vest that has his company's logo embroidered on it on the left hand side. In a strange, thick voice that reminds me of Stephen King's Pet Sematary, the man says, "You want to make sure you don't do something you'll regret, young lady."

"Excuse me?" I reply.

But instead of responding verbally, he simply shoves a roller into my hand and nods. Then he laughs as he walks away, which I find even creepier.

The girl at the front register has a nose piercing. She rings me up, all the while staring at me queerly. Feeling like I am in an episode of the Twilight Zone, I pay the girl then snatch the bag from her hand and leave as quickly as possible.

What is going on?

By the time I get home, I need a break, so I throw on a quick television show before getting started upstairs. My eyes grow heavy and heavier still. I fall asleep and dream of happier days. In my dream I see myself nibbling on a licorice stick and buzzing around like a bee. Ian pulls me into a warm embrace and kisses me sweetly. Then he holds up two shirts and asks which he should wear for his first day on his new job. We are in a different house now, and I am pregnant with our child. "Hold on a minute," I tell him as I lift a finger then pull a box out of a drawer. I present the box to my husband. He turns his back to me as he yanks the wrapper and ribbon off. When he turns around again, I see the Turnbull & Asser tie I stole from Nathaniel's house in Ian's hand. Suddenly there is the pressure of a violent grip on my arm. Damp with perspiration, I wake with a start.

A bomb of blackness, of night, floods the tunnels of my eyes. I slept through the rest of the day.

Right away I recheck the windows and the doors. Then I grab my cellphone off the counter. Ian still has not called.

Why haven't you called?

The battery on my cellphone is low, so I plug it into the charger in the kitchen, all the while pushing the thick sense of dread deep into my gut.

"You're doing it again," I say to myself. Sometimes I get paranoid. I know this.

I trade out my damp clothes for a pair of knee length sweatpants and oversized black tee before pulling my hair up out of my face and grabbing a bottle of spring water from the refrigerator. As I sip on the water, I catch a glimpse of my reflection in the sliding glass door by the dining room table. Beyond the reflection, outside in the dark, something moves. It cuts across the rear of my house. I drop the water.

With trembling hands, I check the lock on the door and switch on the porch light, but whatever was out there is now gone. I watch from the door for the next few minutes to be certain. A cat meows in the distance, and I feel like a fool.

After cleaning up the water, I put on some light music and head to my bedroom to prepare the walls for paint. Because the fumes will still be present by the time Ian gets home, I set aside some fresh linen to make up the guest room. Maybe Ian and I can rechristen the space.

It will be nice.

I pour the paint into the tray and dip the roller into the paint then press the roller against the wall to get started. Afterward, I perform the cut-in method along the top and bottom, where the wall meets the ceiling and baseboards, respectively.

As soon as the first wall is done, I climb off the step ladder to check the result. At this point, I have paint in my hair and a little on my face, sweat above my brows.

The light streaming in from the master bathroom flickers and everything stops, especially the sound.

Turning my head slowly, I do not want to fill my eyes with what I am about to see. I feel as though I already know.

There, standing in the doorway that separates the master bathroom from the master bedroom, not ten feet away, is the man who took me in the space between the trees outside the Paper Nickel. In his hand are my tennis shoes. He throws them onto the floor in front of my feet.

No.

I panic, step backwards and knock the can of paint over. The color spreads out along the plastic like the pool of blood around Wallace's skull on the day of his demise.

Nathaniel's body absorbs most of the light from the other room. He is a substantial presence in dark clothes.

We stare at each other for a prolonged beat, the silence between us like a ten inch thick wall of pure tension.

A wave of heat envelops me; I am paralyzed with fear. I want to run but cannot. I want to scream, but my voice box won't work. My fingers tighten about the handle of the paint roller, and all the while my brain keeps repeating four little words: *Dahlia instead of Delilah. Dahlia instead of Delilah. Dahlia instead of Delilah.*

The heat finally passes. Then the roller flies across

the room in the direction of Nathaniel's head as I make a mad dash for the stairs.

Along the way, I lose my footing. My hip crashes against the corner of a step, my elbow as well. The next thing I know, I am tumbling down the staircase, slamming into the wall, which splinters as my head takes the majority of the knock. The jolt leaves me immobile.

As soon as I come out of the stupor, I try to crawl away. However, I do not get very far.

Nathaniel squats in front of me to block my path. He pushes me up against the wall. Now we are eye to eye.

The foyer is to my right. And beyond that is the front door. But I cannot make the escape. Nathaniel is too close.

With his thumb and his forefinger, he takes hold of my chin. And all I see are his pupils. Oil black and the space between the trees.

I go mad, slapping at his shoulders, wrists, arms, all the while screaming, "Don't touch me! Don't touch me!"

Don't you fucking touch me!

Nathaniel pins my hands.

I spit in his face.

Then my eye explodes with a pain unimaginable, caused by a blow from the back of his hand. Right away the tears roll. I cannot stop them.

"Calm down," he says, faintly.

Eventually, I do. That's when I say, "What do you want, Nathaniel?"

He slips his finger around one of my curls and tugs it like a bell, just as he did that night outside the Paper Nickel.

I scan the room for something I might use as a weapon. No matter which way I turn, though, Nathaniel has me cold.

He smiles and it is a good smile, the kind of smile

that makes others want to do the same, infectious. Only, I am not in a smiling mood.

"Let go of me," I tell him.

He tilts his head as he studies me. "Do you have any idea what you have done, Delilah?"

"Get out of my house."

"What a claim like that does to a man like me? What it does to a man's career? His future? His life?"

"I'll call the police."

"How did you convince her to do it?" he says. It doesn't take a rocket scientist to figure out that he is talking about the intern. He thinks I started it all. And I should have. I wish that I had. But I only got to finish it.

"You have it all wrong," I say. "I don't even know her."

"You know what I think, Delilah?" he replies without raising his voice. "I think you're a fucking liar."

Look who's talking?

"No."

"You're a crazy bitch."

"Nathaniel—"

Before I can finish my thought, his hand comes down to knock the words right out of my mouth. Then he shakes me violently. The fermented odor on his breath makes it so that I can hardly breathe.

His eyes are glassy with intoxication. Oil black pupils like the space between the trees.

Devil.

I try to push past him, but he throws me against the wall once more. Then I yell, "What do you want?! What do you want?!"

Of course, I knew it the moment he touched me outside the Paper Nickel. It was like being touched by the finger of darkness.

Nathaniel studies my features. As he takes my chin between his thumb and forefinger, we hold eye contact.

Then he does something I do not expect. He gets up and sits on the second to last step of the staircase, basically opening the way for me go.

I crawl for the sliding glass doors then get to my feet and run. As soon as I make it outside, though, I feel the sensation of fingers sinking into my hair and experience a violent jerk backwards. The image of my world tips as Nathaniel drags me into the house once more. He throws me up against the dining room table, knocking the wind right out of me. I drop to the floor, unable to perform simple bodily tasks, like breathing.

There is a dining room chair between us. I push it to block him then crawl under the table in an effort to escape.

He knocks the chair over, grabs hold of my leg, and drags me out into the open, climbs on top of me. All the while, I kick and scream, try to fight him.

He tears at my clothes.

No.

I claw at his face in response, my fingernails skinning a track from his ear to his mouth, the gash deep. It leaks blood.

Nathaniel gives me the full force of his hand, and it feels like my eye explodes yet again. I roll over and moan in agony.

Somehow, and I am not sure how, I crawl out from underneath his body and make it to the stairs. Every one of my senses is off, either too strong or too weak, too fast or too slow, distorted.

Nathaniel's hand comes clamping down violently, viciously around my calf. I drop face first onto the steps, my teeth crashing together upon contact. A metallic taste fills my mouth. There is no doubt in my mind it is blood.

He is on top of me once more. The steps dig into my spine. I feel his hands around my neck, squeezing tighter and tighter still. I flail and I thrash like a wild animal. The air leaves the room. There is a flash of my husband in his old beat up truck, singing his heart out, and the two of us pulling the bedcovers over our heads one warm afternoon.

Ian.

My foot makes contact with Nathaniel's thigh. He stumbles backwards, giving me my opening. I make for the master bedroom, lock the door, and push a chest of drawers in front of it, bracing both with my body.

The serrated steel knife is under the mattress, but I can't find it. I fall to my knees and feel around under the bed, panic rising in my chest.

Nathaniel is banging on the door. He is about to break through. And I have nothing to defend myself.

Finally, my fingers reach the knife near the backside of the headboard. How it got there, I have no idea.

I hide in the master bathroom, serrated steel blade in my hand in front of me, and wait. My cellphone is downstairs on the charger in the kitchen. I cannot get to it. Sweat drips into my eye, stinging. And I feel the sticky wet sensation of blood. The only sound I hear is that of heavy breathing and my heart hammering away in my chest. The rest is like the silence before the storm.

Everything that happens next happens quickly.

Nathaniel bursts through the door.

I slash at him with the blade, miss.

He takes hold of my wrist and shoves me against the wall.

The knife falls to the ground.

Nathaniel's vise-like grip closes in around my throat.

I punch at his wrists and arms.

His fingers tighten about my neck.

I see the green door...my pink-eared bunny...color.

The vein on the side of Nathaniel's neck pulsates.

His skin turns a new shade of violent red.

I scratch.

And I claw.

I punch at his wrists and arms to no avail.

But then—then!—for a reason I cannot explain, Nathaniel's hands open. He releases me.

Collapsing onto the floor, I cough profusely.

The serrated knife is a mere few feet away. But before I can get to it, Nathaniel sinks his fingers into my hair and drags me thrashing and flailing into the master bedroom. He throws me onto the floor. My head hits the bedrail. Blood gushes out of the wound. It drips down the side of my face. I cannot see straight, much less put up a fight.

Nathaniel flips me over and climbs on top of me. I close my eyes in preparation for the end.

Behind my eyelids I see my husband smiling; I see him running his fingers gently down the side of my face. And I see myself as in the dream, carrying our child.

Please, God.

I am that little girl, standing at the top of the staircase, staring at the quivering green door again.

How did I get here? Did it start with the space between the trees or long before?

Of course, I know.

Nathaniel slaps me quite hard.

My eyes pop open.

Then he holds up his index finger before he slaps me again.

Though I cannot scream, my fight returns.

Nathaniel's hands tighten to crush the bones inside my

neck. I flail and I flounder. I walk sideways and kick at the air. His hot fermented breath clings to my skin like humidity. The stench fills my nostrils. I feel his body on mine. His knees bear down on my bones. I cannot turn, much less move. He is crushing me. The debris on the floor is digging into my flesh, deep and deeper still. I see color. Yet the black is near.

Somehow, and I am not sure how, my hand makes its way to the place between Nathaniel legs. He is rock hard. I grab hold of his scrotum and squeeze with all of my might.

Nathaniel hollers. Writhing in agony, tears in his eyes, he collapses into a fetal position on the floor while holding his genitals.

I spot the knife in the bathroom and try to reach it. But Nathaniel is faster and stronger than I am. His body lands on top of mine. And the knife goes sliding in the other direction.

Then he punches me in the kidney. Immediately, it feels as though my organ bursts.

A struggle ensues.

We wind up in the bedroom again.

I bite Nathaniel's hand, draw blood.

He knocks me to the ground.

The lamp from the nightstand is on the floor. My fingers reach for it. I swing the lamp around. It makes contact with the side of Nathaniel's head. Blood gushes out of the corner of his brow. The hit disorientates him.

Then I do it again.

And again.

Now it is Nathaniel who crashes against the floor.

I rip the lamp cord out of the wall socket and wrap it around Nathaniel's throat. Dropping with my knees lodged on his shoulders, I haul and I heave on the reigns.

Nathaniel is on top of me face up, his fingernails clawing and scratching at the plastic-coated wire that is digging into his flesh. I pull and I wrench. I give it everything I have.

Die.

Nathaniel kicks off the floor with his feet. He knocks me into the nightstand. I still don't let go. Instead, I squirm out from underneath him to reposition my knees on his shoulders, hauling and heaving on the reigns once more.

A blood vessel bursts in Nathaniel's eye to form a bright red starburst in his sclera. Much like the starburst my father gave me one drunken night.

The cord slices through Nathaniel's flesh.

I strain.

And I wrench.

And I jerk.

Then, slowly, finally, Nathaniel's body goes limp.

I give the cord one last hard yank before letting go.

It's over.

It's over.

Lying on the floor, staring up at the knockdown plaster ceiling, I breathe.

Time passes before I crawl out from beneath Nathaniel's body. I am covered in lacerations and sweat, blood.

Throwing my arms up onto the bed, I pull myself into a sitting position on the floor. Then I stare at the freshly painted wall, my pink-eared bunny sitting right next to me, my head against my forearm.

Fuck.

The paint color isn't right.

CHAPTER TWENTY-FOUR

A victim of certain crimes can only be the victim once in the eyes of the law. Anything more than that draws suspicion. It draws doubt. And anything within weeks of each other, you might as well lock yourself in the cell.

Nathaniel broke into my home. He broke into my home and attacked me, beat the living shit out of me, nearly killed me, ruined the floors in my house. But I cannot call the police.

Imagining Detective Forester's face, I know I will not get support from the men and women in blue. So, I push myself onto rubbery legs and stumble my way into the bathroom to wash up in the sink. The swelling has already started. The water feels like battery acid on my wounds. I suck air in through my teeth as the blood circles the drain. The image in the mirror disturbs me. I cannot look at it for long.

Shutting off the faucet, I return to my bedroom. Nathaniel is dead. He is dead. And I killed him. *What do I do now?*

On the dresser are a stack of plastic sheets. I grab two of them and drop to my knees next to Nathaniel's dead body. Then I sit on my heels and stare at the lines on his face for I don't know how long. His eyes are closed. I cannot see his oil black pupils anymore or the space between the trees inside them.

At some point, my pink-eared bunny leaves the room. I am not sure if or when he will return.

Something has been jarred loose in my mouth. I feel a sharp pain, so I shove my fingers in there to work my way down the bottom gum. My tooth is loose. I taste blood.

Sitting on the end of the bed, I try to figure out how to handle the situation. There is no way I can drag Nathaniel's limp body down the stairs by myself, much less load him into the trunk of my vehicle. And even if I could, I don't think I would on account of the risk of being seen by my neighbors.

Please, God, help me.

The clock keeps ticking. I feel a sense of panic rise in my chest. Something has got to be done.

Pushing my bed toward the wall, I spread one of the plastic sheets out onto the floor next to Nathaniel. Then I roll Nathaniel's body over onto the sheet, grunting all the while because of his weight. He must be close to two hundred pounds. I pull the sheet over his body then roll him again, tucking the ends underneath so that I can yank the sheet tight from the other side. It is a struggle. I need to stop here and there to breathe. Distracted by the task, I fail to notice Ian's return.

"C'mon. Fucking c'mon," I say when my hand catches under Nathaniel's body and I lose part of my fingernail. I cry out in pain. Then just cry.

That is when I sense the presence of another and look over my shoulder to find my husband's blue eyes staring back at me. He is standing near the threshold. In his eyes, I see fear and confusion, disgust, with sadness as the binding force.

Ian's suitcase hits the floor with a thud.

My emotions get the best of me. I weep.

Then I say in a voice that does not sound much like my voice, "I didn't. I didn't."

Ian crosses the room to join me on the floor. He pulls me into an embrace. After a while he says softly, "Is this the man? Is this the one?"

I nod faintly and reply, "He broke in."

Ian looks around the room at the paint and the brushes, the plastic on the floor, the debris. Cupping my face between his hands, he studies me. "Are you alright, Delilah?"

Am I alright?

"Did he—"

"No. No, I stopped him," I tell my husband.

He nods and scans the room once more. "I shouldn't have left," he says.

And I have to agree.

Two layers of milky clear plastic cover Nathaniel's face as well as his body, yet somehow he still looks alive under those sheets. I half feel as though he will attack the minute I turn my attention a different way.

"I don't understand," Ian tells me. "Why didn't you call someone? We need to contact the police."

Without even a second of hesitation, I snap, "No!"

"Delilah—"

"Think about it, Ian. We can't."

Again, he scans the room, stopping on Nathaniel. "What do you want to do then?"

I shake my head because I really don't know.

Suddenly, Ian is walking out of the room. It seems like he is leaving me. I want to call after him, but the words won't come out of my mouth. That fucking cactus.

But then he returns moments later with a box of black bags and some duct tape. "We'll need to move fast," he tells me.

I study my husband for an extended beat. "Are you sure?"

"Help me with this," he growls.

We wrap Nathaniel in the plastic then lug him down the stairs. It is a struggle, especially because of my hands, which probably have nerve damage from how I used the cord.

Afterwards, we clean out one side of the garage so that we can pull Ian's car inside and load Nathaniel into the trunk. By the time we are done cleaning, it is well after 5:00 AM.

"Wait, wait," I say as Ian prepares to slide behind the driver's seat. He is in too much of a hurry. "I can't go out like this. I need to clean up. I need to fix my face."

Oh, God, my face.

He sinks his fingers into his hair before nodding. "No, you're right. Go."

Upstairs, I wash the blood off my skin and change out of my clothes, replacing them with fresh ones. Then I cake a thick layer of makeup on my face and add a bit more. This time I have to use the shellac method.

Meanwhile, Ian does what he told me he would do. He loads lye into the trunk of our vehicle and throws a blanket over everything, Nathaniel included.

When I am done, I sit on my heels next to the stain of blood on the floor in my master bedroom. And the space between my legs tingles.

Shouldn't I feel remorse?

What is wrong with me?

Downstairs, I find Ian waiting for me in the living room with his elbows on his knees and his head held low. He lifts his head as soon as he sees me. "Is there any chance someone will come here looking for him?"

"I don't—I don't think so," I reply.

"You don't think so," Ian mumbles. "Delilah—"

"He came here to hurt me, Ian. I doubt he went around announcing it to the world."

"What does his car look like?"

"I don't know. A black SUV. Why?"

"Alright," he says. "I believe I know where it is. I'll be right back."

"Wait, Ian, where are you going?"

"Where do you think?"

"Ian?"

"Look at me," he says. "You trust me, don't you?"

Trust?

A swollen moment passes before I respond. I have always held the notion that love disintegrates under the strain of certain pressures, and this pressure is intense. But Ian is Ian. So, I nod.

"Then stay here," he tells me. "I'll be right back."

"Ian, please."

"Stay here."

He already has one foot out of the door. There is nothing I can do to stop him now, which is why I wait.

And I wait.

And I wait.

I extract my uncle's letter from the kitchen drawer and burn it with a lit match, watch it turn to dust in the kitchen sink.

My uncle wasn't there the day I left my pink-eared bunny next to the glass turtle ashtray on the table behind the green door. He wasn't there, but my mother's was. And four little words keep playing in my head. *Dahlia instead of Delilah. Dahlia instead of Delilah. Dahlia instead of Delilah.*

Maybe my mother had it right after all.

Maybe she and I are one and the same.

Young.

And dark.
And red.

The End

ABOUT THE AUTHOR

J. L. Michaels was born in Muskegan, Michigan but grew up in various locations in Connecticut. After graduating high school, she joined the U.S. Air Force, where she met and married her husband. The two had two children and traveled across the country and to outside areas. After graduating college with a B. A. in Psychology, J. L. Michaels went on to earn a M. S. in Criminal Justice. She also obtained degrees in interdisciplinary studies and management. Although J. L. Michaels worked in a variety of positions, to include as a Director of Education, Research and Development and Adjunct Professor, her lifelong dream was to write and publish original fiction. Roller Skate Skinny is her first novel.

Made in the USA
Middletown, DE
15 September 2019